ANTIGENIC SHIFT

The Pandemic Series Book 1

Terry L Blackmore

Sasquatch Press

Thank you

[signature]

Writing your first book is not without it's challenges, it's certainly not a lone wolf venture. I have some very special people that I need to thank, because without their help this book series would not have come to fruition. Firstly there are three ladies who read my raw story, offered their comments, suggestions and encouragement. They are my Daughter, Candice, and my good friends, Dawn and Penny. Secondly to my Son, Josh who took on the challenge of my book cover and put up with my comments and criiticism's. In the end it turned out exactly as I pictured it.

This is my first of many books, but let's be clear; I am a wrench and hammer guy. My skills in English prose; quite frankly stink. So finally thanks to Ciska who took an unreadible mass of words and helped me craft it into something digestable.

Thank you so much to everyone.

Antigenic Shift
The process by which two or more different strains of a virus,
or strains of two or more different virus's, combine to a new
subtype having a mixture of the surface antigens of two or more
original strains.

WIKIPEDIA

A BRIEF
AND RECENT HISTORY
OF DISEASE PANDEMICS

The Spanish Flu (H1N1)

The Spanish Flu (H1N1) of 1918 circled the globe ravaging the human population. An estimated 500 million people, roughly 3 to 5 percent of the world's population, lost the battle with this disease.

The deadliest influenza pandemic in modern history killed its victims when their bodies unleashed an uncontrolled immune reaction as a protective response. The lungs of patients rapidly became inflamed, then filled with blood and other fluids, literally drowning people in their own bodily fluids.

Whereas most influenza outbreaks disproportionally kill the youngest, very old, and those with weakened immune systems, the 1918 outbreak was especially deadly to young and previously healthy adults. This flu acted so swiftly victims would often be dead within a day, and people were dying in the streets. Bodies were piling up, so fast emergency services quickly became overwhelmed.

Remember, this happened at a time when there were no effective antiviral drugs to treat the illness. Citizens were ordered to wear masks, quarantines were established, schools and hospitals were closed to visitors, and church services were cancelled. In some cities, business hours were staggered to limit the spread of the disease on public transit. Social isolation was credited with saving many lives.

1

It is believed that the mass movements of troops and armies of the Great War were a significant factor in the broad and rapid spread of this disease.

The worst pandemic in modern history was the Spanish Flu of 1918, which killed tens of millions of people. Today, with how interconnected the world is, it would spread faster.

Bill Gates

The Asian Flu (H2N2)

The Asian Flu arrived on the scene in 1957. This was the first significant outbreak in the era of modern pharmaceuticals. H2N2 was proven to be a mixed species strain, mutating from a bird flu strain in wild ducks, then mixing with a pre-existing human strain.

Originating in China, it rapidly spread around the world. Small outbreaks began in the summer of 1957. When children returned to school in the fall, they quickly spread the disease.

The severity of the illness varied from fever and cold-like symptoms in some to full-blown pneumonia in others. Death rates were highest among the elderly.

Worldwide, between one and two million people succumbed to this pandemic. The combination of rapid detection, reporting, and swift development of a vaccine kept this outbreak from repeating the magnitude of the 1918 pandemic.

During the 1960s, the H2N2 strain underwent several random mutations, resurfacing and causing periodic epidemics. However, after ten years and several more mutations, the virus disappeared. The current belief is that H2N2 mutated into H3N2 and became the Hong Kong Flu.

Pandemic influenza would mean widespread infection essentially throughout every region of the world.

Anthony Fauci

Immunologist

The Hong Kong Flu

The Hong Kong Flu pandemic began in China in 1968 and spread rapidly throughout South East Asia. It was caused by an H3N2 strain of the influenza A virus, which descended from H2N2 through an *antigenic shift*. It arrived in Panama and then in the United States within several months from soldiers returning to California from Vietnam.

The Hong Kong Flu was attributed to the deaths of two to four million people worldwide. The disease was highly contagious, which facilitated its rapid race around the globe. As with the Asian Flu, there were varying degrees of illness among different populations. Japan suffered very little, yet the United

States was heavily impacted. The highest mortality rates were among infants, the elderly and those with weakened immune systems.

Interestingly, those exposed to the Asian Flu H2N2 were not affected by the Hong Kong Flu H3N2. Scientists believe that these people retained immune protection that resisted H3N2. The advent of modern antibiotic medicine was once again the saviour.

When we think of the major threats to our national security, the first to come to mind are nuclear proliferation, rogue states and global terrorism. But another kind of threat lurks beyond our shores, one from nature, not from humans – an avian flu pandemic.

Barack Obama

44th President of the United States

Severe Acute Respiratory Syndrome (SARS)

SARS, the first epidemic of the 21st century, appeared in 2003. SARS did not attain pandemic status. However, the factors surrounding this epidemic deserve mention here.

The SARS epidemic is believed to have begun in the Guangdong Province of China in November 2002. Patient zero, a local farmer, contracted the disease and quickly died. The

Chinese government took some action to control the spread but worked to suppress the outbreak. No notification was made to The World Health Organization (WHO) until late February 2003.

SARS burst on the global scene in February 2003 when an American businessman came down with pneumonia-like symptoms on a flight from China to Singapore. The plane made an emergency stop in Hanoi, Vietnam, where the man was hospitalized but quickly died. Despite following standard hospital procedures, several of the staff contracted the disease.

Dr. Carlo Urbani reported the disease to the World Health Organization (WHO) and died shortly after that. The subsequent infection of hospital staff and the severity of the disease prompted the WHO to issue a global alert on March 12, 2003. By the time the WHO took action, 500 had died, and 2,000 cases had been confirmed worldwide. The disease spread rapidly via social contact. By the time it was contained, 8,422 cases were confirmed, with 775 deaths worldwide.

There is no vaccine for SARS to date. The most effective methods of controlling SARS are isolation and quarantine. SARS took a heavy toll on healthcare workers, with a 20% infection rate worldwide.

China has learned from the SARS experience and has been more open and more willing to respond to disease outbreaks.

Aphaluck Bhatiasevi

The Swine Flu (H1N1)

The Swine Flu pandemic began in 2009, not in China but in Mexico. It was first identified in the United States in a 10-year-old patient from California in April 2009 and recognized as an H1N1 swine flu strain that had never previously been diagnosed in humans or animals.

Initial testing confirmed the virus was resistant to the two antiviral drugs, Amantadine and Rimantadine. However, antivirals Oseltamivir and Zanamivir were effective.

The World Health Organization (WHO) declared a worldwide pandemic in June 2009. By this time, cases were confirmed in 74 countries and territories. Similar to the 1918 H1N1 Spanish Flu, this one attacked the young and healthy and was easily spread among humans.

When the stain died out in 2010, an estimated 18,000 people had died worldwide. The WHO was accused of waiting too long to declare a pandemic when the outbreak clearly met its definition. Later, they were accused of fear-mongering, exaggerating the disease due to pressure from vaccine makers anxious to recoup their investments.

A fast-moving airborne pathogen could kill more than 30 million people in less than a year.

Bill Gates

H5N1

H5N1 is currently listed as the world's most likely pandemic threat. The virus is treatable; however, to date, outbreaks of H5N1 have resulted in 60% mortality.

It is very conceivable that H5N1 will mutate into a form that will efficiently transfer between humans. Should this happen, the death toll could surpass the 1918 Spanish Flu pandemic.

While we cannot predict when or if the H5N1 virus will become a pandemic, we cannot ignore the warning signs. For the first time in human history, we have a chance to prepare ourselves before the pandemic arrives.

Margery Chan

Director General of The World Health Organization (WHO) 2006 to 2017

PREFACE

The upcoming flu season was expected to be the worst in decades. Outbreaks of a mutated H5N1 strain were spreading rapidly all around the globe. The ratio of deaths to infection was lower than in previous H5N1 epidemics at 5% of those infected.

Not wanting to repeat the embarrassment they received for procrastinating during the 2009 H1N1 pandemic, The World Health Organization (WHO) immediately issued a worldwide pandemic warning. Governments with stockpiles of antivirals immediately ordered distribution to dispensaries. They then awarded contracts to large pharmaceutical companies to ramp up production of the latest flu vaccine and antivirals.

Despite their best efforts, John and Elizabeth MacIntyre contracted the flu bug. It was likely from one of the grandchildren who had picked it up at school. As the former Chief Trainer in Canada's Joint Incident Response Unit (CJIRU), John was well ahead of most people regarding understanding and taking the necessary precautions to prevent infection.

This time, however, was different. John and Elizabeth ended up on their backs with the flu at home. Fortunately, they were all healthy two weeks later, having beaten the bug.

Four weeks after that, the flu season of 2019 burned itself out with few deaths and plenty of embarrassment for the WHO, the CDC, and Governments for jumping the gun and starting another panic situation.

We don't know the timing of the next pandemic; how severe it will be. We don't know what drugs will work. We don't have a vaccine. Yet we are telling everyone to prepare for a pandemic. It's tricky... This is scary, and we don't know... That's the message

Dick Tompson

WHO 2005

THE FULFILLMENT OF A LIFELONG DREAM

John and Elizabeth MacIntyre were in their mid-sixties, both 5'7", lean and healthy from living an active life. The MacIntyres happily spent their days tending to a small homestead near Owen Sound, Ontario. They purchased the property just before John retired from the military. While in their 20's, they both got the bug to have a self-sufficient homestead. However, money was very tight as a young military man and a stay-at-home mom with three young children.

Thirty years later and nearing the end of his career in the army, John was the Base Chief Warrant Officer at Canadian Forces Base Borden, a sprawling training facility in southern Ontario. His final posting was a dream position for a man at the pinnacle of his career who loved the army and dedicated his life to it.

Now with a nice nest egg socked away and a generous pension waiting for John's retirement, John and Elizabeth MacIntyre went shopping. They purchased 120 acres of land for cash, north-west of Owen Sound, Ontario. The property was in a sparsely populated area, on a small secondary road off another secondary road, well away from any major routes. The land lay adjacent to the Grey Sauble Conservation Area and consisted of primarily mixed hardwoods with 40 acres of arable land. The outbuildings included a very nice barn, several machine sheds and a large shop heated by wood. To say the house was a dump would not be an exaggeration. That, too, suited their plans very nicely.

John and Elizabeth tore the old structure down during his

days off and built their dream home. The new house was something they had been planning all their lives-a 2,500 square foot brick rancher with four bedrooms, plus a full basement. The home was a super-insulated structure. The 12-inch thick walls consisted of inner and outer 2x4 walls, the gap between them filled with insulation boasting an R-value of 30 plus. The attic, as well, was insulated to R60. John liked to say the home was gentle on consumption.

Roof-mounted solar panels on the house, shop, and barn would absorb the energy from the sun. Two wind generators would harvest the ample winds that blew in off Lake Huron and Georgian Bay. The MacIntyres could live off-grid. However, they remained hooked up and sold excess power back into the grid. A diesel-powered backup generator rounded out the energy production system. Large battery banks stored the extra energy and could provide all their power needs for a week before needing a recharge.

A natural gas furnace and a modern wood cook stove provided the heat. A second wood stove in the basement provided back up. A grey water recovery system and an anaerobic septic system handled all the waste, while a 200-foot drilled well provided abundant water. A backup artesian well north of the barn ran all year round and provided ample water for the livestock. John believed in the safety of redundancy.

The usual livestock consisted of 20 Herford cows, 12 Nubian goats, 24 chickens, and six hogs. The MacIntyres also tended beehives and produced honey. Everything was 100% organic. They planted apple, pear and cherry trees and lovingly tended acres of organic vegetables. They tapped the abundant sugar maples in the early spring and made maple syrup. What they didn't grow or raise for themselves, they traded with neighbouring farmers and any surplus was then sold from their booth at the Owen Sound Farmers' Market. John was often heard joking that he should rejoin the army for a rest. Sure, the MacIntyres were very busy, but they were self-sufficient, healthy, and happy.

As a military man being a prepper seemed second nature to John. Both he and Liz believed strongly in self-reliance. However, Liz often felt her husband took things to the extreme. She could never imagine that our modern technological society would ever come to an end. Liz tolerated and humoured her husband's prepper habit, so when John included a 400-square-foot safe room in the basement plans of their new home, it didn't come as any surprise to her. Liz referred to it as "my husband's bunker. You can take the boy out of the army, but you can't take the army out of the boy," she would tease. To most outside the family, the room was a secret. John was adamant that it remain that way.

John and Liz took the duty of caring for their family very seriously. They both believed that providing for your family should be everyone's primary concern. They chose this before expensive vacations and flashy cars. When others were jetting off to all-inclusive vacation spots, the MacIntyres went camping, hiking, hunting and fishing. When young, the children went to Scouts, Guides, and Cadets. The lessons learned provided a sound foundation for life, which benefited them as they grew older.

To pass basic training, every person that joined the military had to complete a standard-level first aid course. John was one of the most prominent advocates of first-aid training. He earned his instructor level and would teach the class to local youth groups for free. John believed everyone should know first aid; it just made sense. In a civil, caring society, citizens should be willing and able to come to the assistance of others when bad things happen. John worked hard to get first aid training included in the high school curriculum but had no success.

Regrettably, society was moving in another direction. One where not being responsible for oneself and relying on others for safety and well-being was becoming the flavour of the day. John believed the day would come when society would regret that move. However, he sincerely hoped he wouldn't be alive to see it. Humans have become so pampered, so far removed from the natural cycle of life and death that sustained us as hunter-gatherers. Too many believed their food came from the grocery store and water from a plastic bottle. Few people had any idea or cared about how their food was produced.

Large-scale agriculture and factory farms produced cheap food on a mammoth scale, which required transportation over long distances. Robust infrastructure and a fast-reliable transportation system enabled businesses to use a just-in-time (JIT) delivery system. Companies now carry little inventory; the stock goes from the loading dock directly to store shelves. Should there ever be a significant disruption of the modern food and fuel delivery system, most of the western world's stores would be out of inventory in three days.

Once that happens, a pampered population that has become accustomed to having everything available to them all the time will panic. Then, that thin veil that holds us together as a civil society will melt away, and all hell will break loose.

John, Liz and their family had enough food and supplies to provide well for an extended family for over a year. When John and Liz bought the farm, the family came together and made plans. It was agreed that the farm would be their go-to or bug-out location (BOL) if some crisis happened. Food and gear were prepositioned at the farm. All the families needed to do in an emergency was gather everyone up and move to the farm.

Everyone contributed money to a family fund regularly. They sat down and planned out food, gear and weapon purchases so that everything could be standardized as much as possible. This allowed them to buy in bulk to save money, provided interchangeability and facilitated the training.

They understood that they would have to add people to the group if things went bad. People are needed to provide adequate security and labour for their mutual existence. Being military, John had a solid understanding of security. "Think about it," he said, "No one can survive as a lone wolf. One or two cannot provide adequate security and labour." Just providing 24-hour security requires four people at an absolute minimum—one person on security for 6 hours every day, seven days a week. Without the support of a team, one would become exhausted after a few days, and exhaustion leads to vulnerability. To secure an area 24-7, such as their farming community, it would require a minimum of two but ideally three roadblocks, perimeter security by patrols and security at each home. That's a lot of people.

Now consider the need to provide fuel for warmth, plus the health and well-being of the group. Remember, we live in Canada, and winter can last for five months, and temperatures can plummet to -40 and stay there for weeks at a time. Annual winter snowfall can easily exceed 50 cm or 20 inches.

Now let's consider food; there is no chance that hunting and fishing will provide enough for a healthy existence; game animals would be quickly hunted out. Growing your food and having livestock is the only way to sustain a large group. Operating a farm requires a lot of labour, especially without modern labour-saving machinery.

We are talking about a lot of healthy, strong bodies. The family agreed they would have to include the neighbours in their plans. John and Liz made a point of getting to know the folks nearby. Inviting people they could work with and trust into the group. As well prepared as the MacIntyres were, they knew they would have to accept select people into the group. No matter how much a small group prepares or how many skills they acquire, it will never be enough. People with many skills are needed, such as medical, mechanical, electrical, carpentry, plumbing, communications, farming, gardening, cooking and preserving food, teachers, security, hunting, fishing, and so on.

Remember, when disaster strikes, the time to prepare has passed

Steven Cyros

MOTHER NATURE IS ANGRY

The past few decades, the Arctic has been warming up, sea ice has been depleting, ice shelves and glaciers melting, and the permafrost thawing. Climate change is real. The cause, however, is a topic of hot contention. Some claim it's man-made and can produce all the data, and scientists with papers and PowerPoint presentations to back it up. Others argue it's a natural cycle and can equally produce all the data, scientists with documents and PowerPoint presentations to the contrary.

The fact remains; the Arctic is going through fundamental change. With nearly 8 billion people on the planet consuming more and more of the earth's finite resources, humankind is long overdue for a correction.

Nature has always had a way of correcting the balance of things. Wildlife populations peak and die off in regular cycles, and wildfires burn the forests and grasslands of the planet to clean the slate, wiping out disease and sparking new healthy growth.

Humanity has been tampering, abusing, and interfering with mother nature for a very long time. Until recently, humans had been relatively successful at limiting the population, killing one another off through wars of greed. Occasionally, mother nature would step in with a natural disaster or disease pandemic to set humans back a few more decades.

In the past 150 years, however, humans have made extraordinary strides in medicine, industry, agriculture, science, and technology. Deaths by war, starvation, and disease slowed, allowing the planet's population to balloon into the billions.

Human greed has extracted its toll on the earth from the destruction of the rain forests, depletion of the ocean's fish stocks and pollution of the waterways and aquifers.

Recently, Mother Nature has begun to push back. Natural disasters have increased; weather events, earthquakes, volcanoes and wildfires are becoming more frequent.

Antibiotics, the miracle of modern medicine, have been used and abused by the factory farming sector and over-prescribed by doctors for decades. The scientific community warned that viruses were becoming resistant to the current antibiotics, and to ignore this fact was at our peril.

The handwriting was on the wall, yet humankind greedily carried on.

* * *

Every year, billions of birds make an annual migration. In the spring, they fly north into the Arctic regions, mate and give birth. During the Arctic summer, they prepare their young for the fall migration back to the south. A process that has gone on since the beginning of time.

The fall of 2020 was no exception; birds of all types formed up with their young and flew to the wintering grounds in the south. However, this year, they brought a microscopic gift from Mother Nature. A pathogen that, until this year, had been safely contained beneath the Arctic ice and permafrost for millennia.

As the birds settled into their southern range, an antigenic shift occurred between the H5N1 flu virus infecting the local birds and the ancient pathogen brought back with the migrating birds. A new supervirus evolved. A virus that would readily jump the barrier between birds, swine, and humans. A virus that was resistant to any known antiviral. A perfect killer and an ideal tool to chasten and humble humankind.

Sickness is the vengeance of nature for the violation of her laws.

Charles Simmons

---

9 NOVEMBER 2020

Camp Thunder

The MacIntyre moose hunting gang was 200 kilometres north of the small Northern Ontario community of Vermilion Bay at a fly-in hunting and fishing camp. The camp was owned and operated by old friends of John's, Joseph and Pamela Thunder, a native couple born and raised on Wabauskang First Nation. Joseph had served three tours in Afghanistan with Canada's JTF2. They bought the camp when Joseph retired from the army four years ago. Pamela cooked and cleaned while Joseph and their three adult sons guided guests and maintained the camp.

Camp Thunder sat on the north shore of Trout Lake and catered to hunters and fishermen worldwide. Because of Joseph's high ethical standards, Pamela's excellent cooking and the area's abundant wildlife, they were quickly becoming a legend in the business. Customers would book a year in advance to hunt and fish at Camp Thunder. The camp consisted of ten six bunk cabins that surrounded a central lodge. Apart from the electricity provided by a diesel generator, there were few modern conveniences. That was the way Joseph's customers liked it; an escape from the outside world and its many distractions. The Log cabins were cozy, all with a wood stove and electricity. Each cabin had a private dock, an aluminum boat and a motor. Each boat fully stocked with excellent fishing gear.

Doing double duty as Joe and Pam's home, the central lodge was a beautiful log structure with high ceilings. The only building with hot and cold running water and the Internet.

The lodge contained a large kitchen, a warm, inviting dining hall, private showers, and bathrooms. A sizeable floor-to-ceiling stone fireplace in the centre of the lodge sets the atmosphere for people to relax, share stories, and enjoy one another's company.

Hundreds of pictures of successful fishing and hunting expeditions covered the lodge's walls. John MacIntyre, pictured with his Weatherby rifle and a giant moose, adorned a place of honour on the lodge wall as Camp Thunder's first customer and the first to bag a moose. Joseph and John served in Afghanistan with Joint Task Force Two (JTF2). They quickly became and remained close friends.

John assigned either an acronym or nickname to most things. He was military, and that's the way things were done. The MacIntyre clan consisted of three generations of Johns. John, of course, was J1. His eldest son John Jr. was labelled J2. Subsequently, J2's son John was naturally labelled J3. This year's hunting gang included the three J's, Caroline (J1's eldest daughter), her husband Greg, and their only child, Katherine-quickly labelled Kat by her grandfather.

John loved his time in the forest. He taught all his children how to love and respect Mother Nature. The lessons were never lost on the young MacIntyres. They all took to the outdoors like ducks to water. Consequently, the MacIntyres were regulars at Camp Thunder.

14 NOVEMBER 2020

Camp Thunder

They were five days into the hunt with no sign of moose. The weather was just too warm. They need some below-freezing temperatures and a snowfall to make it right. That morning, John and Kat sat on a high rise overlooking a recently logged clearing.

They sat quietly, enjoying the coffee and breakfast sandwiches Pam had made them. They watched a spectacular sunrise spread slowly across the eastern horizon; reds, yellows, and purples, gently pushed the darkness away. They heard a pack of wolves in the distance. They were running something.

"It's likely a moose," John told Kat

"They are getting closer, aren't they, Poppa?" Kat asked.

"Yes, they are," replied John, "Given the direction of the sound, I wouldn't be surprised if they chase the moose into the clearing. It will be easier to bring it down in the open.

Kat, most people think nature is like a Disney movie, all warm and cuddly, everything exists in peace, wolves and bears coexist with deer and raise one another's young. Well-meaning people and animal rights groups pressure governments to restrict or even eliminate our rights to hunt, fish, and farm, preaching that nature is warm and cuddly and that we are cruel killers. I assure you the picture they paint is not reality, Kat. We are about to witness the harshness of nature and how the circle of life works on this planet."

Kat had her binoculars up, glassing the clearing below them. "Poppa look," she pointed.

Sure enough, 800 meters from where John and Kat watched, the wolf pack had chased an exhausted cow moose into the clearing.

She worked hard to escape as the wolves bit at her hind legs tearing away the flesh and tendons. She fell, then tried to get up as more of the pack jumped on her. The wolves tore at her throat and legs as she struggled to get back on her feet. With the ligaments now torn away on her hind legs, she could only raise her front end off the ground. She tried desperately to drag herself with her front legs but to no avail. The pack was on her now.

Kat had a tear in her eye, "Poppa, they are eating her alive!"

"Yes, they are, Kat," John replied. "This is how nature really works. It's survival of the fittest. It's often cruel and brutal. There is always something to feed on something else. It's the way it has always been and always will be."

"Poppa, it's so cruel!" Kat insisted.

"Yes, it is," John replied.

John MacIntyre was a superb marksman. During his four tours in Afghanistan, John pulled his share of sniper duties. Using his laser rangefinder, he checked the range. The struggling moose was 785 meters away. She attempted to stand, large chunks of flesh torn from her face and sides. John shouldered his Remington 700 and adjusted his scope for windage and elevation. He centred the dying moose's heart in his crosshairs and fired. The struggling cow died instantly, ending her suffering.

"Thank you, Poppa, that was the cruellest thing I have ever seen!" Kat exclaimed.

The wolves scattered at the sound of the shot, but not for long. They had a fresh kill. Kat watched through her binoculars as they returned one by one to feed.

"Poppa, how long would she have suffered before she died?" Kat asked.

"It's hard to say, sweetheart. She could have lasted another ten, maybe 15 minutes," John replied.

"My God, what a horrible way to die!" Kat exclaimed.

John looked at his granddaughter, "I think I have seen enough for the day. How be we head back and see what delicacies Pam is cooking up?"

"I'm with you, Poppa," Kat replied. They made their weapons safe, placed them in the scabbards on their quads, started up and rode back to camp.

The week wasn't wasted; they scouted some excellent locations to set up and enjoyed the time together. John was a natural-born teacher who loved passing his knowledge on to his grandchildren, and he never missed an opportunity to teach them survival skills. When they weren't busy constructing traps and shelters or practicing primitive fire-making skills, they would fish and catch their limit daily. Few things in this world are finer than a shore lunch of fresh fish grilled over an open fire.

15 NOVEMBER 2020

Everywhere

Outbreaks began simultaneously around the globe. Cases were springing up so quickly that the WHO and CDC had difficulty assigning a patient zero. Samples sent to CDC for testing confirmed that this was something never before seen.

Not surprisingly, to some in the epidemiological community, tests also confirmed that no known antivirals would have any effect. The unthinkable had finally happened.

Despite the evidence before them, the WHO and CDC were reluctant to make the call that a new pandemic was about to inflict the world. Both feared jumping the gun and feeling the wrath of angry political leaders and bureaucrats.

They were stuck between a rock and a hard place. Declare a pandemic too soon and embarrass the political establishment, they would be punished. Declare a pandemic too late, and they would equally feel the heat from elected officials.

5:00 AM, NOVEMBER 2020

Week two began with a sharp drop in temperature to -15 celcius and a light dusting of snow. Day 10 arrived, and Joseph felt it would be their lucky day. The MacIntyre gang held two bull moose tags between the six of them and hoped to put at least one moose in their collective freezers this winter. Having hunted in this area many times over the years, the MacIntyre group did not need guides freeing up Joseph and his sons to focus all their attention on Camp Thunder's other guests.

Three teams departed before dawn; the father and son team of J2 and J3, Caroline with Greg, and John with young Kat. At fifteen, this was Katherine's first moose hunt. Until now, she hadn't hunted anything larger than the plentiful ruffled grouse that lived on her grandparent's farm. She was the apple of her grandfather's eye, and this was a situation John was determined to make right.

Despite her slim build, the pretty blonde girl was lean and muscular, rightfully acquired from the abundant physical activity of growing up in an active household. Taught and mentored by her grandfather from an early age, Kat was comfortable around firearms. She possessed superior eyesight and keen hearing. Kat was an excellent shot and could easily handle the recoil of a 12-gauge shotgun.

Today, she carried her grandfather's Weatherby Vanguard chambered in the venerable 30-06 Springfield and topped with a Leopold, VX-2 3-9 X 40 Canadian Edition scope. John used his new Remington 700 SPS in stainless steel, chambered in 300 Winchester Short Magnum (WSM) and topped with a Carl-Zeiss, Victory 2.8-20 X 56 scope.

John was an avid reloader who carefully assembled all their ammunition in his reloading room. John had abundant supplies on hand, including the dies and materials needed to reload all the calibres used by the MacIntyres for many years.

John had found fresh tracks the previous day and used them as a training opportunity in tracking for Kat. She spent two hours following the large tracks to an active scrape site. Judging by the height of the rub marks on the surrounding trees, this was a big bull.

This morning they set-up; then enjoyed some coffee while they waited for legal hunting time. They sat silently, taking in yet another spectacular sunrise.

"This was part of the experience," John whispered to Kat. "Even if we don't bag a moose, spending time in nature with the people you love is priceless."

John's phone vibrated, indicating the wait was over. He pulled out his birch bark moose call and made a series of grunts. They didn't wait long. Kat heard the cracking of branches off to her right. She shouldered the Weatherby and waited, her adrenaline rising.

"Try to relax, Kat," John whispered. "Control your breathing, in and out, relax."

John let a short series of snorts from the moose call. Suddenly the big bull appeared. He was huge and pissed. Certain that another bull was at his scrape. Challenge accepted, he shook his giant rack back and forth as he stepped into the clearing. He stopped and sniffed the air, the condensation rising from his nostrils. He shook his massive head again, seeking the intruder.

At 75 meters away, Kat lined him up in her crosshairs. Every lesson her grandfather taught her running through her mind; relax, breathe in, breathe out. Confirm your target and what's behind it in case you miss, and aim for the vitals. Sighted in for 100 meters, she aimed slightly low, knowing the bullet would arc just above the crosshairs as it travelled to her target. Click off the safety, breathe out as you lovingly squeeze the trigger, and BOOM!

The powerful blast propelled the 180-grain Nosler Partition bullet toward the monstrous bull. At 2,847 feet per second, it covered 75 meters, almost instantly impacting him in the heart.

A perfect shot, the giant moose staggered. He turned to his right, took three steps toward the safety of the trees, and fell. Kat chambered another round and waited just in case he rose to his feet. He didn't. Kat snapped on the safety and looked at her grandfather; they were both beaming. She was shaking with a huge adrenaline rush.

"Wow," she said. "The big fella was pissed."

"Let's go look at your moose," John said, smiling. "Move slowly; keep your gun ready in case he is still alive. We don't want that monster coming at us," John cautioned.

The loud report from the 30-06 was impossible to miss, and John's radio crackled to life.

J2's voice was calling, "What's up? Did someone get a moose?"

A smiling John handed the radio to Kat, "This is your ballgame, sweetheart; you give him the news."

"Uncle John, I got a nice bull," she proudly exclaimed.

"Sweet!" came the reply. "We will be right over."

Then Caroline's voice came over the radio. "Good job Kat. We're proud of you. We're on our way."

John and Kat looked at the massive moose in front of them. "Wow!" Kat exclaimed. "He is enormous."

"You're not kidding," John agreed proudly. "That's the biggest moose I have ever seen. He must be 1400 pounds!"

John showed Kat how to ensure the moose was dead. Then they both bowed their heads, saying a silent prayer for the majestic animal that gave his life for them. John hugged his granddaughter tightly; he could feel the adrenaline still running through her.

"Relax," he said, "Let's get a picture of this. Kat, unload your rifle and kneel behind that big bruiser."

Kat did as instructed, then opened the bolt, removing the chambered round. She then removed the magazine and reinserted the cartridge before dropping it into her pocket. She closed her pocket, ensuring it was safely secured, double-checked the rifle chamber and closed the bolt.

The weapon now proved safe. She then placed the Weatherby over the moose and knelt behind it. Both beaming ear to ear, John proudly snapped pictures with his iPhone.

"Yep," John thought, "this little lady can handle a gun.

Caroline and Greg were the first to arrive. They pulled up and dismounted their quads, looking on in awe at the massive moose their daughter had downed.

"Oh my God," exclaimed Greg as he and Caroline collectively hugged their daughter. "We are so proud of you."

The J's were the next to arrive, followed by Joseph, who looked on in disbelief, the size of the moose catching everyone by surprise. John Jr. hugged his niece proudly and told her so.

J3, naturally very envious, hugged his cousin proudly. "Wow, Kat, that is one huge moose!"

Joseph hugged Kat and informed her, "Kat, that is the biggest moose I have ever seen." Coming from Joseph, that was a huge compliment.

The big moose was winched onto Joseph's ATV trailer, almost flattening the four large floatation tires. Joseph looked on and smiled, "Looks like I may need to upgrade if Kat keeps coming up here."

Everyone enjoyed a laugh.

Back at the camp, Kat was the envy of all the other hunters. They looked on in awe at the size of the moose she had bagged.

Joseph had a heavy-duty framework to facilitate the hanging and cleaning of animals. He pulled out a scale and attached it to the block and tackle, and they hoisted the big moose off the ground. 647.7 kilos, or 1,428 pounds.

"Wow," Joseph exclaimed, "Kat, that's one big moose." Everyone hugged Kat, and she was glowing. Everyone at the camp gathered around, heaping on the praise for Katherine, taking photos, handshaking and sharing hugs.

Hatto Masatoshi, who was visiting Camp Thunder from Japan on a fishing vacation, was so impressed he insisted on having a few photos taken with his new heroine Kat and the giant moose.

Kat's father, Greg Young, was a butcher by trade. "We best get the nasty part over with," he announced as he pulled the processing tools off his quad.

Kat jumped in. "Let me, Dad, I shot him; it's only right. You grab me if I pass out."

That brought a collective laugh from the group. Faithful to her word, Kat did the messy work of gutting the moose under her father's and Joseph's careful guidance. Yes, she stopped once to vomit; J3 was by her side, holding her hair.

"Don't feel bad, Kat. I puked the first two times I did it," J3 admitted sheepishly.

Kat wiped the vomit from her face and forced a smile. She quickly cleaned up and got right back at it.

When she finished cleaning up, John, the proud grandfather, was beaming, Weatherby rifle in hand. He walked over to his granddaughter, handing her the Weatherby and said proudly: "This is yours now, Kat. You earned it."

Kat looked at her grandfather in disbelief, "But Poppa, this is your favourite rifle."

"The operative word is 'was,' John said proudly. "Now it's yours."

They shared a hug. More pictures were taken, and everyone

shed a collective tear. Kat proudly slipped the Weatherby into the scabbard of her quad and climbed aboard. Everyone rode back to their cabins to clean up and prepare for dinner. It was a fantastic day.

Like all preppers, John MacIntyre was a news junkie. Even at the hunting camp, John would excuse himself each evening and head to Joseph's office to use the computer. His day ended the way it had for many years, with a thorough gleaning of his news sources.

Two days ago, John began getting leads to flu outbreaks all around the globe. Between the stories from alternative news media sources and his network of fellow preppers, the outbreak was all but confirmed. Not a peep, however, from the mainstream news media.

His curiosity fully aroused, he borrowed Joe's satellite phone and called a former student and colleague from his time at the Canadian Joint Incident Response Unit (CJIRU). Now a General in the Canadian Forces Medical Corps, Dr. Alex Dickson was the head of the Medical Department at National Defense Headquarters in Ottawa, Ontario.

Very few people had Alex's cell phone number, so when his phone rang and an unknown number was displayed, Alex almost ignored it. However, these were troubling times, and he answered, "Alex Dickson here."

"Hey Alex, it's John MacIntyre."

Alex recognized his old friend instantly, "John, how are things at Green Acres?" (A joke between Alex and John comparing him and Elizabeth to the 60's TV sitcom starring Eddie Arnold and Eva Gabor).

"Couldn't be better, General. Lisa is out milking the cow, and I'm still trying to get that damn tractor running. How are you?"

Alex laughed, "John, you know better than to call me General."

After catching up on family and the latest military gossip,

John got to the point of his call. "Alex, what can you tell me about this recent flu bug that's all over the world?"

"John, you never cease to amaze me. How did you learn about this so quickly?" Alex questioned.

"I have my sources," John replied, "and you know, if I told you, I would have to come there and kill you."

After a bit of shared laughter, Alex filled John in on all he knew. "John, the WHO and CDC are both afraid to issue a warning. They took a beating the last two times. The political powers that be want this hushed up until they know with 100% confidence that it's the real deal. There are too many elections next year, and no one wants to look like an idiot. Sound familiar?"

"Sadly," John replied.

"For what it's worth, John," Alex continued," I have spoken with my counterparts at the Pentagon, and they, quite frankly, are worried. This bug is spreading faster than anything any of us has ever seen. John, it's everywhere. The only thing missing, so far at least, are the death tolls, but it's only been a few days.

"The Chiefs of staff from all the NATO countries have been alerted. They don't like what they see either. The Russians are on board with us and making plans if this blows up. China has clammed up tight, and the UN is adopting its typical head-in-the-sand approach.

"My old friend Dr. Kelvin Rich at the CDC told me we are still in the early stages, but this flu bug appears to be acting exactly like the Spanish Flu of 1918. It hits fast. It hits hard. The patient's immune system overreacts to the virus, and the lungs become inflamed, then fill with blood and bodily fluids, effectively drowning the patient. Worse yet, the preliminary tests he has run indicate that not one of the known antivirals in our inventory influences this thing.

"Again, John, it's early. The body count is low, but this could get nasty fast."

"Agreed," John replied worriedly, "Alex, you know where I live. You know I have taken precautions for events such as this. Liz and I would welcome you and Carol if you need a place to go."

"John, that's why I love you. Like only a man can love another man, of course," Alex chuckled. "But seriously, John, I thank you for that. The time may come when I may take you up on that offer."

"Alex, you're always welcome, remember that, and I thank you from the bottom of my heart for sharing this with me. You take care of yourself. You, of all people, know what this could turn into. Please don't wait too long." John said adamantly.

"Thanks, John, I appreciate it. So long old friend."

"So long, Alex," John replied.

John's next phone call was to Elizabeth.

"John, what's up? I wasn't expecting you to call."

John filled Liz in on Kat's fantastic day and how proud he was of her. "You should have seen her, Liz; she was terrific."

Liz filled John in on what's been happening on the farm in the past week. Aside from a bit of snow, nothing was new or exciting, and that's just the way Liz liked it.

"Liz, have you heard of anyone in the area getting a flu bug?" John questioned.

"No," she replied. "I was in town the day before yesterday and stopped at the drug store to pick up a parcel I ordered from Amazon. Sharon never mentioned anything; why?"

"You know me, I was checking my sources and discovered flu outbreaks popping up worldwide, nothing in the mainstream media, of course."

"John, you're not overreacting, are you?" Liz teased.

"Oh, ye of little faith," came John's reply. "I called Alex, and he confirmed that the Governments of the world know about this but are keeping a lid on it. They fear this will affect next year's election, gutless, self-serving idiots."

"John, how bad is it?" Liz questioned.

"It's everywhere, Liz, and it appears to be acting much like the Spanish Flu of 1918, except that few have died so far, but it's only been a couple of days. Alex is worried, and quite frankly, so am I.

Liz, please call the kids, and let them know what's developing. Ask them to stock up on staple foods and gas and plan to get their asses to the farm if this worsens.

Thinking of their youngest son David, John added. "Tell them I expect no argument." John continued, "First thing in the morning, you need to go into town and stock up on all the staples, beans, rice, powdered milk, etc. There is a list in my office. You know the checklists I showed you?"

"Yes, my love, I know the checklists," she replied.

"Good, oh, and please call Karl at the Co-op. Fill him in on my concerns. He needs to take precautions. Ask him to come by ASAP and top off all our fuel tanks," John added.

"Liz, two more things. Please, take all precautions, bring a mask, gloves and hand sanitizer with you, and avoid anyone showing symptoms. I will keep you posted, and I love you."

"I love you too, John," Liz replied.

9:30 AM, 18 NOVEMBER 2020

The MacIntyre Homestead

After Liz hung up the phone. She walked down to the basement and into John's study. John and Liz grew up together, went to the same school, became childhood sweethearts, and enjoyed a loving marriage.

Liz was a farm girl and the eldest of four. Living on a farm and providing for your own was second nature to her. John, however, grew up in town. His Father was a WW2 veteran turned railroad man, and his mother was a stay-at-home mom.

John was the youngest of eight growing up. Money was often tight for the MacIntyres. Liz believed that was the beginning of John's fascination with being prepared. John was a Prepper long before the word became commonly used. Even before they married, John always had emergency money tucked away and never let his vehicle fall below half a tank.

While all the other boys in school drove around in cars with flash wheels and big stereos, John drove a 4-wheel drive pickup. John's truck only had an AM radio. He always carried tools, tire chains, a tow strap and a Jack All jack.

Behind the seat was what John called his emergency bag. Today it would be called a Bug Out Bag or Get Home Bag. It was an old military surplus packsack that contained all the essentials John would need in an emergency. Extra clothes, enough food for three days, water and means of collecting and purifying it, a map and compass, a means to make shelter, a fire starting kit, a sewing kit, a first aid kit, rope, several knives, etc. Also behind the seat was a rifle and ammunition, an axe and a saw.

John would never be caught without his bag of essentials. Even on a date, Liz would often tease him about his obsession.

When Liz, John and a group of high school friends got stranded on a snowmobile trip one weekend, John used his bag of gear to set up shelter, make fire, boil water, and feed them all.

While some of their friends started to panic, John remained calm and held the group together. His confidence was addictive. He knew help would come, and it did. John was the only one that told his parents exactly where they were going.

When the teens didn't show up at supper time, John's father gathered a few friends and searched for them. They were all right where John said they would be, warm, fed and hydrated. They all got back home safe and sound. The event opened Liz's eyes. She was going to keep this fella.

Her husband was organized, bordering on obsessive-compulsive; 35 years in the army would do that to a man. You could set a clock by John MacIntyre. His study and workshop were always immaculate, never a pen or wrench out of place. If someone asked John for anything, he could tell them exactly where it was. God help anyone who didn't put anything back in its rightful place. John's rationale was simple; if something went wrong, if I was injured or blinded, I could find whatever I needed, even in the dark. If I can't get what I need, I can send anyone to get it.

The walls of John's study were covered with awards, plaques and pictures representing his long military career.

A beautiful solid oak bookcase filled one complete wall. John made it when they built the house. John was a compulsive reader and had an extensive library. Liz picked the binder off the bookcase. She studied some of the other titles there; *Where There Is No Doctor, Where There Is No Dentist, How To Survive The End Of The World As We Know It, Back To The Basics, Root Cellaring, Blacksmithing, books on farming, preserving, stocking up, and gardening to name a few.*

Liz smiled, *I married a smart man.* She turned and went back upstairs. She made a cup of tea in the kitchen, sat down and opened the binder.

The first sentence was typical of John MacIntyre. *'My love, if you are reading this, something has gone terribly wrong, and I am not home. See, I'm not crazy after all. LOL.'*

Liz shook her head and giggled.

'We have prepared well for any emergency, so you can take comfort in knowing that. I do regret that I am not there with you. We developed these checklists for just this contingency. You will notice the binder contains tabs for every possible scenario we could think of. Go to the appropriate tab, remove the checklist and follow it through. I know you are laughing right now. Remember, I love you. My number one mission is to get back home to you ASAP.'

Liz shook her head, smiling to herself. *The man can read me like a book.* She opened the tab Disease Pandemic. She drank her tea as she read:

A disease pandemic has broken out, and these are the things you need to know and do ASAP. First and foremost, call all the kids and members of our group. Call our closest neighbours. Fill them in on the situation. Tell them to stock up on food, water, medical, and personal essentials.

Call Karl Hanson at the Co-op at (705) 424-5821. Fill him in on what's going on. Ask him to top up all our tanks and drop off five times our usual order of animal feed and seeds ASAP.

Do not go out in public without an N95 mask, doctor gloves and hand sanitizer in your purse. If you see ANY SIGN of infection in people, use the gear. Wash your hands often and avoid touching your face.

Things can spiral out of control quickly. It's imperative that you stock up on beans, bullets and band-aids before the general public goes into panic mode. I know we are well prepared, but it is wise to add to our preps while there is an opportunity.

We don't know the duration of this emergency or how many

people we will be sheltering. We may need to barter for the goods and services we need. The following will supplement our supplies very nicely. Withdraw five thousand dollars cash in small bills only. Purchase the following in as large a quantity as possible and pay for it by credit card.

<u>Groceries</u>
Cooking oil
Dried beans, peas and legumes
Rice
Coffee
Teas
Sugar
Salt
Pickling salt
Spices
Canned milk
Powdered milk
Honey
Pancake mix
Bisquick
Instant potatoes
Flour
Baking soda
Baking powder
Energy bars
Bleach LOTS
Laundry detergent
Dish detergent
Hand soap
Shampoo
If there is room in our freezers, meats

<u>Medical Supplies</u>
Fill any prescriptions
Vitamins

Band-Aids
Bandages all sizes
Painkillers, aspirin, ibuprofen, Tylenol
Cold and flu meds
Hot packs
Cold packs
Ointments
Alcohol, lots
Hydrogen peroxide
Toothpaste
Toothbrushes
Dental floss
Mouthwash
Hand sanitizer
N95 face masks
Doctor gloves
Feminine products
Condoms
Foot powder
Disposable razors
Shaving cream

Other Items

Booze, lots, all kinds, Richards Red beer and Glenfiddich Scotch, just because a fella has his needs.

Cigarettes and cigars. Excellent barter items.
Anything you feel we could use or need?

Critical Actions

Distance and hand washing are the most effective methods to beat a disease pandemic. Stay away from people, wear a mask and gloves, wash or sanitize hands frequently and keep your hands away from your face.

4:00 AM, 18 NOVEMBER 2020

Camp Thunder

It was 4:00 when Joseph walked into the lodge kitchen. The lights were on and John was sitting at the table with his laptop open.

John, what are you doing up so early? Joseph asked.

"I couldn't sleep, my friend. I wanted to check on a few things," John replied.

"You can't keep a secret from a fellow grunt, I know you to well. What's troubling you, old friend? Joseph quizzed.

A fresh pot of coffee sat on the brewer. Joseph poured them each a mug while John filled him in on his discoveries.

"This could be bad, very bad," Joseph replied.

"Agreed," John said as he added the honey and cream to his coffee, "I will recheck the news tomorrow evening and see how things play out. Then, we can should together."

"Sounds like a plan," said Joseph"

John closed his laptop and stood. "I had better go and get prettied up, there is a moose out there with my name it."

"That's the attitude, John. I had better get breakfast started before Pamela gets in here and gives me an ass whoop'in."

After breakfast, Joseph called everyone around the fireplace, where he proudly produced a large framed picture of his latest hunting heroine, Kat. To thunderous applause, Joseph hung the portrait of Kat and her moose beside her grandfather. The family resemblance was unmistakable, and the same Weatherby rifle was front and centre in both photos. It was the beginning of another fantastic day.

The afternoon was cold and clear. Not a cloud in the sky. John and Kat set up on a ridge where they had seen fresh moose tracks earlier in the morning. With her binoculars, Kat's keen young eyes were glassing the area around a large bog.

"Poppa, I see a moose," as she passed the binoculars to John. "Over there by that tree, about 600 meters."

John spotted the head slowly moving out of the bush next to a half-fallen spruce tree. He checked the range with his rangefinder. Kat's estimate was bang on.

John smiled as he shouldered the Remington 700 and dialled the scope's turrets to compensate for the 10 KPH easterly wind and a range of 600 meters before chambering a round.

After waiting a long six seconds, the moose walked into the open. Condensation rose as the big bull sniffed the frigid air for danger, offering a clear shot to John. He breathed easily in and out, in the relaxed manner of a man who had spent his entire life handling firearms. He centred the vitals in his crosshairs and lovingly squeezed the trigger. BOOM!

The 180-grain Nosler Partition Spitzer streaked from the powerful 300 Winchester Short Magnum cartridge at 3,017 feet per second and buried itself deep into the bull's chest, destroying his heart.

The bull staggered, crumpled and fell to the snow-covered ground. John immediately chambered another round and held the moose in his crosshairs, but the big moose never moved.

"Wow, Poppa, that was a nice shot!" Kat said, her smile from ear to ear.

John looked back at her, smiling. "Let's go check him out."

Once again, the radio crackled to life. This time it was Caroline. Knowing the single shot came from the area where John and Kat were hunting, she knew the answer before asking. "What's going on out there, you two?"

Kat keyed the mic, "Me and Poppa, we're the dream team!"

They all shared a laugh.

J2 keyed up, "Headed your way."

Joseph called that he was also en route.

John clicked on the safety, placed the Remington in the scabbard of his quad, and climbed aboard. Kat followed suit, and they both fired up their machines.

It was a slow trip down to the moose as they carefully picked their way around the rocks and trees. They dismounted and slowly walked over to the moose. Kat carefully checked him out under John's watchful eye; he was gone.

Together they bowed their heads and shared a silent prayer for the second magnificent animal that gave his life for them.

As the others appeared at the crest of the ridge, Kat waved at them. She was easy to spot in her blaze orange, and they slowly descended into the bog.

The gang thoroughly ribbed John about being out hunted by his granddaughter, and John enjoyed the ribbing. He was more than capable of retaliation, but he was enjoying Kat's new status as much as she did.

They loaded the moose on Joseph's trailer, and the team headed back to camp.

5:30 AM, 19 NOVEMBER 2020

The MacIntyre Homestead

As usual, Liz was up early. Her routine was to go out with John to feed the livestock and gather fresh eggs before breakfast. When one of them was away, they naturally filled in for one another.

Liz was a very fit woman. At 65, she didn't look her age. Yes, she had to colour her hair to preserve her natural blonde, but that was a minor detail.

Liz and John were always very active. John being in the army, fitness was part of the job, and Liz naturally went right along. After they attended to the animals, they would walk around the farm.

Today was no different. It was a beautiful November morning. The sun was rising in the east as it had every day since the dawn of time. The air was cold and clear, and the ground was covered with a light dusting of snow. Liz walked quickly around the farm, checking the fences and the animals, then she went back for a hot shower before breakfast.

Over coffee, Liz went over John's checklist again and planned her day. She was worried, but she didn't share John's level of paranoia. Her first phone call was to her daughter-in-law Samantha, John Jr's wife. This conversation would be easy; John Jr was exactly like his father. He and Samantha embraced the whole prepping thing without question. She would be right on board.

"Hi, Mom," and exclaimed, "It's early! What's up?"

"Sam, John called last night; you know he is a news junkie. He has information that a severe flu virus is breaking out globally. He told me to warn you and said you should stock up on staples and prepare to come here should this go bad." Liz replied anxiously.

"Mom, I picked up similar information last night myself on the internet. You're preaching to the converted here. Remember, I worked with Dad and J2 on those checklists. I am looking over ours as we speak," she joked, using John's familiar acronym for her husband.

"You know John," Liz added. "When someone throws him a bone, he runs with it. He even called Alex Dickson and talked to him about it, and they are both very concerned."

"I decided to keep Lauren out of school. We are heading into town after breakfast to stock up," replied Samantha.

"Do you think it's going to be bad, Sam?" Liz asked.

Sam snickered, "I know you believe Dad can seem a little out there sometimes, but something is up, and yes, I am worried. Be safe going to town, Mom. Love you."

"Love you too, Sam, be careful," Liz added.

Liz then called the neighbours and filled them in. Her last call was the one Liz dreaded. Unlike John Jr. and Caroline, David, their youngest, did not embrace prepping. When he was young, David went along with all the family adventures, and he did go to Scouts. He started to distance himself from his family after he met his wife, Chantel. She was the polar opposite of John, and they didn't see eye to eye on many things.

David and Chantel never participated in the family preparedness plans, and Liz knew they would not play along.

David answered on the first ring, "Mom, how are things at the Ponderosa?"

"Things are grand here, David. Is Chantel up?" Liz asked.

"She's still in the shower, Mom. She was up late last night, grading homework."

Liz bit her lip and got to the point of the call, "David, your father called last night. He is worried about a flu virus that is going around. This is a bad one, David; it's all around the world."

"So, Mom, where is he this time? Ah, yes, it's November. Out killing innocent animals again?" David asked sarcastically. He didn't expect an answer. "Mom, I don't need to tell you what Dad's like. You've been married to him for 40 years. I watch CNN every night, not a peep about this so-called flu," replied David.

"He got this information on the internet. Our friend General Alex Dickson confirmed it, and he is worried, too, " Liz explained.

"Mom, those two old warhorses are as bad as those tin foil hat-wearing conspiracy theorists they listen to on YouTube. According to the news, nothing is going on, and I have received no information from the University whatsoever," David argued.

"David, I don't like your tone. You will speak respectfully of your father. I know he can sometimes be a little off the wall, but he knows about these things. You should take him seriously," argued Liz.

David cut her off, "A little off the wall? Mom, the man has a bunker with guns in the basement of the house, enough ammo to take on China, and enough food to feed an army. That silliness should have stopped when the Cold War ended."

"David, please; he wants you to stock up on food, water, and medical supplies, to watch this situation and be ready to come to the farm if it gets worse, that's all." Liz pleaded.

"Ok, Mom, I will pick up a few groceries on the way home tonight. I hope that makes him feel better, but we are staying put. Unlike him, we have lives to lead." David conceded.

"David, he loves you. We love you," Liz said sternly.

"I know, Mom; I'm sorry. Look, I need to be at the University early today. Love you." And he hung up.

* * *

After that call, Liz needed another coffee before she called Karl at the Co-op. Karl and John were good friends. Karl would take this seriously. She filled him in on John's phone call and placed the order.

"Thank you so much for the heads-up, Liz. Anita and I appreciate this. We trust John's judgement. We will get ready."

Karl promised the order would be delivered today. Karl was a man of word, so Liz had no doubts he would make it happen.

When she calmed down, she dressed to go into town, putting four N95 masks, four pairs of surgical gloves, plus hand sanitizer in her purse. After locking the house and setting the alarm, she looked in the back seat of her Suburban. The get-home bag John always had packed in each vehicle was sitting in the rear. She could hear her husband's words when he put the bag in the new Suburban they had just brought home. *There is enough gear and food in there to last a minimum of 72 hours. Should anything go wrong, this will get you home.'* That gave Liz comfort and made her smile. She opened the garage door and backed out. She closed the garage door, and then she drove into Owen Sound.

Her first stop was the bank. Withdrawing five thousand dollars in cash required going to a teller.

"Good morning Mrs. MacIntyre. How are you today?" asked the young man behind the teller's window.

"I'm very well, thank you, Gordon. Why are you working up front today?" questioned Liz.
"Mr. Allison asked me to fill in. We had three tellers call in sick today; some flu bug is going around," Gordon replied casually.

Liz's eyes widened at the news. "Gordon," she said, reaching into her purse, "You take this mask and gloves and wear them today. Please think seriously about calling in sick tomorrow. John warned me about this bad flu going around, and you should do some research online."

It was Gordon's turn to be shocked. Gordon Cameron was a Reserve Officer with the Owen Sound Army Cadets, The Grey and Simcoe Foresters. Gordon knew John well. John had spoken many times at Cadet functions as a guest speaker. During Cadet training camps, he would also help out with cooking and first aid training. Gordon had a world of respect for John MacIntyre. Gordon took the mask and gloves from Liz, passed her the envelope full of cash and thanked her.

That conversation spooked Liz. *John is right, I had better take this very seriously.* Her next stop was the local big box store, where she could get almost everything she needed in one location. She parked, donned the N95 mask and gloves, grabbed two oversized carts and headed inside. She was on a mission.

A few people were coughing while they shopped, and the pharmacy lineup was long; even more coughing people were searching for flu meds. Many people looked at her, figuring she was a nutbar. Liz, however, would not be deterred. This was getting real.

Thirty minutes later, she checked out. She wrestled the carts to the back of her Suburban, and with mask and gloves on, she loaded up. People whispered to one another as they walked by. *Yep, I probably did look like a lunatic.*

Liz repeated the scenario at Costco and again at the liquor store. All tolled $7,358.39 on her Visa.

Liz was back home by noon; she had an overwhelming need to take a shower. She felt unclean.

Once clean, Liz made another coffee. Leaving the cup on the table, she closed her eyes and breathed in the aroma through her nose, her hands still shaking as she tried to digest what she had just witnessed.

Liz picked up the now-familiar checklist and put it back in its rightful place in the binder. *I married a good man.*

6:00 PM, 19 NOVEMBER 2020

Camp Thunder

After supper, John excused himself to check on the news. He was anxious and was trying not to show it before he got a good handle on the situation. His internet sources reported infections and deaths were increasing globally from the mystery flu strain. Numbers were still small; however, growing deaths were the confirmation John sought. Any loss of life so soon after infection was a very bad sign.

The WHO finally declared a pandemic watch but stressed the situation was under control. Under pressure from the US President, the CDC reluctantly followed the lead of the WHO and issued the same statement word for word. The mainstream media reported the very same prepared release from the WHO and CDC that stated there was no immediate need to be concerned.

When questioned, government spokespeople all parroted a similar message. The public does not need to be worried. Those statements caused familiar alarm bells to go off in John's head. He was concerned, very concerned.

John quickly called Liz to update her and check on her preparations.

"John, I got the checklist and did everything you had written down." She also filled him in on her conversation with Gordon Cameron and the sick people around Owen Sound.

"Excellent, I'm not a lunatic after all," he chuckled.

"That's why I love you so much. I will update everyone," she promised.

"I have to run, Liz. We have to light a fire under everyone here, and they will need to fly out in the morning. Stay safe. I love you."

Liz replied, "I love you too, John."

Returning to the lodge, John found everyone gathered around the fireplace. Franz Roske, one of Joseph's regulars, was on retirement leave from the German special forces, the Kommando Spezialkrafte or KSK. Franz had the entire lodge in stitches as he played his guitar and sang in broken English. The man may very well have missed his calling as a comedian.

John looked at Joseph. As former operators, they both knew the look that something was up. Joseph nodded in return and walked into the kitchen, followed closely by John.

Joseph made coffee while John filled him in and started writing the information in point form on a notepad. It was like old times as the two ageing soldiers studied the data and laid out a course of action. First, they agreed to inform everyone of the world's dangers and insist that they make immediate attempts to return home.

Back during their days in the military, an Operations Order or Ops Order would be drawn up as a means of communication through the chain of command. A simple format was used that listed all the relevant points logically, ensuring nothing was left out. The acronym was SMEAC, and it stood for Situation, Mission, Execution, Administration, Command and signals. Using the familiar format, John and Joseph wrote up the information they would share with everyone in the camp.

Satisfied they had covered everything, Joseph went into the lounge area. Using a loud commanding voice, Joe called for everyone's immediate attention. The singing stopped, and everyone looked at Joseph with a look of concern on their faces.

"Everyone, please, listen very carefully! You are ALL to gather around the fireplace in 15 minutes for an important meeting. Ensure everyone in your cabin is also in attendance. Grab a quick bathroom break and be back here at 8 PM, don't be late!"

Joseph then turned and went back into the kitchen.

The tone of Joseph's voice and the look on his face made it abundantly clear that he was dead serious. Everyone quickly dispersed

At 8:00 PM sharp, John and Joseph walked out of the kitchen.

A group of sombre faces stared back at them as Joseph checked the numbers and confirmed everyone was there.

John began, "Thank you all for being here on such short notice. We have vital information to share with you. This situation is gravely serious, and we require your undivided attention. Please hold any questions until I am finished.

THE SITUATION:

"There is a severe flu pandemic breaking out all over the globe. The rate of infection is out of control worldwide and growing exponentially. Up until yesterday, no deaths were reported. However, the death rate is now beginning to climb rapidly—any deaths this soon after infection is unprecedented and must be taken very seriously. We have no information yet regarding the ratio of infections to deaths.

"So far, the Governments of the world are playing down this situation. We believe this is a grave mistake. I repeat, Governments are containing this information in an attempt to keep the panic down. Very little is being reported in the mainstream media so far this evening.

"Reliable sources close to us have confirmed that this flu is acting exactly like the Spanish Flu of 1918. It hits hard and kills fast. Worse yet, no known antivirals affect this flu. I repeat, no known antivirals have any effect on this flu. No one knows where this flu started or how it spreads. However, given the rate at which infections are growing, we do not doubt that it is airborne and spreads easily between humans."

THE MISSION:

"Everyone here is to make plans and preparations to return

to their respective homes and families as expeditiously as possible."

THE EXECUTION:

"Joseph has contacted Red Lake Air Service, and they have confirmed that no one there is infected. As of 7:30 this evening, no one in Vermillion Bay has been infected. They will send three float planes to ferry us all to Vermillion Bay. The aircraft will arrive at 0600 hours in the morning, and departure will be as soon as we are loaded. Ensure you pack all your gear tonight. Check and double-check everything."

ADMINISTRATION:

"Joseph will make his satellite phone available for anyone who needs to make travel arrangements. The planes will leave here as soon as we load up in the morning. If you cannot make travel arrangements here, you must do it en route or in Vermillion Bay. Is that perfectly clear?

John looked around the room at all the heads, silently nodding in confirmation.

"Joseph has a supply of N95 face masks and rubber gloves. He will issue some to everyone after breakfast. Please see us when we wrap up if you do not know how to wear them. If you travel via personal automobile, I strongly recommend you fill up on fuel before leaving Vermillion Bay. Fuel stops are few and far between up here. Purchasing extra fuel containers and filling them in Vermilion Bay is strongly recommended. Again, before you leave Vermillion Bay, ensure you have plenty of cash on hand. You do not want to get caught unprepared. Ensure you charge all your electronics before you leave, and if possible, purchase a backup battery pack and get it fully charged. Pamela will have breakfast ready at 0430 in the morning. As well she will prepare travel lunches for everyone. Be sure to pick some up as soon as you finish breakfast.

"The aircraft will all be filled to capacity; therefore, Joseph will arrange to have any meat and fish shipped to your homes as soon as this thing passes.

"Lastly, Joseph and Pamela will happily refund everyone for their unused time here.

COMMAND AND SIGNALS:

"Once in Vermillion Bay, everyone will be in control of their travel arrangements.

"Travel safely, and God bless you all. Are there any questions?" asked John.

Everyone was stunned into silence. Franz Roske being military, understood fully. He quickly rose and addressed John.

"John, this is worldwide and spreading fast, have you or your contacts any information regarding border closures?"

"Excellent question Franz. No one we spoke to this evening had heard of any countries closing borders or initiating quarantines. That, however, could change quickly. This situation is very dynamic, and Governments never react as we expect them to. This is why everyone must get back home as soon as possible. We will monitor this all night, and if anything changes, we will let everyone know ASAP. I know Joseph and I will not get much sleep tonight," John replied.

"May I help?" Franz asked, "I have reliable contacts in the German military. Germany is five hours ahead, and that may be beneficial."

"Thanks, Franz, that would be super," replied John.

With the only question answered, everyone hurried off to pack and make travel arrangements.

The MacIntyres were already scheduled to leave in the morning, so they were packed. The MacIntyre gang swarmed John as soon as they returned to the cabin. John let them know

Liz was busy contacting the family and filling them in on the situation.

With that, everyone ratcheted down several notches. He explained the extent of his research and his conversations with General Alex Dixon. John looked at them all one by one; the trip home could get interesting. Given the gear they brought, they had driven up to Vermillion Bay in three separate vehicles.

"Our return will be a little different, and we will need to pair up," John informed them.

Kat immediately spoke up, "I'm with you, Poppa." That brought a collective smile.

Then it's settled. We will pair up in our hunting groups," John concluded.

Everyone agreed.

"Next, when we get to Vermillion Bay, J2, can you go on the hunt for gas cans and gas?" John asked.

"Sure, thing Dad," he replied.

"Greg, Caroline, can you two run to that little grocery store and pick up as much water and extra food as possible and maybe grab some rechargeable battery packs for our devices if they have any?"

They both nodded in unison.

"Kat and I will hit up that outfitter in town and buy as much ammo as we can. Does everyone have their Bug Out bags in their vehicles," John gave them an evil stare? "I better not hear a no from anyone?"

"Yes, Dad," came the collective reply.

"Good, I raised bright kids," John said, smiling. "I suggest we try to drive right through, and it's a long way, and the one that's not driving can catch a nap."

Caroline looked at her father. "Dad, Kat doesn't have her license!"

"I know," he replied, "she can keep me entertained, and if I need a break, one of you can spare me off."

"I could drive Poppa; you let me drive at home," Kat added excitedly.

"I know he does, sweetheart," Caroline replied as she glared at her Father.

"Guilty as charged," John said, holding his hands up to surrender.

"There is a big difference between the backroads of Owen Sound and up here. Besides, it may well get nasty out there. I would be happier if you didn't drive Kat," Caroline ordered.

"Ok, Mom," Kat replied, looking defeated.

Caroline looked at John, "Dad?"

"Yes, ma'am, understood. Oh, one last thing," John said as he stood, "Keep at least one rifle close, in the case, of course, but close."

J2 and Greg both nodded in agreement.

"I'm going to the lodge. Joe, Franz and I will monitor the situation all night on the computer and shortwave radio. I love you all."

"Goodnight," came the collective reply.

John, Joseph, and Franz were huddled around the computer, taking turns, checking with contacts and taking notes. The one constant was the rapid rise in cases of the flu being reported, along with an exponential increase in deaths.

As the night went on, the three men took turns between napping and using the computer. At 0300, Franz was on the computer with his contacts back home. I was 0800 hours in Germany, five hours ahead of Camp Thunder

"Damn," Franz called out, "the Russians just announced they are closing the border at 0900 Moscow time. Shit, shit, shit, this situation is unravelling fast."

John and Joseph were asleep. They leaped to their feet, almost banging heads with one another. As they gathered around the computer to read the message, Joseph's satellite phone rang.

Joseph picked up on the second ring. "Hello, Joseph Thunder."

"Hello, old friend, it's Alex. Is John with you?"

"Yes, he is, and we have Franz Roske with us, a trusted friend retired from the German KSK," Joseph replied. "I will put you on speaker Alex."

"Good morning, gentlemen," Alex sounded like he hadn't slept in days. "I have bad news. Listen carefully. I only have a few minutes, and this is highly confidential." I just got off the phone with Calvin Rich from the CDC. Infection rates are still out of control worldwide, and the CDC fears that with no workable antiviral available, the mortality rate of this bug will exceed 50%." Alex paused to let the reality of that statement settle in. "At 0800 New York time, the WHO, the CDC and the UN will declare a full-blown pandemic. I know I don't need to explain that to any of you."

The three men let out a collective, "Damn!"

"You got it," Alex agreed, "this shit is getting real. Godspeed, my friends, I have to go."

"Thank you, Alex, and remember my invitation. God bless you and Carol," John added as the call ended.

The three men looked at one another. "Ok," John said, "Joseph, can you call up Red Lake Air Service, get old Charlie out of bed and see if he can be here earlier?

"Franz, you and I better go and wake up the cabins. Everyone needs to get up and moving right now. We will meet back in the kitchen to help Pamela with breakfast."

The three old soldiers headed out with purpose. Fifteen minutes later, they met back in the kitchen. All the campers were up and lugging their gear to the docks. As Joe poured the coffee, he announced that Charlie would get the ball rolling on his end.

One by one, the folks started rolling into the kitchen with looks of shock on their collective faces. Over breakfast, John filled everyone in on the changes. It was NOT a good day.

* * *

At 0530, Joseph lit up the dock lights and called out to Charlie on his handheld radio. There was a hint of a glow from the sun rising on the eastern horizon. Five minutes later, the unmistakable drone of three de-Havilland Beaver aircraft circled overhead. In the almost complete darkness, the three veteran bush pilots gently dropped the old Beavers down onto the lake's calm surface and pulled up to the docks.

Joseph, John, and Franz tied them off while 15 sombre faces looked on, their future uncertain. Goodbyes were exchanged, and the MacIntyres and Thunders shared a group hug. John and Joseph lingered in that hug for a bit longer, both knowing what was to come.

"Godspeed," waved Pamela and Joseph as everyone boarded the aircraft.

Not a single one of Camp Thunders's customers asked for a refund.

7:30 AM, 20 NOVEMBER 2020

The Journey Home

The flight to Vermillion Bay went smoothly, arriving at 0730. By the time everyone was offloaded, more countries had followed Russia's lead and closed their borders. Germany was one of them.

John approached Franz. "You are welcome to join us at the farm Franz. We have plenty of room, plenty of food and gear. A man with your skills would be a real asset to our group."

While they were together overnight, the men had plenty of time to get to know one another. Franz was 55 and a widower. His wife had lost her battle with cancer two years before, and they had no children. Franz was officially on retirement leave, and his last day of service was in two weeks.

Franz looked out over Eagle Lake, inhaled deeply of the cold, clean, pine-scented air and thought silently for a moment. "John," he replied, "they may let me through, cancel my retirement and put me back on active duty."

Franz paused for another moment looking out over the lake as the sun rose. There was no time for long thought or debate. *God, I love Canada.* He turned to face John. "It will be hell over there, John. I would be more than pleased to accept your offer."

The two men shook hands and loaded Franz's gear into John's F150.

The other man that was stranded was Hatto Masatoshi. Japan closed its borders to the world only seconds after Russia did. Hatto was single and living alone, and both his parents were deceased. Hatto was a self-employed martial arts instructor, and John knew Hatto would be another valuable addition to the group.

John made the same offer to Hatto, who, without hesitation, bowed slightly and said: "John, I would be honoured. Thank you so very much."

They loaded Hatto's gear into Greg and Caroline's SUV.

Everyone else was determined to make it home, border closing and quarantines be damned. They all said farewells, and the expanded MacIntyre clan climbed into their vehicles and headed south.

7:30 AM, 20 NOVEMBER 2020

The MacIntyre Homestead

L iz had just got off the phone with John. This morning's update was outright scary. She was happy that they were making their way home. She was also pleased to hear that Franz and Hatto would join them. *The more, the merrier and these two sound like competent men.*

John Jr. had already called Sam. Liz wasn't worried about her; Sam was on board. David and Chantel concerned her, and she hoped he would accept this news and come to the farm.

Seeing his Mother's name on the call display, David picked right up. "Good morning, Mom," he said somewhat sarcastically.

"David, I don't like that tone," she replied.

"I know, I know, I'm sorry, Mom, what is it now? Are UFOs landing?" He asked sarcastically.

"David, this is serious. People are dying from this flu. I was in Owen Sound yesterday, and people were off work sick, and some were out and about coughing, spreading the damned flu around," Liz informed him.

"Mom, yes, there were some faculty and students down with the flu, and I saw something on the news. The government is telling everyone not to panic. I did as you asked, I got food, water and stuff and filled the car with gas, but Chantel and I are staying here. The government has a handle on this thing, and it will be fine."

"Son, you both have sick days. Why don't you take them and come up here? If this all blows over, no harm done," Liz begged.

"Sorry, Mom, we can't. We have careers, and we need to be here," David insisted.

Realizing the futility of continuing, Liz gave up. "Ok, David, I hear you. You two, be careful. Wear masks at schools, ok?"

"Yes, Mom, we will wear masks," he said, as he shook his head in a no gesture.

7:30 AM, 20 NOVEMBER 2020

Vermillion Bay, Ontario

Armed with their list of items to pick up, the MacIntyre gang went their separate ways, agreeing to meet in 20 minutes at the gas station.

Twenty minutes later, they filled up the vehicles and gas cans and did a quick inventory of the new supplies. John, Kat, and Franz had scored 20 boxes of 30-06, 21 boxes of 308, 10 boxes of 300 WSM, three battle bricks of 7.62X39 Russian, and 2,000 .22 rounds.

"We even got 250 12-gauge slugs and another 300 of double 00 buck, and, as a bonus, 1 case of MREs. The shop owner thought I was a lunatic," laughed John.

"He was right," joked Caroline, to the collective laughter of all.

Hatto helped fill ten 20-litre plastic fuel cans and insisted on paying for everyone's fuel.

Caroline and Greg managed to pick up a bag full of premade sandwiches, jerky, energy drinks and cliff bars, plus 3 of those USB rechargeable power cells. Everyone withdrew as much cash as they could from the ATM.

The group secured the bulk of fuel in John and J2's F150s, then secured three of the 20-litre plastic fuel cans to the roof of Greg's SUV. The food and ammo were divided between the three vehicles, so everyone had some of everything.

"Remember what I said last night about keeping a gun handy?" John reminded everyone.

They all nodded.

"Ok, I will lead. Greg, let's put your SUV in the middle. Everyone put your 2-way radios on the home channel 154.100

MHz. Keep your eyes open and stay close," John said. "Let's roll!"

It was 08:10 on a beautiful bright morning when the MacIntyre convoy pulled out onto Hwy 17. Thunder Bay, with just over one hundred thousand souls, was five hours away. That was one of John's worries; a lot can go wrong in five hours. Hoping to catch any developments, he turned on his satellite radio, alternating between the channels as they drove.

* * *

Despite the Americans closing all the borders, Canada's Prime Minister delayed closing the border with the US. Due to the vast amount of trade between the two countries, she didn't want any Canadians trapped there. She opted instead to have the Canadian Military set up screening posts to check returning Canadians for infection and hold those they suspect in 48-hour quarantine.

All international airports were to stop accepting flights by midnight. Citizens were asked to shelter in place, restrict their travel and report to the Hospitals if they developed any symptoms. John was thankful there was no mention of road closures and citywide quarantines.

The time switched from Central to the Eastern time zone an hour west of Thunder Bay. It would now be 1400 hours local time when they hit the city. The MacIntyre convoy circled Thunder Bay on the Hwy 102 bypass. There was a heavy police presence but no roadblocks.

John studied the scene as they drove. *Things are starting to heat up.*

One hour later, they crossed the bridge in Nipigon, the last major barrier and John's biggest concern. Trans-Canada Highway 17 runs through Northern Ontario from the Manitoba border to Quebec. In northern Ontario, there is only one alternate route: Hwy 11.

Roughly 1-hour west of Thunder Bay, the two highways

intersect and become one. At this point, there is only ONE road through Northern Ontario. Hwy 11/17 parallel the shoreline of Lake Superior until they arrive at the small town of Nipigon. The Hwy 11/17 bridge spans the Nipigon River and is the only way through. Had that been closed, the MacIntyres would have been swimming across. Once past the Hwy 11/17 bridge, the highway splits again. Hwy 11 takes the northern route, and Hwy 17 follows the rugged shoreline of Lake Superior.

The convoy would follow Hwy 17. The first leg consisted of roughly eight hours driving around Lake Superior to the City of Sault Ste. Marie, Ontario, a spectacular, beautiful drive during better circumstances. The area was sparsely populated, with only a few small towns. The most significant hazard here was hitting a moose on the road.

John was breathing easier now, having crossed the bridge at Nipigon. An hour east, Nipigon, Caroline and Greg's Jeep Cherokee was getting thirsty. The group stopped at the picturesque little town of Terrace Bay for fuel. Terrace Bay sat high above Lake Superior and offered an impressive view of the mighty lake.

Electing to preserve the fuel cans for emergencies, they pulled into a Shell fuel station. The little town was quiet, so John quizzed the kid at the gas station for news regarding the flu pandemic, but he had no idea what John was talking about. So far, so good. A coffee and quick bathroom stop later, and they were moving again.

From Terrace Bay, they drove another three hours of rugged Lake Superior shoreline straight through to Wawa. Both the MacIntyre F150s were equipped with the 2.7 Liter Eco Boost engine, giving them an impressive fuel range of 1,300 kilometres before needing a fill-up. The Cherokee, however, was almost down to half a tank. Again, they elected to conserve the fuel cans and join the short lineup at Wawa's Esso fuel station.

Kat and J3 hit the coffee shop while the adults fueled the fleet.

"This will be our last fill-up, folks. If the lineups are starting here, people are beginning to wake up to what's happening —getting around, Sault Ste. Marie may be challenging," John informed the crew as they shared drinks and snacks. "It's 1900 hours, and we will make the 220-kilometre run through to the Soo in the dark. Keep an eye out for moose, everyone and stay sharp."

The night was dark, and snow started falling heavily as they made their trek through Lake Superior Provincial Park and on to Sault Ste. Marie.

"Let's see what is happening around the world," John announced as he pressed the volume up on the F-150s radio.

Good evening, this is Peter Mansfield from the CBC newsroom, and this is The National.

Tonight, we continue our special coverage as this worldwide pandemic unfolds.

We have breaking news. Health Canada confirms that 12 hours after a pandemic was declared, there are over one million confirmed flu cases in Canada. Worse yet, they have confirmed the death toll to be over one thousand.

The Prime Minister has just released the following statement.

Fellow Canadians, this is a sombre day for our nation and the entire world. This flu pandemic that has struck so quickly is presenting us with infection rates never before seen.

So far, the death toll is low compared to infection rates, but sadly we expect that to get worse. As you have heard, most countries have either closed their borders or put strict screening and control measures in place.

I called an emergency session of Parliament earlier today. The danger we are facing is unprecedented. Given this, a unanimous decision was made to invoke the Emergencies Act.

With this announcement, Canada will close all international airports to international travel, effective at midnight tonight. Our border with the United States will remained open to Canadian citizens returning from the US.

Under the Emergencies Act, all the Provinces and Territories have requested aid from the Canadian Armed Forces to assist in the operation of screening stations at US borders, Provincial borders and other strategic locations across the country.

Screening is mandatory, and those who fail the screening will be placed in quarantine and under medical care.

Please bear in mind that under the Emergency Act, our military will be aiding our police forces. They will have all the powers of a police officer and he armed. Please give them all the due respect you would any law enforcement officer.

All our reserve forces have been placed on 24-hour notice of deployment, and all military leaves have been cancelled.

The Provincial Premiers have also ordered all schools and non-essential public services closed. At this time, we are also asking all businesses to voluntarily go to minimum staffing to prevent the spread of infection.

Social distancing, wearing an N95 mask and frequent hand washing is the most effective means to prevent this virus's spread. We recommend Canadians shelter at home and ensure they have plenty of food and water. Please do not hoard food and supplies.

Only by pulling together can we beat this virus.
Thank you, Merci.

Peter Mansfield's familiar voice returned to the radio. We are indeed living in troubling times. The last time Canada had armed troops on the streets was in 1970 during the October

Crisis.

Please stay tuned for breaking news as it happens.

This is Peter Mansfield, and this is the CBC News for this 20th day of November 2020.

Good night.

"Oh, my God, Poppa that sounds scary. Were you born when that October Crisis happened," Kat asked.

"In 1970 I was a just a young fella, about your age. I'm older than dirt, remember," John chuckled.

The three enjoyed a moment of laughter.

"We learned about that event at school. The separatist movement in Quebec was powerful back then, and those people killed a man didn't they Poppa?"

"Yes, they did," replied John. "They kidnapped two men, Pierre LaPorte, a Quebec Provincial politician who they murdered. James Cross, a British diplomat, was held but eventually released. Prime Minister Trudeau immediately invoked the war measures act and put the army in the streets. Those were scary times." John stated.

"Do you think it could happen again? I mean, people killing people?" Kat asked.

"Yes, it very well could," Replied John.

A frightened look crossed Katherine's young face.

"Don't let this trouble, you sweetheart. We are together, and we are prepared," John replied confidently.

Both he and Franz knew full well that perilous times lie ahead.

* * *

The heavy snowfall added an hour to their drive to the Soo. As the group approached the truck inspection station just west of the city, the traffic came to a stop.

John could see the flashing lights in the distance. He picked up his hand-held radio. "There goes the neighbourhood, everyone. It looks like the police are routing all the traffic into the inspection station. Have your IDs ready, and make sure your rifles are not loaded and are adequately stowed. Everyone put on those N95 face masks Joe gave us."

Fifteen minutes later, at 10:00 PM, they approached the roadblock. Portable light towers bathed the area in a brilliant white light. Three large military trucks and two Ontario Provincial Police cruisers, lights flashing, blocked the highway. The roadblock was manned by two soldiers and two police officers. A heavily armed soldier stood slightly back, apparently the senior rank. All were wearing N95 masks. Off to the right side, John noticed another six soldiers in full battle gear, armed with C7 rifles, standing by should something go wrong.

John could make out a quarantine area, a large green military tent in the centre, and armed soldiers posted at the entrance. A paramedic vehicle and an army ambulance were stationed just outside the quarantine area, where a smaller military tent was set up. Two unarmed soldiers were stationed there, ushering the occupants of vehicles into a secondary screening area. Two more armed soldiers and a police officer watched over them.

There was also a police van parked off by the ambulances. Two armed soldiers and one police officer guarding it. John could make out two people inside the van.

The car in front of John pulled up and stopped. One police officer and one soldier took the left side of the vehicle, while another police officer and soldier took the opposite side. The police officer at the driver's side did the talking while the other three carefully studied the vehicle and the occupants.

John had his window lowered. There was a hint of diesel in

the air from all the generators, and the steady droning made hearing difficult. John could just make out the conversation, which didn't sound cordial. The people inside refused to show IDs and informed the officer they had rights. John noticed both occupants were unmasked and coughing. The officer politely asked the driver to pull to the right.

"Fuck you!" the man yelled back. "We have rights, and you can't hold us here." He then started to roll ahead.

The soldiers by the car quickly stepped back. The soldier in charge signalled the armed guards. Four armed soldiers immediately surrounded the car; rifles pointed menacingly at the occupants. Two more pulled open the doors and dragged the two out of the vehicle.

Kat watched the scene unfold in front of them, wide-eyed and mouth opened, having never witnessed anything like this before. "Oh shit!" She exclaimed. "Sorry, Poppa."

Within 15 seconds, the couple was zip-tied and carried to the waiting police van. Another police officer drove the car into a holding area.

When things settled down, the police officer signalled for John to pull up.

"I'm sorry you had to witness that, sir. May I see your IDs, please?

John passed his ID to the officer, his veteran's ID card on the top.

"I will not ask anyone to remove their masks. Is anyone experiencing any flu-like symptoms?" asked the officer.

"No, officer," they each replied.

"Sir, I see your ex-military."

"Yes, Officer, I served in JTF2," Replied John proudly.

"Thank you for your service Sir, and this young lady is?"

"My granddaughter," Replied John. "Her father and mother are behind me, and my son and grandson are behind them in the pickup."

The officer looked at Franz, "Sir, I see you're a German citizen and a military veteran, is that correct?"

"Yes, Sir," replied Franz. "When my government closed the borders, John offered to put me up until this blows over."

"Thank you for your service Sir. The officer looked at John questioningly.

"Yes, officer, Franz is a friend and is welcome to stay with my family as long as needed."

"I see you have quite a bit of gear in here. Where are you folks coming from?" asked the officer.

"We had just spent the past two weeks at a fly-in hunting camp north of Vermillion Bay," stated John.

"Nice," replied the officer. "Any luck?"

Kat opened her phone and proudly showed him the picture of her moose.

"Wow!" the officer exclaimed. "That's the biggest moose I have ever seen."

"Ditto," replied John and Franz in unison.

"Then I assume you have firearms in the vehicle, Sir."

"Yes," John replied. "All secured and stowed away properly."

"Very well," the officer replied. "Pull up in front of the ambulances there, and the medics will quickly check you out. Have a nice evening."

"Thank you, officer, same to you."

As instructed, John pulled his F150 up in front of the ambulances. One of the soldiers approached and asked everyone to step into the tent. The medics asked if anyone had flu-like symptoms and checked their temperature, eyes, ears, and throats. Upon giving them all a clean bill of health, the medic announced they were free to go. John pulled up to the end of the inspection station lot and waited for the others to catch up.

"Wow, Poppa, that was intense!" exclaimed Kat.

"Sure was. Let that be a lesson for you, Kat. When I pulled up, I had all our IDs ready and handed them to him as soon as he asked. Make his job easy, and things will usually go your way. When I handed him our IDs, I made sure mine was on the top, and the very first piece he saw was my retired military ID. That will usually set the mood on a positive note. Franz and I both addressed him as Sir. We were polite, to the point and let him lead the questioning," instructed John.

"I was afraid after the previous car, he would be pissed," replied Kat.

"Police are trained to handle those situations, Kat," Franz added. "It's no different in Germany; most are professional and know how to handle themselves. I was a bit worried, but he never questioned my German citizenship. Military IDs carry a lot of credibility in most countries, and we quickly established trust. Yes, he was a real pro."

Ten minutes later, the others were through screening. They gathered around John's F150.

"That was interesting, Dad. Can they do that? I mean, drag those two out of the car like that and arrest them," Caroline asked.

"Yes, they can," John replied. "Even under the Emergency Act, certain rights are protected under the Charter of Rights and Freedoms. However, verbally assaulting and not following the directions of a law enforcement officer is a dumb move. Using a vehicle as a weapon is a serious offence, no different than pulling a gun.

"Trudeau's war measures act is no longer. It was replaced by the Emergency act in 1988. Under the act, the military has the same powers as the police. The entire incident will be on video. They will be entitled to their day in court. We better roll," John concluded as he glanced at his wrist watch.

* * *

Aside from the snow and massive police presence, Sault Ste Marie was busy. There were lineups at all gas stations, and the grocery store parking lots were full. The food stores were working on extended hours to address the situation.

The fact that two security guards were at the front doors didn't escape John's trained eye. "Look over there," he said, pointing to the right, "That's the third group of punks I've seen since we entered the city. Even the weather doesn't deter these good-for-nothings."

"They look like they are up to no good. Waiting for an opportunity," replied Franz.

"Agreed," said John, and he picked up the hand-held radio, passing the message on to the others to stay sharp.

The F150's satellite radio was reporting outbreaks of looting in cities worldwide. In Canada, Toronto seemed to be hit the hardest. The Golden Horseshoe, as it is termed, runs from Oshawa through Toronto, circles around the west end of Lake Ontario and back east to Niagara Falls and the US border. This area boasts the country's densest population: nine million people, roughly 26% of Canada's population. If the proverbial shit were to hit the fan, it would no doubt begin there.

"Nothing like a good disaster to bring out the dregs of humanity," John stated.

"Oh my God," yelled Kat when a window exploded in some electronics store just as they drove by.

John and Franz went on full alert. Three young men wearing balaclavas ran into the store.

"Shit is getting real," said Franz.

"Sure, is," replied John. "It's been one day, and that thin veil that separates civil society from anarchy is already beginning to crumble."

John checked in with Liz, using the hands-free calling feature of the F150. She had seen the latest infection and death numbers, the Prime Minister's address and the looting in Toronto on the news.

"I'm scared, John; this is getting worse," Liz said nervously.

"I know, my love, we just left the Soo. We saw looting there as well. The police and army stopped and checked us out just west of the city, and they were detaining anyone infected. Where are the kids?" John asked.

"Samantha and Lauren arrived four hours ago. David and Chantel wouldn't leave Toronto. I tried John. I'm sorry I couldn't convince them," Liz insisted.

"Damn, stubborn fools," John grumbled.

David, of course, was John and Elizabeth's youngest. He and his wife, Chantel, live in a condo in downtown Toronto. David is a professor of liberal studies at the University of Toronto. Chantel is an elementary school teacher. Chantel was a sweet girl, and John and Liz loved her like their own.

It was apparent she and David loved one another deeply. Chantel, however, was very urban and stubborn; she adopted a vegan lifestyle at a young age. David being head over heels in love, went right along. To say John locked horns with them regularly would not be an exaggeration.

"I better call him," John replied. "Don't worry; we will be home soon. Love you, Liz."

"Love you, John," replied Liz.
"I love you, Gramma," Kat added.
"Love you too, Kat," Liz replied. "Drive safe."

John pressed the voice command button on his steering wheel, "Call David MacIntyre," he spoke.

"Calling David MacIntyre," the F150 replied.

Knowing how this conversation would play out, Kat picked

up the two-way radio off the centre console and gave Franz a mischievous grin. She keyed the mic. Franz clued in immediately. Everyone in the convoy heard the phone ringing and stifled a laugh.

David finally picked up. "Hello, Dad." David had been dreading this call, and the tone of his voice made it clear.

"David, how are you two?" asked Joh cheerfully.

"We are okay, Dad, Mom called. I know you want us to go to the farm, but we don't need to worry. We have plenty of food and water here, and we have security at -"

"Security!" John cut him off. "You have one guard at the front door. He's older than me and three times my weight. If anyone tried to get in, he would keel over and die. The biggest threat he would present is falling on someone."

Kat and Franz both stifled a snicker.

"Listen, David, infection rates are out of control, and people are dying from this thing within days of infection. Your mother and I are worried to death about you two, and I can't emphasize enough how dangerous it is to be in that city right now."

"Dad, we will be fine. Please, it's ok. The government has a handle on it, and I promise to keep an eye on things," David insisted.

"The government has a handle on it," John barked sarcastically. "Now that's a contradiction of terms. I worked for these idiots for almost 40 years. Those fools couldn't organize a two-man piss parade."

"Dad, calm down. If it gets worse, we will drive up to the farm, ok?" David reassured him.

John pleaded, "David, you two must get out of the city now. I'm serious, and this situation could spiral out of control quickly."

"Dad, we are not your soldiers. You can't order us around. We will be fine, don't worry."

"Ha, don't worry," John snorted. "Does a bear shit in the God damn woods? You know bloody well we are going to worry."

"Dad, we will talk about it in the morning, ok?" David replied stubbornly.

"Suit yourself," John replied.

When he pressed the hang-up button, John was fuming. He ranted on. "God damned liberal-minded fools! They have no bloody idea what they are doing. Oh, everything is warm and fuzzy. No one means to do anyone harm. No one can enter our safe space because we have a sign-up. We can't hurt anyone's feelings. The GOVERNMENT will look after us," he ranted. "Those two snowflakes are going to be the death of me yet."

Kat and Franz were beside themselves, trying not to burst into laughter; the others were in stitches.

John looked over at them, "What the hell are you two chuckleheads laughing at," he asked with a grin. Then he noticed the two-way radio in Kats' hand. "Ahhh, you think that was funny, eh," John grinned.

Unable to hold it in any longer, they both burst out into laughter, the laughter of the others clearly heard over the radio.

"Dad, you're hilarious," Caroline said through the radio, wiping the tears from her eyes. "Let me call them in the morning; maybe I can get through to them."

This is a serious situation. Like so many others, David and Chantel have their heads in the sand," John barked.

"Let me call him, ok, Dad?" Caroline asked.

"Ok," John agreed. "I don't need to get my heart rate up like that. The Goddamn thing may just give out on me," he laughed.

The hourly news was back on the radio at midnight. The group listened intently as the announcer read off the latest statistics.

Good evening, this is Peter Mansfield from the CBC News Room, and this is The National.

Tonight, the worldwide death toll from the flu rises. Law and order have begun to break down as looting breaks out in cities all around the world.

The World Health Organization has confirmed that this pandemic is raging out of control.

We are a mere sixteen hours into this most recent pandemic, and worldwide infection rates now exceed 2 billion. More shockingly, worldwide deaths were rapidly rising and reported to be over 2 million.

Health Canada confirms the death toll from the flu pandemic has now taken the lives of 1,200 Canadians. Infection numbers have also jumped to a staggering 1.5 million.

Within the past twelve hours, grocery stores and fuel stations across the country have been completely overwhelmed.

Janie Handley reports from a Costco location in Brampton, Ontario. Janie?

Hello Peter, I arrived here at the Costco located at Hwy's 7 and 427 at 10:00 PM. Costco have extended their closing time to accommodate shoppers wanting to stock up on needed supplies to ride out this pandemic.

Peter, the store manager, told me that at 7 pm the store was busier than usual, but everything was ok.

After the Prime Minister appeared on TV and announced the border closings, and asked everyone to stock up and shelter at home, all hell broke loose.

Shoppers streamed into the store. By 11 PM, fist fights had broken out over parking spaces and shopping carts. By midnight the shelves were mostly bare.

Peter, it is pandemonium here. I spoke to a lady loading goods into her car when a man and woman ran up, knocked her over and stole her supplies. When we tried to intervene they pulled knives and threatened us.

Costco had hired two security guards to assist in crowd control. Peter, tonight, they are both in the hospital with serious injuries.

Back to you, Peter.

That was CBC's Janie Handley reporting from Brampton, Ontario.

This very scene has been repeating itself not just in Canadian cities but in cities all over the world this evening.

To make matters worse, the absenteeism from the flu among police, military, and emergency workers is currently estimated at 8%.

We are witnessing the breakdown of law and order just hours into this crisis. The picture couldn't be bleaker when you factor in the still out-of-control infection rates and the rising death toll of this flu.

This is Peter Mansfield, and this is the CBC News as the day ends on this 21st of November 2020.

Good night.

The grim news report resulted in a quiet drive through to Espanola. The bright note of the evening was that the snow had stopped. Kat nodded off in the back seat. Franz was sitting on the front passenger side, his eyes closed but still awake.

When the heavily laden convoy passed through the small town of Blind River, they didn't go unnoticed. Three men in a black pickup pulled out behind them and followed at a distance. J3 noticed right away and picked up the two-way radio.

"Poppa, a pickup was sitting at the end of that side road we just passed with his lights out. As soon we went by, I saw his lights come on, and he pulled out."

"Thanks, J3," John replied. "Look alive, everyone. This may get interesting. Whoever isn't driving, load up a rifle."

Franz uncased his rifle and put in a loaded clip, as did Greg and J3. John called over the radio, "J2, you slow down a little. Let's see if he passes you. Caroline, you and I will speed up."

A few minutes later, J3 keyed the mic on his hand-held radio, "Poppa, he is not passing. He switched on his high beam lights and is tailgating us."

"Ok," John replied. "Here is the plan. Three kilometres ahead on the right is an abandoned fuel stop. Caroline, you and I will pull in there. When we do, you stay right, and I will go left. You stop at a 45-degree angle. As soon as we stop, Greg and Franz jump out, get behind the vehicles and ready your weapons. J2, you go between us and stop. Kat, you stay low. Everyone got that?"

"Yes," came a collective reply.

"Good," replied John. "Let's see if these pricks want to play hardball."

John and Caroline swung into the pull-off. John went left, spinning the F150 around quickly on the snow. He was now facing the entrance. Caroline went right, stopping at a 45-degree angle. Franz and Greg quickly jumped out behind the vehicles, levelled their rifles over the hoods and chambered a round.

Seconds later, J2 pulled in, passing between the two stopped vehicles. He stopped at an angle. J3 leaped out and ran behind the F150, chambering a round as he ran. He then lowered his rifle over the hood.

As the pickup pulled in, John switched on his high-beam headlights and a brilliant LED light bar. The pickup skidded to a stop. Bathed in light, the three men were clearly visible, sitting open-mouthed in a black, jacked-up Dodge pickup. No one moved.

Realizing their mistake, the pick-up slowly backed onto the

highway and sped back toward Blind River.

John stepped out of his F150, "Who wants to bet at least one of them worthless assholes pissed his pants?"

They all laughed while everyone stretched their legs for a few minutes allowing the adrenaline to wear off.

"This shit is getting real," John announced. "We have a long night ahead; let's roll."

* * *

There was a parking area right next to the police station in Espanola, and John figured that would be a safe place for a quick stop and to top off their tanks from the plastic jerry cans. Across the road, at a fuel stop, cars were lined up back to the highway. Ten minutes later, all filled up, they were back on the road. As they approached the city of Sudbury, they came across the next roadblock. Two military trucks blocked the eastbound lanes of Hwy 17; a single police cruiser parked in front of them, lights flashing. Only one police officer and one armed soldier manned the blockade; both wore N95 masks.

There were six vehicles in front of John. As he studied the roadblock. *Only one cop and one soldier; the damn flu must be severely thinning their ranks.* "Mask up everyone, ID's ready," John called over the two-way.

The officer chatted briefly with the occupants of the vehicles and waved them through. She looked as though she had been there all day with no break. She waved John forward and looked around the F150 as she spoke. "Good evening. I see everyone is taking precautions this evening. You folks appear to be well stocked up. Where are you headed?"

"Good evening, ma'am," John replied. "We are headed home to Owen Sound. My daughter, her husband, and a friend are behind us, and behind them are my son and grandson.

"Thank you, is anyone experiencing flu-like symptoms she

asked?"

They gave a collective, "No, ma'am.

We were all checked out at Sault Ste. Marie," John added.

"We are having a little trouble with looting in town," the officer continued. "We are just making sure it doesn't spread out this way. You folks have a good evening; you're free to go."
John asked Kat to pass him a six-pack of energy drinks and two packs of MREs from the back seat. John then gave them to the officer. "Here, you two look like you could use these."

The tired officer smiled smiled, "Thank you so very much. You have no idea how much we appreciate this. There is another roadblock just after the Hwy 69 exit. I will radio ahead and let them know you're coming."

"Thank you, we appreciate that, and stay safe," John replied. Then he drove through the narrow gap between the two trucks.

"Poppa, why didn't you tell the police about the men in the truck?" Kat questioned.

"Kat, the police don't look too favourably on people pulling guns on others. Even if the situation was warranted, and I certainly believe it was, the law doesn't see it that way. The last thing we want is to have our weapons confiscated."

"I understand now," Kat replied. "I agree it doesn't seem right. God knows what they could have done if those people wanted to harm us, and no one would have come to our aid."

"Exactly, if only that meathead David could see that clearly," John grumbled.

They rolled around the bypass at Sudbury at 0245 in the morning. From the high vantage point, they could see plenty of flashing lights in the city as they passed. As they exited to Hwy 69 south, the police and military barricade came into view. While they waited for their turn in line, John asked Kat for another two energy drinks, some cliff bars and some Jerky.

When the lone, tired-looking police officer waved John

forward, he looked in the window. "I've been expecting you," he said. The officer smiled when John passed him the food and drink. "Thank you so much for your generosity. Drive safe"

"Thank you and be safe," replied John as the officer waved all three vehicles through.

* * *

The drive down Hwy 69 was ok. Traffic was heavier than usual for that time of night. The road was snow-covered, and there was no sign of any snow plow activity. Turning onto Hwy 400 at Parry Sound, the road conditions improved. It was now a 4-lane divided highway. The road was primarily bare due to traffic volume, not from snow plows.

Traffic was getting heavier, and people drove much more aggressively than usual the further south they went. This was partly due to the higher population density of Southern Ontario and partly because people were beginning to wake up to the reality they were now facing.

Every fuel stop they passed by had long lineups of agitated people. Panic now seemed to be the flavour of the day. The 6 AM news didn't do anything to brighten the solemn mood of the convoy's occupants.

6:00 AM, 21 NOVEMBER 2020

Just North of Barrie, Ontario.

Good morning. This is Allison McLean with the CBC, and this is the 6 O'clock hourly news.

This morning, infections and death numbers sharply spike upwards as the day dawns around the world.

Law and order deteriorate further as panic sets into the worldwide population.

The World Health Organization reports that the latest worldwide infection figures have skyrocketed overnight to 2.5 billion. Global deaths are now approaching a shocking 30 million.

Andrew Roberts picks up this story from Health Canada's headquarters in Ottawa. Andrew?

Thank you, Allison. Christine Lemay, the spokesperson for Health Canada, laid out the horrifying details to the news media gathered here this morning.

The first is those shocking statistics you just mentioned. This pandemic has not spared Canada. Our numbers are 2.5 million confirmed infections and 175,000 deaths. Allison, these are staggering numbers. Christine confirmed that the average time from infection to death is between 48 and 72 hours. She also confirmed that no known antivirals work on this flu. Not since the Spanish Flu of 1918 has the modern world seen a pandemic so lethal.

Allison, back to you.

Thank you. That was the CBC's Andrew Roberts reporting from Canada's Health Agency in Ottawa.

The CBC has just received word that the Prime Minister will make a televised statement at 8:00 AM eastern time. The CBC will air that statement as soon as it becomes available.

Overnight, the world's hospitals became filled to capacity with the sick and dying. Morgues are also filled. Here at home, some hospitals have been forced to store the dead in tents provided by the military. The situation continues to deteriorate due to sickness and high absentee rates among medical personnel.

Worldwide, police forces, bolstered by the military, struggled overnight to contain the looting and violence in the major cities.

Here in Toronto, the police and military managed to round up just over 500 looters. However, with absentee rates now approaching 10%, they cannot keep up with criminal activity. Calls to the police are being put in a priority sequence with long wait times before police arrive on the scene. Regrettably, this fact has not been missed by the criminal element.

Many of the nation's shops stayed open late last night to accommodate people needing to stock up on food and water. Sadly fights have broken out over parking spaces and shopping carts. Inside the stores, clashes broke out over goods, and there were too many people injured to count.

Again, police and paramedics were utterly overwhelmed. The mayor of Toronto, Nancy Steinman, announced that effective at 8:00 PM tonight, the city will be under a mandatory curfew order. Anyone caught outside will be arrested on the spot.

As the sun rises across the country, a bleak picture is being painted.

The CBC's Halifax Bureau Chief, Christopher Burke, picks up the story from Halifax, Christopher.

Thank you, Allison. The dawn in Halifax this morning was nothing like anything in recent history. Windows were smashed, stores looted, fights broke out, and dozens were arrested. Sadly, this scene repeated itself in towns and cities across the Maritimes and will only worsen as food runs short and the death toll rises.

Back to you, Allison.

Thank you. That was the CBC's Christopher Burke reporting from Halifax.

We have just received a cell phone video showing a Quebec City store owner shooting and killing four men attempting to loot his store overnight. Six hours after the 911 call went in, the Police and Emergency Services had not yet arrived on the scene. The four men are still lying in the street, which is unbelievable.

Stay tuned for more developments as they happen.

This is Allison McLean for the CBC news.

John picked up the hand-held radio. "Did everyone hear that news?""Yes, we did," both Caroline and J2 replied.

"How is your fuel holding up, Caroline?" asked John.

"I'm below half a tank, Dad, starting to sweat."

"We better look for a safe place to fill up. When that's done, it's hammer down all the way home," John replied.

They drove past several pull-offs on Hwy 400, passing on them because they had cars and desperate people moving about. The convoy took the Horseshoe Valley Road exit from Hwy 400 and followed Horseshoe Valley Road west. John planned to head west, join up with Hwy 26, and then continue west. They would be zigzagging cross-country to the family farm via secondary roads avoiding larger centers. There were a few small towns to deal with, but they could be avoided if necessary.

They were approaching a forest road, part of Simcoe County Forest, just past a power line right of way. The road presented a suitable area to pull off and fuel up. John knew the area well because he had hunted wild turkeys there in the past. He picked up the hand-held radio, "Let's pull in here. We will fill up Caroline and dump any remaining fuel into the Fords. The area looks clear so far, but stay alert."

"Ok, Dad," came the replies.

They pulled onto the bush road and continued for 50 meters. The ground was snow-covered but not deep, and there was enough room to circle around and face back in case they had to escape quickly.

John called again, "You ladies, please stay inside. Us Johns can do the fueling. Franz, Greg, and Hatto, please ready a weapon and keep a lookout for any trouble."

The four remaining fuel cans were unstrapped and offloaded. With the Jeep now full, the remaining fuel went into the two Fords. Before they climbed back in the vehicles, Hatto excused himself for a piss break and walked behind J2's pick-up to take care of business.

Randy Green and David Allen had been left stranded. The pair of petty thieves from the small city of Midland were returning from breaking into farms. They had been stealing high-end items they could quickly resell for drug money when their car ran out of gas. The two had been outside all night and had walked the last six kilometres. They were cold, hungry, desperate and not overly bright.

The two petty thieves remained hidden behind the trees just behind where the convoy parked, waiting for an opportunity. The slightly built Asian man taking a piss by himself gave it to them. They grinned at one another. The plan was to grab him as a hostage so they could get a vehicle.

They struck when Greg turned the other way.

Hatto had just zipped up and was about to return to the others when he noticed movement to his right. Franz saw it, too and yelled a warning. He raised his rifle and started to run toward Hatto.

Before either of the thieves knew what hit them, Hatto had broken both their noses and dropped them painfully to the ground. Lying on their backs on the ground in disbelief, bleeding and in pain, they looked up at Hatto standing above them, waiting to strike. The others quickly gathered around. Caroline held Kat and J3 back at a safe distance. Franz had his rifle barrel pointed between Randy's eyes.

John walked up and looked over the two, shaking his head. "You mutts didn't see that coming, did you?"

David then pissed himself.

"Listen and listen good. You two assholes better march yourselves back down that road," John said as he pointed back toward Horseshoe Valley Road. "If you so much as turn around, you will be shot. Do I make myself perfectly clear?"

The two defeated men nodded in agreement.

Franz and Hatto stepped back, giving the men room to get up and walk off. They never looked back.

"That was close," J2 said.

"Too close," replied John. "We had better be a lot more careful. This is NOT the same world we left two weeks ago."

"People are starting to get desperate," remarked Greg, his hands still shaking from the adrenaline rush.

Everyone took turns praising Hatto while he cleaned up with hand sanitizer. Then the crew loaded up.

* * *

It was now 7:30 AM. John pressed the voice command button on his steering wheel and said, "Call Liz."

F150 replied, "Calling Liz."

Liz picked up right away. Concerned, she asked, "John, where are you?"

"Good morning, my love. We are just south of Midland, following the secondary roads, is everything ok?"

"John, we just had two cars driving by slowly. People were looking in, I'm afraid."

John replied in a calm voice, "Liz, is the driveway gate closed?"

"Yes, it is," she answered nervously.

"Good," John said calmly. "Remember, we have a security system that will alert us if anyone comes up the driveway."

"Yes, I remember," she replied. "Sam went down and took three shotguns and some 00 buckshot out of the gun safe."

The MacIntyre family had 10 Mossberg 500 tactical 12-gauge shotguns, each equipped with a Streamlight TLR2 light-laser sight unit, stored in John's gun safe. The look alone should be enough to deter most petty criminals.

"Good," John replied. "All three of you know how to use them, and I sure hope it doesn't get to that. Where is Higgins?"

"He is on the front porch standing guard. He wouldn't come in, he knows something is not right," replied Liz.

"That's good," John cheerfully replied.

Higgins, the MacIntyre's Jack Russel terrier, is a real little firecracker and intelligent. He does a fantastic job of keeping the livestock in line. On top of that, he is a hell of a watchdog.

"He doesn't miss a trick, that dog. We should be there before noon if all goes well," John replied confidently.

"I can't wait to see you, all of you," Liz replied. "Sam is on the phone with J2 right now. What kind of trouble did you have?"

"Nothing really, just a couple of thieves figured they could get the jump on us, and it didn't end well for them."

"My God, John, you didn't kill them?" Questioned a nervous, Liz.

"No, no, Hatto broke their noses for them. Then we sent them on their way. They are likely looking for a place to change their shorts," John chuckled. "We are on the road now, my love." John's tone changed to one of concern, "Liz, I think it would be wise to call the neighbours. Let them know someone may be casing us. Call me back right away if they show up again. We will be there as quick as we can."

"Ok, John, love you."

"Love you too, Liz."

7:45 AM, 21 NOVEMBER 2020

The MacIntyre Homestead

Liz called Margret and Dan Clary; they owned the farm next door. Marg answered the phone. She recognized the name MacIntyre on the call display, and knowing John was away; she picked up. "Good morning Liz. How are you?"

"Good morning Marg. I'm sorry to bother you, but I'm worried. Two cars have drove by slowly twice today. I think they are casing us. I wanted to warn you and Dan. People are going crazy with this flu pandemic."

"Thanks, Liz, Dan is out in the barn, and I haven't seen anything. I know; it's scary out there. We are worried too."

"John will be home in a few hours. They drove right through from Vermillion Bay last night," Liz replied happily.

"I will let Dan know. He has been worried about looters and what has been happening in the cities." While they talked, Marg walked over to the front window to look at the road. She pulled back her curtain and looked out toward the road. "I will call you," she hesitated. "Liz, the two cars, they're at our gate. Oh my God, I must warn Dan," and she hung up.

Liz yelled for Sam and Lauren, and the two came running with shotguns. "The two cars are at the Clary farm," Liz told them.

"Mom, you and I should go over there to back up the Clarys. We don't know what these people want," Sam suggested nervously. "Lauren, I want you to stay here, lock the door and don't let anyone in unless you know them, call me if you see anything."

"Ok, Mom," Lauren replied, as she rechecked that her safety was on and chambered a round of 00 buckshot.

Higgins looked up at the women as they walked out of the

house. Liz stopped and patted him on the head, "You keep watch on Lauren, Higgins."

Liz and Sam climbed into Liz's Suburban and drove down the driveway. Sam jumped out at the gate, shotgun in hand, to open it. Liz pulled through, and Sam closed the gate then slowly walked out to the road and looked both ways, nothing. She climbed back in, and they drove carefully to the Clary's laneway.

When they arrived, they spotted the two cars parked on the side of the road at the Clary's gate. Liz pulled up slowly behind them. No one was in the vehicles.

Their adrenaline was rising as they both got out, Liz covering. Sam double-checked that the cars were empty, except for a mess of beer cans, junk food bags, bottles and boxes of what looked like drugs littered the backseat

"It looks like we are dealing with a bunch of druggies. We need a plan, Mom, Sam stated nervously."

The Clarys lived in a single-story rancher that sat on a slight rise 100 meters from the road. The ground leading to the house was clear open land, with the barn another 100 meters back and to the right. Aside from the chickadees chirping away, everything was quiet.

Sam and Liz chambered a round of 00 and double-checked that they both had extra ammo. Sam looked at Liz, "I will lead Mom. Follow me, but stay back a bit. Not too close."

Liz nervously nodded her agreement.

Sam seemed calm and collected, but inside she was terrified. Her heart was running a mile a minute. They stalked quietly up the driveway, Sam's head on a swivel, shotgun at the low ready, taking in everything. Liz, ten paces back. Every few steps, she would look behind.

The sun was rising, the sky was clear, and the air was cold. The ground was covered in about three centimetres of fresh light snow. They got to the left side of the house. Hugging the side wall, they worked their way to the rear. Sam carefully looked around the corner. She had a clear view of the barn door from here. It was open. She could see a lot of tracks around the door.

The men had driven up from the city of Guelph overnight. They were all meth heads, taking what they wanted from whom they wanted. The defacto leader of the group, Billy, had grown up in Owen Sound before he went to Guelph to attend university. His parents provided generously, paying for a decent apartment and giving him a generous allowance.

Billy had never held so much as a part-time job for more than two days. He was spoiled, entitled and selfish. He partied hard with his friends and drank heavily every night. Drugs just came naturally, one leading to another. It didn't take long, and he became hooked on methamphetamines.

After his second term, he dropped out of university and squandered the money his parents sent him for the next term's tuition on drugs and booze.

The others came from different cities but shared very similar backgrounds. When things started going bad in Guelph, Billy convinced the guys to go with him to Owen Sound.

They had all the gear needed to set up a sweet meth lab. They even hit a few pharmacies and stole all the drugs they could carry on the drive-up. They planned to find a quiet farm to hole up until things improved.

The men had caught Dan by surprise as he was tending to the 20 hogs he had in the barn. They snuck in and hit him over the head with a bat. Marg ran in as the men dragged Dan into a stall. Billy grabbed her, pinning her against the wall, then sniffed her neck. "You smell really nice, sweetheart."

"You stink," Marg replied definitely as she struggled.

While Sam studied the barn, Liz looked in the house's side door. She had a clear view into the kitchen and living room, and there was no sign of Marg, Dan or anyone else.

Liz carefully made her way to Sam's side. "There is no one in the house," she whispered.

Sam whispered to Liz, "they may be holding the Clarys in the barn. We need to check it out"

Sam studied the wooden pasture fence ran from 20 meters behind the house to the corner of the barn. *That will make perfect cover while we run to the barn.* "Mom, we will cross behind the fence and follow it to the barn. Maybe we can hear something. You cover me while I cross and go under the fence, then I will cover you."

"Ok," Liz replied as she knelt and levelled her 12-gauge at the barn. Ten seconds later, Sam was under the fence and in position to cover her mother-in-law. Liz sprinted across and crawled under the fence. To Liz, it felt like she was running forever before she got to the fence and crawled under it. She knelt beside Sam breathing heavily.

Looking at Liz, Sam asked, "Are you ok, Mom?"

"I'm good, Sam. Scared shitless, but I'm good."

"I hear you, Mom. I've never been more afraid in my life," Sam replied. The women ran to the barn, knelt close to the door and listened.

* * *

Billy had his hand over Marg's mouth as he pinned her against the wall, "I think me and the boys are going to enjoy you." He reached around with his other arm and grabbed Marg by the breast. Marg bit down hard on Billy's hand He yelped, spun Marg around and punched her right in her head. The other men laughed as Marg fell to the barn floor unconscious.

"Fuck you, assholes," Billy complained. "The bitch bit me. We're gonna teach her a lesson. Get her over there on that hay and pull her clothes off."

One of the men grabbed Marg's arms and dragged her to the hay piled in the centre of the stall. The other two started to remove Marg's clothes.

As her sweatshirt and bra came off, Billy whistled, "Boys, look at those hooters! She has nice tits."

s her pants came off, Marg started to come around. Marg was strong, and she thrashed like a tiger. "Freddy, hold the bitch's hands. Joey, you and Ben hold her legs. I get first go at that cute shaved beaver," Billy grinned.

Marg, realizing she was naked and seeing Billy dropping his pants, realized her fate and screamed.

"Shut that bitch up," Billy yelled.

Not wanting to get bitten like Billy, the man called Joey grabbed her sweatshirt and held it over her mouth. Marg struggled as best as she could, but she was simply overpowered.

Liz and Sam heard Marg screaming. "We have to move, Mom. I will go in the door, and you follow, covering me. Let's switch on our laser sights. It's going to be close in there, and we may not get time to aim."

Liz nodded in agreement.

Sam quickly glanced around the opening. The barn interior was dark, the air heavy with humidity and scents of livestock. She crouched low and went in, the shotgun at the ready. A second later, Liz followed. It took a few seconds for their eyes to adjust to the darkness of the barn interior. Both women were terrified, but they had to act and had to act now.

Sam turned to Liz, who was breathing quickly, her adrenaline rising. "I see them ahead 3rd stall on the right."

Liz nodded in agreement.

The two women crept along the stalls. The hogs were making enough noise to cover their advance easily. Marg thrashed about, making it hard for the three to hold her down. She was a slight woman, but farming had made her strong.

Billy stood over her, his pants around his ankles, his hard

penis in his right hand. "See this bitch," as he shook it at her. "I'm going to stuff this right in that pretty shaved pussy of yours. Joey gets sloppy seconds, and then Ben gets a go. Freddy will finish you up because he wants to roll you over and stick it your ass."

Billy dropped down on top of Marg. "Open up for me, bitch," he said. The others were all excited, cheering him on while Marg continued to struggle.

Sam and Liz knew what was going on and were both angry. This was every woman's nightmare. They positioned themselves right outside the stall. Uncertain how this would play out, Sam and Liz looked at each other and silently mouthed, *I love you*, then Sam moved.

"Be still, bitch." Billy snarled menacingly in Marg's ear, "You're gonna enjoy this."

Marg was the only one that saw Sam move in behind Billy. She stopped struggling and closed her eyes.

Billy smiled, showing off his meth-blackened teeth, "That's right bitch, lay back and enjoy," he taunted.

Sam moved like a cat. She was up into the stall and shoved the barrel of her 12-gauge hard into the back of Billy's head. Liz followed Sam in and levelled her shotgun alternating between the two men holding Marg's legs and the one holding her arms. "Freeze, every one of you," Sam ordered.

Billy froze, and no one moved. Sam nudged the barrel into the back of Billy's head, "You hold still. The rest of you assholes get over in that corner," as she nodded her head to the right. "lay on your stomachs and don't move."

The sight of the two women coming from nowhere with serious-looking firepower and the tell-tale red dot alternating between their chests gave them pause. They did as directed. Liz followed the three with her shotgun as they moved.

Sam shoved Billy again. "You get into the opposite corner, lay down on your stomach, and don't move," Sam ordered.

Billy did as directed.

Marg curled herself into a ball, terrified and crying, but neither of the women could go to her aid. Liz started to sob. The situation's intensity was beginning to take its toll on the older women's emotions. She had never witnessed anything like this.

Sensing weakness, Joey moved to get the 9 mm he had tucked in the front of his pants. Joey managed to pull the gun free and quickly rolled over, swinging the 9mm toward Liz.

Seeing Joey's sudden movement toward her mother-in-law, Sam swung her 12-gauge, centring the red dot on Joey's chest and fired. At that range, the full effect of the double 00 buckshot was devastating, throwing him back against the barn wall. Blood and flesh splattered the wall as he slumped to the floor, dead.

The blast from the 12-gauge inside the barn was deafening. For a moment, time stood still. Then either from fear or stupidity, the other two men thought this was their chance, and they moved toward Liz. She fired the instant the red dot centred on Ben's chest, blasting him back onto the barn wall beside Joey. Sam had already chambered another round and dropped Freddy beside his two comrades.

The barn looked like a horror show. The blasts, noise and the stench of blood and death put Billy in complete panic mode. He made a run for Sam. He was fast, but not fast enough. Sam was rock solid. She had chambered another round before Freddie had hit the floor. Billy was less than a meter away; the red dot was on his face when she pulled the trigger. The blast knocked Billy off his feet and dumped him on the floor.

Sam bent over and threw up, deafened by the blast and overcome by the metallic stench of spilled blood. She had to get herself back together. Uncertain if the barn was secure, she gathered her strength. "Mom, help Marg. I will look for Dan." Sam quickly refilled the tube magazine of her Mossberg and cautiously went looking for Dan.

Marg was in shock, sobbing violently. Liz refilled her

magazine, thumbed on the safety, and lay down her gun. It was her turn to throw up. Knowing her friend needed her badly, she quickly gathered herself together and went to Marg, holding her close. The two women cried together.

Thankfully there was no sign of any other intruders. Sam found Dan lying in a heap three stalls further along. Unsure that Dan was alive, she cautiously kneeled and checked him for a pulse. He had one, but it was weak. "Mom," she called. "Dan is in here, and he is unconscious."

Sam and J2 had taken paramedic-level training as part of their preparedness plans. She engaged the safety on her shotgun, laid it down and continued examining Dan.
Liz helped Marg gather her clothes and dress. A few minutes later, they joined Sam.

Oh my God!" Marg cried out as she knelt beside her husband.
Sam took Marg's hand, "Be careful, Marg. He is hurt badly and has a concussion, possibly a neck injury." Liz knelt beside her friend and held her as she sobbed.

Sam got to work treating Dan's wounds. She wore a fanny pack that contained her IFAK or individual first aid kit and other survival items. Dan was bleeding badly from a wound on his scalp from the hit he had received. A small amount of straw-coloured fluid was in his left ear. Sam knew that meant a severe head injury.

She opened a package of Celox and poured the granules into the head wound. Celox acts to form a gel-like plug, sealing the wound quickly. Sam quickly cleaned the area around the wound, dressed it with a sterile dressing, and then wrapped it tightly with gauze. Lastly, she wrapped him in a mylar emergency blanket to help preserve his body temperature and prevent him from going further into shock.

Sam knelt beside Marg, "We need to make a stretcher to move Dan into the house. I will look for some things to make one." Sam put a hand on Liz's shoulder, "You ok, Mom?"

"I'm fine, Sam," she replied, "You be careful."

Sam picked up her shotgun and headed for the door. Outside, she pulled out her cell phone and called Lauren.

"Mom," Lauren answered in a panicked voice, "I heard shots!"

"Sweetie, we are ok but Dan is hurt. I need you to bring my big first aid roll over here. Bring your shotgun, and be careful. Do you understand?"

"Yes, Mom, I'm on my way." Lauren grabbed her mother's red first aid Bug Out Roll and her shotgun and went out the door. She looked around carefully, droppeddown beside Higgins and told him to stay and watch

After Sam hung up, she went inside the house. She found the blanket she needed to make an improvised stretcher. She grabbed some towels from the bathroom and headed back to the barn. Once in the barn, Sam called out. "It's me, Mom. I'm coming back in." Sam dropped the towels and blanket in the stall by Dan. I need to find something to use for a stretcher, something solid like a door."

"Dan was refinishing some closet doors. They are inside his workshop. Would they work, Sam?" Marg sobbed.

"Perfect," exclaimed Sam. "I will go check them out." Sam went out to Dan's workshop, and sure enough, two closet doors were stripped, ready for staining. She picked one up and felt its weight. *Excellent, this should do nicely.*

Back in the stall, Sam laid the door next to Dan, spreading it out like a bed. She then placed the blanket over the door to use as padding. Sam knew Liz had been first aid trained and could count on her. However, Marg was in shock and hoped she could count on her. "Marg, I will roll Dan towards me onto his side. When I do that, I will need you to slide the stretcher under his back as tight to him as you can, do you understand?"

Marg, still sobbing, nodded in agreement.

"Mom, I need you to hold Dan's head steady. When I roll Dan, you follow with his head. We can't let his head flop around, just like we learned in first aid."

"I remember," Liz replied.

"Ok," Sam ordered as she gripped Dan to roll him. "On the count of three, one, two, three," and she pulled him onto her knees. Marg did as instructed, sliding the improvised stretcher under her injured husband. "Excellent," praised Sam. "Now, Mom, on the count of three, we roll him back, one, two, three." Sam and Liz gently rolled Dan back onto the stretcher. With Dan lying flat on his back, Sam tucked the towels she brought beside his head to cushion it and prevent it from moving. "Mom, Marg, you two take the foot of the stretcher, standing on the outside and drop down to one knee."

They did as Sam instructed.

Sam would take the front. She lowered herself to one knee and grabbed both sides of the door. "Ok, on three, we lift. One, two, three." The three women raised Dan off the barn floor and carefully carried him to the house. It wasn't a perfect setup, but they managed to get him into the bedroom and onto the bed. They repeated the rolling process to separate Dan from the stretcher.

Lauren knocked on the door as Sam made Dan comfortable in bed. Liz let her in and led her to the bedroom. The women gathered next to Dan's bed and hugged one another, and they all cried and shared, "I love you."

Sam had put together extensive emergency medical kits that were equal to anything a paramedic would have. Each household had one, except, of course, David and Chantel's. When Sam discovered the Bug Out Roll made by Canadian Prepper, she ordered three in red. These rolls are exceptionally well built. With them, she could organize all their first aid gear in see-through compartments for easy access. They turned out to be perfect additions to the family preps.

Having calmed down, Sam set to work on Dan. Liz took Marg

for a shower while Lauren made some coffee; they all needed it. A half-hour later, the four women, still shaking, sat at the table with fresh coffee.

The shock of the day was still evident on their faces. Dan was still unconscious. Sam had stopped the bleeding and bandaged him. His blood pressure was low, and he had lost a good bit of blood, but he was stable. They decided that Sam would stay with Marg while Liz and Lauren went back to wait for the others to arrive home.

"Mom, call me before you call Dad. I should be on the phone with J2 at the same time. We don't want anyone panicking," suggested Sam.

"Good idea," Liz replied.

Liz and Lauren drove back to the house. At the gate, Lauren got out, opened it, and Liz went through. Lauren closed the gate and jumped back in. As they approached the house, Higgins still waited on the porch as commanded. His tail was wagging so hard the little dog swayed.

Once inside, doors secure, Liz knew she needed to call John.

8:00 AM, 21 NOVEMBER 2020

Collingwood, Ontario

T he occupants of the convoy listened intently to the 8:00 AM news anticipating the Prime Minister's announcement.

Good Morning. This is Allison McLean with the CBC hourly news at 8:00 AM.

Any moment now, the Prime Minister will be making a statement. We go directly to the CBC's Andrew Roberts at Parliament Hill in Ottawa, Andrew?

Good morning Allison. We are anticipating the Prime Minister to speak at any moment. Please stand by.

Good morning. Today, our nation is facing a crisis that few Canadians have ever witnessed. The Canadian Health Agency handed me the latest figures just minutes ago, and I must warn you, they are shocking. As of 7:30 AM today, Canada's infection numbers stand at 2.7 Million, and the death toll has claimed 200,000 Canadian lives.

Worldwide known infections stand at 4.2 Billion, with a shocking death toll of 45 million. Worse yet, the Worldwide Health Organization informs us that infection rates are still out of control and rising. The Centers for Disease Control in Atlanta has confirmed that this is a mutated form of the H5N1 flu virus, similar to the 1918 Spanish Flu that ravaged the world over a century ago.

The CDC had confirmed that an Antigenic Shift occurred when the common H5N1 flu virus came into contact with a yet unknown virus brought back this fall by migrating birds.

So far, the CDC has been unable to break this new virus's genetic code. Sadly, I regret to announce that, to date, no known antiviral has any effect on this flu. The WHO, the CDC, Canada's National Microbiology Lab, and other worldwide bodies are actively seeking an antiviral to control this. At this time, we ask for everyone's patience and cooperation while we do our jobs. Make no mistake. We will defeat this virus.

Last night, cities and towns across the nation experienced looting and violence never seen before in our nation's history. The Police, military and emergency services are understaffed because of sickness, and they are overworked trying to cope with the lawlessness.

Violence and lawlessness are unacceptable and will not be tolerated. Therefore, I regret that we must take the following actions. Beginning tonight at 8:00 PM, mandatory nationwide curfews will be enacted. Anyone caught outside between 8:00 PM, and 6:00 AM will be subject to immediate arrest and detention. This is necessary to keep criminal activity in check.

Quarantine areas will be established at hospitals and medical centres in all cities and towns to prevent people from spreading infections. The only proven method we currently have to defeat this is to isolate the sick.

We ask anyone with flu-like symptoms to report to these centres for treatment. Remember, the curfew still applies.

Food and fuel stores across the nation and, for that matter, the entire world are suffering shortages due to transportation delays, staff shortages and theft. Therefore, beginning tomorrow, the 22nd of November, The Canadian military will begin establishing emergency food and fuel distribution centres throughout the nation. Your government requires you to be patient. Food and fuel will be made available for those that need it. I remind you once again violence will not be tolerated. Food and fuel shipments will be redirected to these secure sites for fair distribution. Your local government agencies will inform you where the locations will be set up.

Municipal water supplies are safe; please continue to use them.

Effective immediately, zero-tolerance rules will come into effect for any criminal activity. Anyone caught will be immediately arrested and jailed. These measures are temporary, necessary and will be enforced. Your government asks for your cooperation and understanding as we work to support all Canadians.

Thank you, Merci

There you have it, Allison. The Prime Minister paints a very bleak picture of the immediate future for Canadians. This is Andrew Roberts. Back to you, Allison.

The Prime Minister did not take time to answer any questions on this latest announcement. The statement, however, has left us with far more questions than answers.

Stock markets worldwide have taken a severe tumble overnight as more and more people call in sick for work and the world economies grind to a halt. There have been reports of runs on banks as the day dawns in nations around the world.

Lastly, Environment Canada has issued a severe winter storm warning for South and Central Ontario. Within the next 36 to 48 hours, a low-pressure area will dip down from Hudson's Bay, bringing with it cold temperatures in the range of -25 Celsius with high winds and snow. Accumulations of 30 centimetres are expected in traditional snow belt areas.

This is Allison McLean with CBC hourly news.

10:00 AM, 21 NOVEMBER 2020

Westbound on Grey Road 18, South of Owen Sound, Ontario

The convoy was roughly a half hour away from home. So far, the final leg of the drive had been drama free. A few abandoned cars were littering the sides of the roads, and they had seen desperate-looking people walking. It was heartbreaking not to stop, but the group had family members worried and scared at home.

The primary concern was that if they made contact with infected people, they risked infecting themselves and bringing it home to their families. Unable to help, they carried on. It was hard but necessary. The road was bare of snow but wet; the temperature was right around freezing, with the potential for black ice, front and centre.

John's phone rang. His wife's picture, name and number appeared on the F150 display screen. John thumbed the call answer button and put Liz on speaker. "Hello, my love," he spoke cheerfully.

Liz sobbed, "John, we have big trouble."

Knowing that her Mom and Dad needed to hear this, Kat grabbed the hand-held radio and keyed the mic.

"What is it, Liz?" John asked, concerned.

Liz was still shaken and upset. Between sobs, she blurted it out as the others listened in shock at the story.

"John, I called Dan and Marg. Dan was in the barn when I was talking to Marg. She looked out the window, and the cars were at her driveway. Marg hung up to warn Dan. Sam and I grabbed our guns and rushed over. Oh, John," she sobbed, "I killed a man, and Sam killed three. Dan is badly hurt, and Marg was almost raped.

She is a wreck, John. It was terrible."

"Liz, are you, Sam, and Lauren ok?"

"Yes, yes, we are ok. We are all shaken up, but ok."

Relieved, John replied, "Thank God! What happened to Dan?"

"The men surprised him in the barn. He was hit over the head and knocked out. Marg came running in to warn him, and they grabbed her. Liz sobbed again. "John, they had her on the ground naked. They were... my god John, it was horrible," she sobbed.

They all heard Caroline gasp over the hand-held radio, "Mom, we're glad you're all ok."

"We are Caroline," Liz replied.

John spoke up, "It's ok. You girls did well, and you did what you had to do. Most important, you're still alive, and that's what's important."

Liz sobbed some more.

Kat, too, was sobbing. She called out, "we love you, Gramma!"

"I love you, too, sweetheart," Liz replied.

The reality of the event was sinking into John, "I am sorry we weren't there, Liz. I am. You should never have had to deal with that. I am sorry."

"It's not your fault John. How could you know this was going to happen?

"I know," he replied. "It's just that I never expected to see you in harm's way."

"We are ok, John. We are ok. I am worried about Dan. Sam is with him, and Marg. Lauren and I are home."

"Liz, we are just south of Owen Sound and should be there in half an hour. I love you, Liz."

"I love you, John. I am exhausted. I need a shower," Liz replied.

"Ok," John said. "You go get your shower. We will be there in 30 minutes. I love you."

"I love you too," replied Liz.

John pressed the hang-up button, his hands shaking. "That was scary," he said.

"Oh my God, Dad," Caroline called over the radio. "That must have been horrible. Poor Mom, poor Sam."

"I know," John replied. "I can't imagine."
Kat was still sobbing. "It's ok, sweetheart," Caroline said calmly. "We will be home soon."

J2 came over the radio, "Dad, I assume you got all that?"

"Yes, we did, son. I can't imagine what they are going through right now."

"I know," answered J2.

"We better push it a bit harder," John ordered.

❉ ❉ ❉

Twenty minutes later, they pulled up to the gate. Kat got out and hurried to unlatch the gate. Higgins sat on the porch fully alert; he never left his post. Eyeing the familiar girl and John's pickup, his tail wagged so hard the little dog shook.

Kat climbed back in, "I never imagined the farm would look this good," she said.

"I hear you there," John replied and drove to the house.

After Greg pulled in, Caroline got out and closed the gate. She climbed back in, and they drove to the house. John Jr. and J3 went straight to the Clarys to see Sam. The reunion was like no other, with many hugs, kisses, and tears.

Introductions were made between Liz, Lauren, Franz, and Hatto, while Caroline and Kat made coffee and sandwiches for everyone. Liz was still in shock, and John never left her side. Lauren was handling things well, having not witnessed the gory parts.

Finishing up lunch, John asked the others if they would bring all the gear from the vehicles into the living room. "I need some time with Liz."

Everyone agreed, understanding what Liz must be going through right now. John took Liz into their bedroom and held her close. "Liz, you did what you had to do. Please don't feel bad about it. I don't need to tell you what would have happened to Marg and Dan if you and Sam didn't intervene."

"I know," said Liz, still shaking.

"Everyone who experiences combat goes through this. You have to work through it and learn to let it go. It's not easy," John said, comforting her. "You need to rest, Liz."

"John, I am exhausted," she said, "I do need to lie down for a while." John kept some melatonin in the master bathroom cabinet for those occasions when sleep didn't come easy; this was such an occasion. He gave some to Liz and tucked her into bed.

When John returned to the living room, the others had just finished bringing in all the gear. He asked everyone to find a seat in the living room, and they all gathered around. "Ok, everyone, I believe we can all see the seriousness of the situation we now find ourselves in. I need to get together with the others at the Clary's, but I do not want the farm left unguarded. It will take a little time to make a plan, especially with us spread out.

"We must get in touch with all our close neighbours and determine if anyone is showing symptoms. If so, we will have to deal with that. We need to activate our mutual assistance group (MAG) to secure the area and help one another out. Caroline and Greg, can I ask you two to stay back here, keep an eye on Liz, and set a guard?

"Yes, Dad," they replied and nodded.

"We can't take any chances after this morning. From here on in, anyone going outside must be accompanied by at least one person, and both will be armed, John ordered."

"I will start gathering things for supper," Caroline offered.

"Excellent," replied John. "Kat, I need you to stay and help your parents. Lauren, you need to see your father and brother."

The girls nodded in reply.

"Greg, we have two loaded shotguns up here now. I will take Franz and Hatto downstairs and make sure they are suitably armed. I will bring you up a rifle and some ammo."
"Ok, Dad," Greg replied.

"Franz, Hatto, on me," John said smiling, and the two guests followed John downstairs. "This is my study," John said proudly. The two men looked around the room at John's extensive military awards, honours and pictures. Hatto spotted a beautiful Japanese Samurai sword with two matching tanto knives on a wall display. John noticed him looking, and he removed the sword and passed it to Hatto.

"May I?" Hatto asked humbly.

"Certainly," John replied.

Hatto then pulled the sword from its sheath, examining the steel. He held the sword and checked the feel and balance. He nodded at John approvingly. "This is a beautiful sword. Made in Japan by a true craftsman." He sheathed the sword and handed it back to John.

John held the sword turning it over in his hands. "It was a gift," John continued, "I worked with some American special forces soldiers in Afghanistan. One of them, Jason Greene, was into Japanese martial arts. He was an excellent swordsman. We were working as sniper teams picking off the local Taliban leadership.

"We were very successful, but one day Jason's team came under heavy fire from the Taliban. Eight fighters had Jason's team pinned down and were advancing on them. We were 1,500 meters away and had a clear view from where we were positioned. My spotter, Joseph Thunder and I took out all eight fighters, saving their asses."

Franz and Hatto both smiled.

"Hey," John laughed. "We can do more than just play hockey here in Canada."

They all laughed.

"Anyways," John continued, still turning the sword in his hands. "After we returned home, this arrived. Joseph has an identical sword." John passed the sword back to Hatto. "I'm a gun guy, Hatto; I would be honoured if you used it. You could bring out its true potential."

Hatto bowed toward John. "My ancestors were Samurai, and I am a master swordsman. I taught swordsmanship at my dojo back home in Japan. John, I am truly honoured." Hatto replied in his thick Japanese accent. "I am not good with gun."

"Nor I with a sword, Hatto," John added.

That settled, John led them over to the huge oak bookcase. He removed a set of three hardcover books, revealing a deadbolt lock with a numeric keypad and a backup key slot.

Franz looked at John. "Nice."

Hatto, too nodded his approval.

"The combination is the number of my basic training course when I joined the army, 7818."

The men both nodded, registering the combination in their brains. "Should that fail, the key is inside the back cover of," John picked up a book from the top shelf. "What else," he smiled. "The Art of War, by Sun Tzu." John replaced the book and then keyed in the number. The lock made an audible click, and he pulled the hidden door open. "Welcome to my safe room," he grinned proudly and led them inside.

The entrance lights were on a motion detector, and John reached around the corner and switched on the main lights. The two men looked around in awe. The safe room was a 400-square-foot warehouse, and the walls were lined with shelving containing food, water and gear.

"The walls," John said, "are 12 inches of solid reinforced

concrete. The room is self-contained with heat and hot and cold water. We have a small cooking stove, a sink, and a bathroom with a shower.

"Impressive," said Franz smiling widely.

"Very much so," added Hatto.

"Thank you," John replied. "We came here for weapons." He led them over to his reloading area. A large solid oak bench held a top-of-the-line RCBS reloading system and a huge gun safe next to that. John placed his thumb on the electronic thumb reader, and the lock slid open. John then pulled the heavy locker door open.

"Wow!" exclaimed Franz. "You don't fool around, do you, John."

John smiled, "It's a family affair, Franz. I have been into preparedness since I was a teenager, and you could say it rubbed off. We all pooled our money and shared in the purchase of gear, food and weapons. We wanted to standardize our choices as much as possible. That, of course, allowed us to bulk buy and standardize our ammo."

Franz and Hatto both nodded in approval.

Inside the gun locker was an extensive collection of weapons. Three Remington 700s on tactical chassis chambered in 338 Lapua magnum and topped with a top-of-the-line Carl Zeiss V8 4.5-35X60 scopes.

"Come to Poppa," praised Franz. "I am very familiar with that rifle and a real tack driver, and that optic is superb." It was his turn to grin.

Let's talk about that later, Franz," John smiled, patting Franz on the shoulder. There were six more fierce-looking Mossberg 500 ATI tactical, 12-gauge, pump-action shotguns, all equipped with the Streamlight TLR2 light/laser sights, identical to the two upstairs.

Next, twelve Russian SKS semi-automatic rifles, bayonets removed. Each gun was equipped with an ATI stock and

Picatinny rail scope mounts made by Addley Precision, a local shop in Midland, Ontario. They were all topped with Vortex Stikefire red dot sights.

"We bought those SKSs," John continued. "Because Canadian laws list them as non-restricted. In Canada, the AR15 is restricted and requires lots of paperwork. Owning too many of those would set off alarm bells. These, however, do not need to be registered. I don't need anyone thinking I am a lunatic," he grinned.

Lastly stood an impressive McMillan TAC 50 sniper rifle, topped with another Carl Zeiss V8 4.5-35X60 optic and chambered in 50 BMG. "Don't get any ideas there, soldier," John grinned, looking at Franz. "I see you eyeing that MacMillan with love in your eyes. This is my personal weapon."

Franz grinned from ear to ear, holding his hands up in surrender. John handed him an SKS, "Franz, these are all zeroed for 50 meters." He then passed Franz three Tapco 20-round magazines. "In Canada, we are restricted to 5 rounds in the mag. I removed the plugs from these; they now hold 20 each," John explained while Franz checked out his weapon.

John grabbed an SKS for himself, one for Greg, plus three magazines for each. He then led them to a shelf containing body armour, belts, and pouches.

While Franz selected his gear, John handed him a Battle Brick containing 100 rounds of 7.62X39 Russian ammo and five stripper clips.

John opened the setup menu of the gun safes lock and typed in Franz's name. "Franz, place your thumb on the pad, and we will set you up."

He repeated the process once more. "Ok, Hatto, it's your turn." John exited the setup menu and closed the door, locking it.

"Let's verify," he said.

Franz thumbed the reader, and the safe unlocked. Then Hatto did the same.

"The backup key is inside that Nosler reloading manual on the bench," John instructed.

The men nodded.

"Great," John said. "One more thing." After he secured the gun locker and put on his body armour, the men followed John out of the safe room, and John secured the hidden door.

Back in the study, John opened another large gun locker. "This is where I keep all my registered firearms and hunting guns," he said. "These our government knows about." Pointing to the safe room. "Those they do not.

Inside the safe were eight handguns and several long hunting guns and shotguns. "In Canada, handguns are restricted and must be securely locked up and ONLY allowed out to be transported to an approved range, then directly back home again. Under our current circumstances, I think the rules need to be flexible. From now on, we will all carry a sidearm," John informed them.

John picked up a stainless steel 1911. "This is my personal weapon and my favourite," he said. "It's made in Turkey by Tisas and imported into Canada by a company called O'Dell Engineering. Naturally, they market their guns under the brand name Canuck," John grinned. The 1911 was in stainless steel; it had beautiful rose-coloured wooden grips with carved maple leaves.

"I am familiar with Tisas," added Franz. "They are excellent firearms."

John strapped on the holster and dropped three magazines into his vest. "I have put 1000+ rounds through it, never had a single stoppage." John then pocketed 100 rounds of 45 ACP. The other seven handguns were Glock 19's. John passed one to Franz along with three mags.

"Thank you," replied Franz as he checked his weapon. "I love the Glock 19. It's German you know," Franz teased as he strapped on the holster.

John and Hatto laughed.

"Would you like one, Hatto?"

"No, thank you, John," he replied, patting the pair tanto's strapped to his side, "This is all the sidearm I need."

John handed Franz 100 rounds of 9MM, "Remember, my friend. Walking around with these is strictly illegal. Any sign of the law, and we had best use discretion."

"Got it," Franz replied, grinning.

❋ ❋ ❋

Returning upstairs, John handed Greg the SKS, mags and another battle brick of ammo. He then checked on Liz, please she was sleeping soundly. His next stop was the kitchen, where Caroline and the girls were busy preparing supper. John hugged his only daughter tightly. "We are ready to go over to the Clary's. Please keep watch on my sweetheart," he said.

"I will, Dad," Caroline replied, "I love you."

"I love you too," John said.

"Us too," Kat said as she and Lauren wrapped their arms around their Grandfather.

"I love you both," he hugged them back, kissing them each on the cheek.

Greg, John and Franz had loaded their mags and installed one in their weapons; they were ready to go. John put his hand on Greg's shoulder. "We will be back soon. If you see anything, call me on my cell."

Greg nodded his approval.

When John, Franz, Hatto, and Lauren walked out the door. Higgins was still faithfully on guard duty. John stooped to pet his friend, "You guard the farm, old buddy." Higgins replied by licking John's hand.

The men climbed into John's F150 and headed over to the Clary's. They passed the two cars and pulled up to the gate. J3 was in the window on watch. John waved, and his Grandson waved back. Franz opened the gate while John drove in then secured the gate behind them.

Inside the house was another reunion. John hugged Sam and told her how proud he was of her and how much courage it took to do what she did. Sam had tears in her eyes as she hugged John back. Despite being exhausted, Sam refused to go to bed, wanting to spend time with her husband and son. Hatto and Franz were introduced to Sam. Sam, J2 and J3 were reunited with Lauren; many I love you's were shared.

While Franz and Hatto assumed guard duty, Sam led John to see Marg. She was asleep, thoroughly sedated. She had a nasty bruise on the left side of her face where Billy had punched her. They then went in to check on Dan. Sam quickly filled him in on Dan's condition. "He has a concussion, but the bleeding has stopped. I cleaned up the wound. He needed ten stitches to close it up. His vitals are better, and I started him on an IV to replenish his fluids."

"You have done a super job here, Sam," John said, hugging her. "I can't emphasize that enough. I am so proud of you. I cannot imagine what would have happened if you and Liz didn't intervene."
They turned and left Dan's room.

"Ok, everyone," John spoke up. "The world as we know it is quickly changing for the worse, and we need to sit down and discuss where we go from here."

Lauren and J3 passed mugs of coffee around while everyone took a seat around the kitchen table. Franz remained on security detail in front of the kitchen window, which looked toward the gate. He was close enough to hear the conversation and provide input.

John pulled out a notepad and pen. "As of right now, we need

24-hour security on both farms. We have injured people to look after and animals that need attending. To do this, we will have to split up."

They agreed that J2, Sam, Lauren, and J3, backed up by Franz and Hatto, would remain at the Clarys. John, Liz, Caroline, Greg, and Kat would hold down the home farm.

"Now, with the security arrangements made," John added. "We have two items of business that require immediate attention. First, we must get those two cars off the road and out of sight, and we need to inventory the contents as they may contain some useful pharmaceuticals. Second, there appears to be some trash in the barn needing disposal. Franz, would you help me search the trash for car keys?"

"Sure, John," Franz replied, a sinister grin appearing on his face.

"J2, can you, J3, and Hatto head down to the road and make sure the area is secure?"

The three nodded in agreement.

"Sam, I need you to stand guard here at the house."

"Sure thing, Dad," she replied.

"Great, grab your weapons and let's clean up this mess," John ordered.

John figured it would be best for him and Franz to deal with the dead since they were both soldiers and the most accustomed to gore. Entering the barn, the lingering smell of death was immediately apparent as they quickly made their way to the stall.

"Wow!" exclaimed Franz, looking at what remained of Billy's head, "Remind me never to piss off those women."

"I second that," replied John.

Within two minutes, John and Franz were on their way down the laneway with two sets of car keys. The gate was open. J2 called out, "All clear, Dad."

John climbed into a late model Lexus SUV and Franz a Toyota Highlander. The stink and filth of the two vehicles ran a close second to the barn. "Shit these people were pigs," John remarked as he drove off.

Once inside the gate, John exited the Lexus and placed his hands on his grandson's shoulders. He looked him in the eyes, "J3, I don't think you need to see this."

"I agree with your grandfather," added J2. "Son, I would rather you stand guard at the house with your mom."

J3 nodded, "Ok," he agreed. He had never seen a dead person before. Part of him wanted to, and part did not; what if he puked? That would be embarrassing. J3 closed the gate and returned to the front porch while J2 and Hatto walked out behind the barn to help with the inventory.

The car trunks were full of all the needs to build a meth lab. "What isn't useful we will bury out back with the rest of the garbage," John remarked.

The back seat of both vehicles was a treasure trove of painkillers and antibiotics that could be very useful. These were boxed up to carry back to the house. There were also 225 rounds of 9MM ammo to add to their stores. The emptied cars were driven behind Dan's machine shed, locked up and covered with a tarp.

"Now, the messy part," said John. "I will go get Dan's tractor. We can load the dirtbags in the bucket, and I will take them out back and bury them." John climbed onto Dan's Kubota tractor and pulled it up to the barn door.

Franz and J2 had already dragged two bodies out to the door. The bucket was only big enough to hold two at a time, necessitating two trips to the back of the property. While John made the first trip and dug the hole, J2 and Franz shovelled the gore into a wheelbarrow and wheeled it to the door. They then got a hose and used the water to wash out the stall.

"Good as new in there," J2 said to John as he pulled up for load two.

"We collected four older Glock 17's, each with a full mag and four folding knives," Franz added as he and J2 tossed the last of the bodies unceremoniously into the tractor bucket. They then followed with the wheelbarrow load of gore and straw. Lastly, the meth lab garbage was dumped on top of that.

John drove back to the grave site, raised the bucket then dumped the last body and debris on top of the other two. Lastly, he backfilled the hole. Back at the barn, the tractor was washed and put away. When everyone washed up, John called Caroline.

"Hi, Dad, dinner is almost ready. How do you want to do this?"

"Thanks, sweetheart, we worked up a hell of an appetite cleaning up the barn," John said excitedly.

Oh my God, Dad!" Caroline exclaimed. "You're a sick man!"

"Just saying," replied John laughing.

The men all laughed at John's dark humour. They agreed that Franz and Hatto would return to the home farm with John to gather their gear. Caroline would prepare dinners for everyone staying at the Clary's, and John would drive the men back over and drop off the food.

"We all need a good rest," John said. "We will meet at 8 AM to re-evaluate."

When John got back to the house, Liz was up. She and John hugged for a long while. After dinner, they sat and talked over coffee. By 8:00 PM, John was nodding off. Greg and Kat would share the first watch and agreed to wake Caroline at midnight. Caroline was to wake John at 4:00 AM. John had been up for close to 40 hours. When his head hit his familiar pillow, it was lights out.

6:00 AM, 22 NOVEMBER 2020

The MacIntyre Homestead

John woke up feeling well rested. He looked at the clock. It was 6 AM. No one woke him at 4 for his turn at guard duty. Liz was still sleeping; yesterday was a traumatic day for her.

John dressed, put on his pistol belt, picked up his SKS and walked to the kitchen. Caroline and Greg were both up. Hearing him rummaging around, she knew her father would look into why no one woke him at 4. She poured him a coffee and handed it to him as soon as he walked in.

"Good morning," John said. "Why didn't you wake me?"

"Dad, we all got to catch a nap on the way down. You drove right through, needed the rest, and mom needed you. No argument got it, soldier," Caroline scolded him.

John stood straight, "Yes, ma'am, understood." They shared a hug.

"Any action Greg?" John asked.

"Not a thing, Dad. Just the way I like it."

"Good," replied John, "I'm starving."

"I'm already on the breakfast thing Dad," Caroline replied. " There is more coffee in the pot."

"You're a good woman Caroline. Your parents must be decent people," he joked.

Caroline shook her head, "Whatever, Dad."

John grinned, "Caroline, have you called that brother of yours?" John asked.

"I will, as soon as breakfast is cleaned up, Dad. You know they like to sleep late."

John nodded, "Hmmm, understood."

Liz was the next up. She shared a hug with John, then Caroline and Greg. "How are you, my love?" John asked.

Liz smiled, "I'm ok. John, I am sorry I doubted you all these years. If it wasn't for you teaching me things I wasn't interested in learning, yesterday might have had a much different outcome." She paused, "I wish I didn't have to shoot that man, but he deserved it.

John hugged her hard, "That's my girl."

The last up was Kat. She looked well-rested, and everyone shared a hug. Kat helped Caroline with breakfast. Eggs, bacon, home fries and toast, they all ate hungrily. Right after breakfast, John's phone rang. It was J2.

"Hello, son," answered John. "How are things over there?"

"Super Dad. Marg is up and looking well. Best of all, Dan woke up this morning. He is groggy but ate a little and asked for you and Mom."

"That is great news, son. We will be over shortly. There are many things to discuss."

The morning news on TV contained even more gloom and doom than yesterday; infections up, deaths up, crimes up, and shortages up. To make matters even worse, that storm front was still barreling down on them and should arrive within the next 24 hours.

After breakfast, Kat and Caroline cleaned up while Greg stood watch. John and Liz resumed their morning routine of tending to the animals. It was just like old times; however, now they were armed. The chores completed, John waved at Greg to let him know they were headed to the Clarys.

Greg waved back.

John called Higgins, and the little dog came running, leaping right into John's pickup and cozying up beside Liz. When John and Liz entered the Clary's, Marg practically jumped into Liz's arms, holding one another for a long time.

"Thank you so much for all you did yesterday, Liz. Thanks to all of you," Marg praised.

Sam joined them in a group hug, "She hasn't stopped thanking us, Mom."

"I'm so happy everyone is ok and Dan is awake," Liz said happily.

"How is everything here, fellas?" John asked the men.

"All is good, Dad," J2 replied.

Franz and Hatto rubbed their bellies. "Sam is excellent cook," Hatto replied, smiling broadly.

John laughed. "Good. Now that you are all well-fed and rested, we must plan to go forward. Put your brains in gear, and we will discuss it after I see Dan."

Marg led Liz and John in to see Dan. Dan smiled when they walked in. Marg sat beside him on the bed while John and Liz each held one of his hands.

"Liz," Dan said groggily, a tear running down his cheek. "I can't thank you and Sam enough for what you did here yesterday, and we owe you both our lives."

"You're welcome, Dan. I am thankful we were here," Liz replied.

"So are we," Dan added. "So are we."

"He is doing so much better today," Marg added happily. "Sam and John Jr are great medics. We are blessed to have so many watching over us."

"You get yourself well, Dan. We will take care of everything around here," John reassured him. "That goes for you too, Marg. You take it easy for a few days."

Marg smiled. "I can keep an eye on this fella," she said, pointing at Dan.

They all shared a smile.

Everyone gathered around the table in the kitchen while J3

stood watch. "Ok," John said, "Firstly, are you all ok with staying here a few more days to help Marg and Dan?"

They all agreed that would be for the best.

"Good," John replied. "We can reassess in a few more days and go from there. We must contact all our neighbours and discuss establishing a MAG Mutual Assistance Group. When we finish here, I will get right on that. Next, we need to do a supply run for you folks here to pick up more ammo. Marg, you and Dan have radios, correct?"

"Yes, we do, John. I will get them."

"Thanks, Marg," John replied. "That will give us backup COMMs."

J2 agreed to do the supply run, and Franz agreed to help.

"Marg, how are you set up with food and fuel?" John asked.

"We are good on food, John. When Liz called, we rushed out and stocked up, and Karl topped up our tanks and restocked our feed and seed. Even with the extra help, we can get by until summer."

"Excellent," John replied. "We have a storm front moving in, so let's ensure we all have all the gen sets fueled up and enough firewood close at hand in case we need it. Anything else?" John asked.

"John, would you mind if I used one of the Remington 700's? I want to set up some targets in the field out back, get to know her and check my zero," Franz asked.

Poppa, could I shoot some too?"J3 added excitedly.

John smiled, "That sounds like an excellent idea." Looking at Franz, "I saw that hungry look in your eye when I showed you 700s yesterday. Once a grunt always a grunt"

They both laughed loudly.

John looked at J3, "Franz would be an excellent mentor. We should send Kat with you; you know she can shoot, John, winked."

"Excellent idea," nodded Franz. "We will check out all three rifles and get comfortable with them."

"Super then, let's make It happen," John replied happily.

Three other farms shared the road with the Macintyres and Clarys. John called the Bennet farm first. William and Karen Bennet lived about 1 KM east of John, on the north side of the road. The Bennets were both in their late 60s; they had two adult male children and six young grandchildren.

Will picked up on the third ring, recognizing John's name on the call display. "Hello, John. Am I glad to hear from you. How was the hunting?"

"We did very well. Kat got herself a monster of a moose, her first one, and I got a nice one as well. We had to leave them behind, however, with this pandemic. We packed up, left in a hurry, and got back yesterday at about noon. Will, how are things at your place?"

"We are good, John. Both Ed and Glen showed up yesterday with their families. No one is sick, at least not yet. As agreed, we stocked up on food, fuel, feed and seed. We have seen a few shady characters driving around, so we have been taking turns standing watch."

"I'm happy to hear that," replied John. "We had a little drama yesterday. Dan and Marg are both hurt, but they will be fine. The problem has been taken care of."

"I don't need to know any more than that," Will chuckled.

"Will, we need to get moving on forming the mutual assistance groups (MAG) we discussed. I want to establish a roadblock at each end of the road and have it manned 24-7; it would keep us all safer."

"Smart move John," added Will. "We are up for that."

"Great," replied John, "We can also aid one another with medical needs and any other work that needs to be taken care of."

"I like it," said Will, "How do you want to handle it?"

"I think we should have a meeting at 2 PM today. We will meet in the conservation area parking lot. Will, I'm going to ask everyone to wear a mask and to keep apart. We don't want to take any chances regarding infecting one another. I hope you don't mind."

"Not at all, John. Under the circumstances, that's a wise move. On another note, I called the Emersons yesterday. Rob and Mae are not feeling well, and I want to drop by to check on them now that Ed is here. Ed is a reserve medic and anxious to talk with you."

"Yes, I remember that, Will. Another medic will be an asset. If you don't mind, hold off until I call them. We will need to make a plan to check on them safely. We can't afford to have anyone infected."

"You are right, John. We will follow your lead, you know this pandemic stuff. We will see you at 2."

"Excellent, see you then," John ended the call.

John's next call was to the Emerson farm. They were next to the Bennets and opposite the Conservation area parking lot. Rob and Mae Emerson were both in their 70s and still working the farm Rob's parents owned and operated until they passed away. The phone rang and rang, and no answer. Now John was worried.

Lastly, he called the Campbell farm. They were the first farm off the main road, next to the Emmersons and across from the conservation area. The Campbells were in their late 40's and had three adult children, Brent, Kara, and Jessica. The phone rang twice.

"Hello," Pauline Campbell's soft voice said over the phone.

"Pauline, it's John MacIntyre. How are you and Cory?"

"Oh, John, it's good to hear from you. We are fine but worried to death about this pandemic."

"I hear you," said John. "I want to talk to you both about getting our mutual assistance group going so we can keep an eye on things and help one another out when needed."

"That's a great idea, John," she paused. "Hang on, John, Cory just came in. Cory, it's John MacIntyre."

"Hello, John," Cory said. "I hope you are all well?"
"Right as rain," John replied. "Cory, I think we should get the ball rolling with this mutual assistance group we spoke about."

"Good idea John. How can we help?" Cory replied.

"I want to meet at 2 PM in the conservation area parking lot."
"Sounds good. We will both be there. Jessica is on the way. Brent has his hands full with the army, as you can imagine. Kara will be staying in Halifax with her in-laws."

"Tell them to be extra careful," John warned. "We had a little drama on our trip home, and Cory, given this pandemic going around, I am asking everyone to please wear a mask to the meeting."

"We are good with that, John. We know you're the expert on that stuff, not a problem. One more thing, Pauline talked to Mae Emerson yesterday. Both she and Alan were under the weather; we need to check on them."

"I spoke with Will a few minutes ago," John replied. "He told me they were sick; when I called, I got no answer. Cory, we will make a plan to check on them at our meeting."

"Ok, John, we will do as you see fit. We will see you at 2." They both clicked off.

"The meeting is all set for 2:00 PM," John relayed the news to the others.

Liz was visibly upset; "Mae Emerson is a lovely lady. I hope they are ok."

"Me too," replied John. "Me too."

Caroline picked up her phone and tried David for the fourth time. The phone went to voicemail. "David, it's Caroline, please call me, ok. We are worried about you, please." She clicked off.

Behind the Clary's barn, Franz, J3, and Kat had positioned themselves on a hay wagon. Using a laser rangefinder, Franz placed targets at 300, 400 and 500 meters. "Ok, J3, call your target."

J3 called 300 meters and chambered one of John's reloaded rounds into the 700. Franz coached him on holding the powerful weapon and adjusting the windage and elevation scope. Franz and Kat looked on through spotting scopes as J3 relaxed his breathing, clicked off the safety and lovingly squeezed the trigger.

BOOM! The 250-grain Nosler Accubond bullet exited the muzzle at 2902 feet per second, instantly impacting the target.

"One inch to the right and one inch high," Franz reported. "Correct and fire again."

J3 adjusted his scope, chambered another round, breathed in, and relaxed. BOOM!

"Bull's eye," yelled Kat.

"Excellent," praised Franz. "Your turn Kat."

Until this point, Kat's longest shot was a target at 300 meters, which was with her grandfather's, now her, Weatherby 30-06. This was a different class of weapon altogether.

"Tuck that stock into your shoulder securely, Kat," Franz instructed. "The 338 has a bit more kick than your 30-06."

Kat adjusted the rifle into her shoulder. "300 meters," she confirmed as she centred her optic on the bullseye. Kat adjusted for windage and elevation. She relaxed and breathed in and out several times. She breathed out once more and lovingly squeezed the trigger. BOOM!

The bullet impacted the bullseye. The recoil of the 338 Lapua Magnum was like nothing she had ever experienced before. Her shoulder hurt, and it showed on her face. "I think I just dislocated my shoulder," she said, rubbing her right side.

"The 338 has a bit of kick to it," Franz smiled. "That was excellent, Kat. You are both excellent. John has taught you well. All the mechanics that lead up to the shot are the most important part. I can see that you both know that part well," Franz smiled. "Let's up the game, shall we? J3 the 500 meters, please."

Like his cousin, J3 had never done any shooting beyond 300 meters. John was a good teacher, ensuring they could easily master a lighter calibre before advancing upwards. They were both young, and John was a patient man. Franz sensed as much, but this exercise proved it to be true.

J3 lined up his target and made his adjustments for windage and elevation. He relaxed and controlled his breathing. Despite the cold air, a bead of sweat dropped off his brow. He breathed out slowly, and BOOM!

The bullet impacted the 500-meter target at the top right-hand corner of the bullseye.

"Excellent. J3, your nervousness is obvious, and you may not realize it, but you did flinch just a little. All the same, excellent shooting."

J3 and Kat high-fived one another, smiling.

"I know that the last shot hurt a little. You are young, Kat, but you are strong. The 338 is a powerful cartridge, make no mistake." Franz made a few adjustments to the stock of the 700. "Try that, Kat, tuck it in snug but not too snug. How does it feel a little better on your cheek?"

"Yes," she replied, "I'm ready."

Ok, Miss Katherine, 500 meters. Your trigger control is excellent, so don't fear the recoil; concentrate on the pull," Franz encouraged.

Kat lined up the shot and made the adjustments for windage and elevation. She relaxed her breathing. BOOM!

Like her cousin, her bullet impacted the top right of the

bullseye.

"Excellent, Kat. Just like J3, you both are reacting to the added recoil of the 338. Just a little flinching is keeping you both off your game. A good sniper fires thousands of rounds in practice," Franz smiled approvingly.

"I hope my shoulder can stand up," replied Kat.

"You've got this, Kat. Now, let's take the centre out of those 500-meter target, shall we?

2:00 PM, 22 NOVEMBER 2020

Grey Sauble Conservation Area

The neighbours arrived at the parking area of the Grey Sauble Conservation area at 2:00 PM. Everyone wore face masks and kept their distance as agreed. Greetings and introductions were made, but no handshakes were shared.

Attending were John, Franz, Liz and Caroline, representing the Macintyres. Will Bennet, his eldest son Ed and his wife Anna represented the Bennet farm. Cory and Pauline Campbell, their youngest daughter Jessica who had just arrived home, attended for the Campbells. Despite repeated calls from everyone, there was no answer at the Emerson's.

John called the meeting to order, "I would like to thank you all for coming. For those that don't know me, my name is John MacIntyre. My wife Liz and I live just up the road. I spent 35 years in the military in the Canadian Joint Incident Response Unit or CJIRU, Canada's version of Special Forces. I served four tours in Afghanistan.

My colleague, Franz Roske, also retired from the military after 28 years. Franz served with the German Kommando Spezialkrafte or KSK, Germany's version of Special Forces. He served three tours in Afghanistan. Franz will stay with Liz and our family until the world returns to normal."

John continued, "I do apologize for the circumstances; they are necessary. Dire times have descended upon the world, my friends, and it will be up to us to help one another through this. First and foremost, are any of you or your families experiencing flu-like symptoms?"

Everyone replied, "No."

"Thank God," John responded. "Now, we have to keep it that

way. I have prepared two sheets of notes for everyone." While John spoke, Franz passed out the sheets. "The first itemize all the steps we must take to prevent infecting one another, as well as the steps to take when coming in contact with others. They are obvious: masks, rubber gloves, frequent hand washing, distancing yourselves from others and quarantining the sick. I cannot stress these measures enough. Again I apologize if I am being a bit anal here, but the survival of ourselves and our loved ones is at stake here.

The second contains the names, contact information and skills of my family, our guests, plus Dan and Marg Clary. My daughter Caroline is handling the administrative duties. We would appreciate you all giving Caroline your contact information, skills and areas of interest that could help us all.

"OK, we have come together today to form a MAG or Mutual Assistance Group. The purpose is to help one another and pool our skills and resources for our mutual betterment. I believe we are well represented with farming and raising livestock and crops, so I won't waste anyone's time with that issue. Save to say that if extra labour is needed, we should be ready to pitch in and help as soon as possible. We must address our mutual security and medical needs first and foremost. May I ask if anyone here has any police, military, security or medical experience?"

Ed Bennet stepped forward. Ed was 38, 5'8" and in excellent shape. "John, I work as an engineer in the automotive industry, and I was a Reserve Force medic for 20 years, now retired."

"Excellent," replied John, "My son John Jr and his wife Samantha are also trained paramedics. Ed, can I assume you are comfortable with firearms?"

"Yes, I am John. I served one tour in Afghanistan. I brought all my weapons, ammo and medical gear with us when we came."

"Super," replied John.

Caroline walked over to Ed and wrote down all his information, skills, and phone number.

"Your engineering skills will come in quite handy as well. Thank you, Ed," John added.

Will Bennet spoke up. "John, Ed's younger brother Glen is some kind of computer expert, and he is also a ham radio operator. He is standing guard duty right now, and his wife Christine is a damn good school teacher."

"Very good," John replied. "We need to keep education going for our young ones, and I would like to get together with Glen. We need to set up communications and train radio operators."

Caroline went right over and gathered the info from Will.

Jessica Campbell was the next to speak. Jessica was 26 and single, having never met the right person. "John, As you know, I am a veterinarian, and I would be happy to help out in that regard. When Dad called, I loaded up all the supplies I could carry. I would be able to help out with us humans well. The anatomy of two legs or four is similar, and we all bleed red. A lot of the medications I have can do double duty."

"Thank you, Jessica, John replied."

Caroline hustled over to exchange information with her.

"We have a lot of talent here, which is very good. Others are still coming, so please have them contact Caroline when they arrive. She can gather the information over the phone and update our lists."

Everyone agreed.

"Next item is security. I cannot stress enough; how important it is to have someone standing guard at your farms 24-7. I would also stress that no one should go outside alone and unarmed. To put this in perspective, I have a story to share with you all." John quickly went over the unfortunate incident with Marg and Dan but left out the gory details.

Everyone was shocked by the story and immediately understood the need for security.

John, we have seen a few vehicles entering the Conservation

Area," cautioned Cory Campbell.

Thanks, Cory," John continued. "There may be people taking refuge there that may or may not be dangerous. Once we have our roadblocks in place, I suggest we check this out."

"This leads us to my next topic—access control. I would like to see a manned roadblock set up at both ends of our road, ideally, they would be staffed 24-7. Handling two roadblocks and securing our farms 24-7 will stretch us to capacity. The only way we can do this is to have everyone, male and female, take a turn. We agree that young children should be exempt, of course, and anyone with health issues."

Everyone agreed and volunteered to take turns.

"I will set up the details and do my utmost best to ensure family members share the same duties."

They all nodded in agreement.

"Let's get to work on the roadblocks first thing tomorrow. My gang can supply six bodies. We will need four more without leaving anyone's farm unsecured."

Will, Ed, and his eldest son Chad volunteered. Cory agreed to help.

"Excellent. We have five bodies for each end. We need to make the roadblock moveable, and I'm thinking of a couple of vehicles. We will also need shelters to keep people out of the elements. We do have a storm coming in, and winter is upon us. We can use the two surplus cars at Dan's for one roadblock. Can anyone else help out here?"

"We can use my loader, John, nothing will get by that, and I have a small camper we can use," Cory added.

"Perfect," replied John. "Dan has an old camper he uses for hunting, and I imagine he will let us use that. How about we meet here at 10:00 AM tomorrow after everyone's chores are completed?"

They all agreed.

"In addition to security, we must ensure everyone is trained and armed. The attack on the Clarys reinforces our need to have every capable body armed and every residence guarded. This brings me to my next topic, weapons and training. Most of us in the country have weapons and know how to use them.

"Franz has volunteered to help out with weapons training. There is a big difference between hunting and self-defence. We strongly encourage everyone to attend. Franz is a capable weapons instructor. He would like to spend ninety minutes every day on training.

We also have Hatto Masatoshi staying with us. He is a competent martial arts instructor and master swordsman. Hatto has volunteered to teach anyone who has the desire to learn. He will set up a schedule in a few days. I will keep you all posted.

"I know you all have two-way radios at your farms. Check them out and set them at our agreed home channel, 154.100 MHz. We need to have someone monitor the radio at all times, preferably whoever is on guard duty. If we are all on the same channel, we can use them to alert everyone in an emergency. We will also need one radio at each roadblock. I would also like everyone to stand by their radios at 8 AM and 8 PM. That way, we can check in on one another, make announcements and do a radio check. I have extra radios if anyone is in need. Please give your name to Caroline, and we will get you one ASAP.

"One of our priorities is to set up a communication network and train qualified operators. We will keep everyone posted on this once Glen Bennet and I have a visit.

"Lastly, we need to check on the Emerson's. We are all worried about them. They are both sick, and we cannot risk more people than necessary. Franz and I are willing to go there."

"I will come to represent the medical side, " Ed Bennet offered.

"Thanks, Ed," John replied. "Before we depart, are there any questions?"

No," was the collective reply.

"Very well then, we can all check in at 8:00 PM beginning tonight. Thank you all for coming."

✻ ✻ ✻

"Ed, you can ride with us to the Emerson's, and we will run you back home when we finish," John suggested.
"Sure," Ed replied. "I will grab my gear."

John, Liz, Caroline, Franz, and Ed climbed into John's F150 and drove to the Emerson's driveway. The gate was open, so John pulled in and stopped. Two men wearing Tyvek suits sat on the front porch. Each had a beer in their hand, and neither was Alan Emerson.

"Franz, what's your feeling here?" John asked.

"I don't see any weapons, and they don't look aggressive, John. I recommend we approach cautiously and talk to them."

"Agreed," replied John. "I will drive a little closer and get out. I will keep my sidearm holstered. You cover me, Franz."

"John, be careful," Liz said nervously.

John pulled up and stopped. He exited the pickup wearing his N95 mask. He left the door open and stepped to the side, his holstered pistol visible. John's posture was relaxed and non-threatening, but ready to react if things went bad. "Hello, gentlemen. My name is John MacIntyre, and I live on a farm to the east of here. Who might you two be?"

They both slowly stood, facing John. The older man was a heavy fellow who obviously enjoyed his beer and good food. His face was deeply wrinkled, and his hands showed signs of hard work. He looked to be in his late 50's.

The younger man appeared to be in his mid-30s and looked a lot like the older, obviously family. Like the older man, he was heavy set, more muscle than fat, John thought. His hands, too, showed signs of hard work.

The elder addressed John, "I am Calvin Emerson. Alan and Mae were my parents. This here is my son Carl."

"Pleased to meet you both," replied John. He paused, "You said Alan and Mae were your parents?"

Calvin nodded, "Sadly, they were deceased when we arrived. We buried them this morning."

"I am so sorry," said John. "I heard they were sick, we came by to check on them."

"I appreciate that, John," Calvin replied. "Carl and I arrived late last night and found them both. They passed late yesterday afternoon; we didn't get here in time."

"Again, Calvin, I am truly sorry. I wish we, too, had come by sooner. Do you mind if we walk up there?" John asked.

"Sure," Calvin replied. "Come on up."

Liz, Caroline Franz and Ed donned their masks and walked up with John. They stopped roughly 10 meters from the porch. "Calvin, forgive me if we don't come closer. With this pandemic, it's wise to keep some distance."

"Understood," replied Calvin.

"Calvin, Carl, this is my wife Elizabeth, my daughter Caroline, and our friends Franz Roske and Ed Bennet. Ed is the eldest son of your neighbour to the east, Will Bennet. We are pleased to meet you, folks."

"Our wives and children are in the shop, and we are living there until we get the house disinfected," Calvin added. Calvin then asked Carl to go and bring the ladies out for introductions, and Carl excused himself to do that.

"Calvin," John asked, "do you folks have any weapons?"

"Yes, we do, John. We have several rifles and shotguns between us. Carl is an avid bow hunter, and his wife Arlene, well, let's say she can kick some serious butt," Calvin said, smiling.

"Excellent, Calvin." John filled him in on the drama at the Clarys and suggested they should be armed at all times and not be out alone.

Calvin agreed.

Carl arrived with the others, and introductions were made. John filled everyone in on the mutual assistance group, and Emersons were happy to join in.

"None of us here are farmers, John," Calvin said apologetically. "We can use a lot of help here. Carl and I own and operate a heavy equipment shop." Calvin gestured toward the two service trucks parked at the side of the shop.

"No worries there," replied John. "We have plenty of good sturdy farm help, and adding two heavy equipment mechanics is a blessing. Again, while John spoke, Caroline took everyone's contact information and skills and shared what information she had.

Calvin and Carl agreed to meet at 10:00 in the morning to help set up the roadblocks.

"Carl is also a talented shortwave radio operator and brought his equipment with him," Calvin offered.

"I will have that all setup and operating as soon as the house is squared away. In the meantime, I have several hand-held units," Carl added.

"That is excellent news, Carl. Ed's brother Glen Bennet is also a Ham. We will have to get you both together. We need to get some training on COMMs to bring everyone up to speed. Can you help us out there?" John asked.

"For sure, John," Carl replied. "I would be happy to."

"Our radios will all be on our home channel, 154.100 MHz. We have designated check-in times at 8:00 AM and 8:00 PM daily," John added. "We are all delighted to have everyone aboard here."

Please accept our condolences for the loss of your parents. Alan and Mae were good friends," added Liz.

"We best get on our way," John announced. "Calvin, we will see you and Carl at 10:00 AM in the parking lot. Good night folks."

They drove Ed back home and then returned to the farm.

Greg and Kat had supper ready when they arrived home. Franz was joining them for roast beef, vegetables, potatoes and gravy.

"I even baked an apple pie," Kat said proudly.

"Mmmm, that's why I love you both," John replied rubbing his belly.

Liz thanked them both and apologized for not being there to help.

"Gramma, you needed a break today. You have been through a lot," Kat told her.

They shared a hug and then sat down at the table.

Over supper, Kat filled them in on their shooting. After Franz left with John and Liz, she and J3 kept practicing.

"We are getting better, Franz, and we even moved a target out to 600 meters and hit the bullseye."

"That's excellent, Kat. You two keep up the good work," he praised.

"That's great," exclaimed John. "How do you like the 338?"

"Poppa, that beast has a punch. It took us both a while to get a feel for it and to hold it properly, so it didn't tear our shoulders off," Kat smiled, rubbing her shoulder.

After supper, Franz excused himself to relieve Hatto on watch at the Clary's farm. John turned on the evening news. He wanted to check that and then check his internet sources before the 8:00 PM radio check-in.

> Good evening, this is Michael Anderson filling in for Peter Mansfield, and this is the National.
>
> Tonight, worldwide infections and death tolls rise sharply, and as the sun sets on cities around the world, curfews fail,

and anarchy rises.

The worldwide infection numbers surpassed the 3.5 billion mark today, and the death toll has reached a staggering 1 billion.

Here at home Canada's infections are 5 million, with the death toll climbing to over 500,000 souls.

Food and fuel shortages worldwide have led to panic in the streets in all major cities. The police and military have been unable to keep up as their numbers fall due to illness and death. It has gotten to the point now that some police, military, and emergency health workers are just not showing up for work for fear of infection.

Riots have broken out at food distribution centres, hospitals and emergency medical facilities as desperate people clash for dwindling resources. Things have deteriorated to the point that people's homes are being broken into, their food stolen, and the homeowners are often beaten or killed.

Video clips were aired from around the world showing people clashing with police and military at food distribution centres and medical facilities in the world's major cities. Looters ran out of stores with TVs, computers and trendy fashion items.

In cities across Canada, the story repeats as curfews go unheeded and riots break out at food distribution centres. Desperate people are resorting to violence to feed themselves.

With winter setting in and a major storm on the way, we are getting reports that utility workers are not showing up for work. Some areas are seeing power brownouts as failing equipment cannot be replaced quickly enough. It is expected that this situation will only get worse.

The CBC's entire Ottawa staff is down with the flu. The only news we are getting from the nation's capital this evening is that the Prime Minister's family, staff and senior government officials have relocated to a secure site.

The Prime Minister is expected to speak to the nation tomorrow evening. Stay tuned for that.

We also regret to announce that CBC's own Peter Mansfield and Allison McLean have come down with the flu. Both are in critical condition.

This is Michael Anderson with the CBC news, this 22nd of November 2020. Good night.

At 8:00 PM, John called for a check-in on the radio, and everyone replied. "My first order of business is to inform all of you about Alan and Mae Emerson." John briefly filled them in on the deaths and meeting Calvin, Carl and their families.

"I hope everyone had a chance to watch the evening news. The pictures on TV and internet sources are horrific. Thankfully living out here in the country has spared us from the worst. I want everyone to be aware that desperate people will be heading our way when the food runs out in the cities and towns. As you witnessed tonight on the news, people will do whatever they have to and take what they want.

I cannot stress enough about having 24-7 security at your farms. We will also need to beef up security once these roadblocks are complete tomorrow. This weather front is still coming at us. I hope we can get these roadblocks operational before it hits us.

I have been going through the information we gathered today and will have updated copies for everyone tomorrow. I will put together a roster of names and times for roadblock duty. Again I will do my best to keep family members together. If there are any conflicts, please let me know immediately so we can rectify them. Our safety here demands we have these roadblocks manned 24-7.

"Franz has suggested he would like to lead a patrol into the conservation area tomorrow. We believe that people may be sheltering there; if so, we want to know who they are. We are all exposed here. Franz, Hatto and my son John are going from this end. Is there anyone else interested in joining?" asked John.

Carl and Arlene Emerson agreed to go. Ed Bennet also signed up

"Good," replied John. "Franz wants to go there right after lunch at 1:00 PM sharp. Bring your gear and meet at the parking area just off the main road. That's all I have for tonight. Any questions?" John asked.

Everyone was good. They all signed out.

9:30 AM, 23 NOVEMBER 2020

The Grey Sauble Conservation Area Parking Lot

John pulled into the lot a 9:30, Dan's old hunting trailer hooked to his F150. Right behind were Franz and Hatto in the vehicles liberated from the meth heads. J2 followed them in with J3, Lauren and Kat. In the rear of the pickups were six full 30-pound propane cylinders that would heat the old RV, sandbags, a gas-powered Honda 2000 gen-set that would keep the batteries charged and four 20-litre fuel cans to service the genny. John also brought along a pair of hand-held radios with chargers.

Cory Campbell was the next to arrive, the old Detroit Diesel engine of the massive green loader was screaming and spewing out a blue fog. The bucket was filled with sandbags and tools. Jessica followed in the pickup, her father's hunting trailer hitched to the bumper. In the pickup box were three 30-pound propane cylinders, a Generac gen-set and five 20-litre fuel cans.

Calvin and Carl Emerson pulled in at 9:45 with their service trucks behind them; they towed two portable light units. Arlene Emerson drove a pickup and a trailer loaded with two older quads plus five 20-litre fuel cans. Will, Ed, and Chad Bennet followed them.

Will Bennet had a load of lumber on a trailer behind his pickup and more sandbags.

As Cory climbed down, Calvin Emerson looked lovingly at the giant green loader. "Mmmm, mmm, I do love the wail of a two-stroke in the morning," Calvin praised as he admired the beast. "1978 Terex 72-61 rubber tred loader powered by a 350 horsepower 8V71 Detroit diesel with a bore of 108 mm and a stroke of 127 mm," Calvin reported proudly.

"In my 48 years on this earth, I have never met anyone who could spout off specs like you, sir, and they are 100% accurate. Cory Campbell," Cory announced as he bowed in admiration.

"Calvin Emerson, diesel engineering specialist and Detriot Diesel aficionado," Calvin replied proudly.

John laughed as he looked at the two men. "Gentlemen, if this love affair is over, may we please get down to business?"

"You most assuredly may," replied Calvin grinning.

The entire group broke out in laughter.

"Good morning, everyone," welcomed John cheerfully. "So far, we have dodged that storm," looking to the west at the large billowing grey clouds. "But not for long, I expect."

John introduced Hatto, J3, Lauren and Kat. Then he introduced Calvin, Carl and Arlene Emerson. Ed Bennet introduced his son Chad.

Kat caught Lauren looking at Chad and bumped her with her foot. Lauren looked at her, blushing. "He is cute," she smiled shyly.
"Ok," John spoke. "We need to set these roadblocks up to stop traffic but still be moveable to let vehicles through.

We will set an RV at each roadblock, so people can warm up, make coffee etc. Let's keep the trailers back about 10 meters from the roadblock on the side of the road.

Keep the gen-sets as far back as possible behind the RV to reduce the noise; we need to be able to hear. Keep the fuel away from the gen-sets to prevent any chance of fires, and let's set a fire extinguisher up by the gennies.

At night, we need light discipline. If you're in the light, it will ruin your night vision. Smokers, that glowing cigarette at night will ruin your night vision, so let's remember that. Set up your flood lights facing away from the roadblock towards traffic. We want anyone approaching to be blinded, not ourselves. Questions, concerns?" John asked.

"We brought these two quads along so each roadblock would have a secondary means of transportation. They are old but in top-notch condition," added Carl Emerson.

That is very kind of you, Carl. Thank you," John replied.

"Cory, can you and your crew take the west roadblock?"

"Sure, John," Cory replied.

"Will, Calvin, can I ask your people to work with Cory?"

"Sure, thing John," both Will and Calvin agreed.

"Excellent. My gang can handle the east side. Ok, let's get it done," said John cheerfully.

An hour later, John looked at the roadblock they had just assembled approvingly, "It will do for now. When we have opportunities to beef it up, we will," he said happily.

John drove to the west end to check on the progress.

Cory had the big loader parked across the road. John smiled, "Not much will get past that he said."

"Everything is set up and tested, John," Cory replied proudly.

John and J3 would take first watch on the east roadblock, while Cory and Jessica would take the west. The next shift would take over at 6 PM and run until midnight. The midnight shift would run until 6 AM.

At 12:45 J2, Franz and Hatto pulled into the parking area. Carl and Arlene Emerson were already there, and Ed Bennet pulled in a minute later.

Hatto immediately noticed Arlene carrying a Ninja-style short sword on a sling behind her back. He smiled approvingly and bowed, and Arlene responded with a bow toward Hatto.

Carl chuckled, "Looks like the mutual admiration society is alive and well with the group."

They all shared a laugh. Everyone had a small patrol pack with food and emergency items that could tie them over for at least 36 hours should something go wrong.

J2 and Franz carried their SKS rifles with three spare 20-round mags. They each had a 9MM Glock as side arms with three spare mags. They each took 100 extra rounds of ammo for each weapon and a fixed-blade knife. Hatto, of course, only carried the katana sword and two tantos. Ed had his AR 15, three extra mags, a Sig Sauer 9MM as a sidearm, plus a Ka-Bar knife. Carl and Arlene Emerson carried matching Ruger mini 14's chambered in 223. They had three extra 20-round mags each, and both wore matching Glock 19s and Ka-Bar knives.

Franz addressed the group. "Thank you all for coming. I am not anticipating any trouble, but we know people are in here, and their disposition we do not. Please everyone, be on alert. We will walk in a single file, keeping about 10 meters between one another. We will not talk. I will take the point, and Ed, if you don't mind, could you take the rear."

"Yes," replied Ed.

Franz had a detailed map of the conservation area. He handed out a copy to everyone and went over their route. "Should we get separated for any reason, we will rendevous at the locations I have marked on the map 1st, 2nd, 3,rd. Should those areas be compromised, head for home.

"Should we experience any people, I want us all to remain non-threatening. I will attempt to speak with them. Be alert if they make any threatening moves, then take action but don't shoot unless we are in danger.

"We have three radios between us. We should all be on 154.100 MHz. Let's check them out now," asked Franz.

Everyone checked their settings and did a radio check.

Our home stations monitor the same radio frequencies and will come to our aid if necessary. The temperature is -5, and the weather front is approximately two hours away. We should be back before then. Watch one another for any signs of frostbite or fatigue."

Franz reviewed the standard military hand singles, ensuring everyone knew them. "Any questions?"

"No," everyone replied.

"Let's move out," ordered Franz.

Franz set a comfortable pace as they followed the road through the conservation area. After about 20 minutes, they encountered their first group of people; three large campers and three late-model pickups parked in a picnic area. Six adults and five children sat around a fire warming themselves. It was below freezing but not too cold. The site was well sheltered here, and not much wind made it through the thick trees.

Franz held up his hand, giving the patrol the halt signal. The team went on high alert. Franz had his weapon shouldered as he looked over the area, seeing no guards or surprises.

Franz lowered his rifle and called out, "Hello there."

Everyone at the campsite jumped. The women grabbed the children and led them behind the trailers. One of the men stood. He held a hunting rifle, but he didn't raise it. The others all had hunting rifles close by. They were scanning the area looking for the owner of the voice.

"Hello," the man called back.

"May I come forward?" Franz asked.
"Yes," replied the man.

Franz and his team moved into the open then Franz moved cautiously, taking in everything he could see as he advanced. The others stayed back, ready to react. Franz stopped about 10 meters away. "Good afternoon. My name is Franz Roske. I am staying with friends at one of the farms out on the road. My friends behind me are all neighbours. Is anyone in your group infected or showing symptoms of the flu?"

"No, we are all healthy," the man with the rifle replied.

"Excellent," replied Franz. "We are attempting to secure the area to keep ourselves all safe. We knew there were people here, and we felt it wise to get to know one another."

The man holding the rifle answered, "My name is Ken Hodgson, and these are my brothers, Christopher and Roger."

"I am pleased to meet you all," Franz replied politely. "There is a storm heading this way. Do you have enough food and supplies?"

Not wanting to reveal to much to this heavily armed stranger, Ken Hodgson cautiously replied. "We have enough for now, Franz. Thank you."

"Excellent," Franz replied. "We also have trained medical personnel if needed."

"That's very kind," Ken replied. "We are good for now."

"May I ask if you know of others staying in the park?" Franz asked politely.

"We know of another group with three trailers and a tent further down the road. There are four families there," Ken replied.

"Are they friendly?" asked Franz.

"They stopped and talked to us when they arrived, and I told them about the other campsite. We all felt it better not to mingle because of the pandemic, but they seemed like good folks. All are families with children; we don't know of any others. No one has driven by here," Ken replied.

"Excellent," said Franz. "Keeping a distance is a wise thing. We feel the same way and can't take any chances with this killer flu. We want to meet these folks, introduce ourselves and make them the same offer we made to you. I will give you our phone number should you need anything or an emergency arise. Please do not hesitate to call us."

"That's very kind of you," replied Ken. He and Franz

exchanged phone numbers.

"One last thing," Franz said. "I would recommend having an armed guard standing by 24/7. We have had trouble back at the farm."

"Thank you for that advice, Franz. We will do that."

"Very good," said Franz. "It was nice meeting you all, and please do not hesitate to call if you have any need."Franz turned and walked back out to the road. The Hodgsons watched as the group walked away.

* * *

1.25 kilometres into the park, they came across the next group. Two older travel trailers, one foldup hardtop camper with canvas sides and a small tent were set up in another picnic area. Two pickups and one car were parked off to the side. Franz signalled the halt and surveyed the area. The buzz of a generator could be heard in the background; no one was in sight.

Franz spoke quietly with the others. "Cover me and be vigilant," he ordered. Franz walked closer and called out, "Hello in the campers!"

The two campers rocked as the people inside hustled around. Both doors flew open, and two men pointed shotguns out the doors.

Franz didn't move. The others quickly shouldered their weapons, and Hatto slipped quietly into the woods.

Franz kept his weapon slung over his shoulder and raised his hands. "We mean you no harm," he called out. "My name is Franz Roske, and I am living with friends at one of the farms up on the road."

One of the men called back, "We have nothing for you, and we want to be left alone."

"May I approach?" Franz asked.

The man spoke to someone inside the trailer, "This guy is either an idiot or one cool customer. I'm thinking the latter."

The others nodded in agreement.

"Let him come closer," said a woman.

"Ok," the man called out. "But not too close. You may be infected."

Franz walked in and stopped 10 meters back. "We mean you no harm," Franz spoke. "My friends and I are all neighbours. We live in the farms out on the road. We are trying to secure the area to make it safe for ourselves and you folks. We knew there were people in the park and wanted to introduce ourselves."

The two men began to relax and lowered their shotguns. The one doing the talking spoke up, "My name is Tom O'Gorman. This here, pointing to his right at the other armed man, is Scott Sabovitch."

"Tom, is anyone in your group infected or showing flu symptoms?" Franz asked.

"No, we are all fine. We came here to get away from crowds," replied Tom.

"Do you folks need any food or supplies?" asked Franz.

Tom looked at him like he was crazy, "You're offering us food and supplies?"

"Yes, Tom, there is a storm headed this way, and it's] expected to dump a lot of snow and be very cold."

"We don't have much, but we should be ok," replied Tom.

"We plan on hunting for food if we have to," added Scott.

Franz glanced at the tent and fold-up camper. "Can you stay warm?" Franz asked.

"We have extra propane, enough to last a week," Scott replied.

"Very good," Franz replied. "We have medical staff should anyone need care. May I leave you my phone number? Should any needs arise, give us a call." Franz asked politely.

A voice inside the trailer asked, "Tom, who are these people?"

"I don't know, but they sure as hell know what they are doing," Tom answered.

The conversation went back and forth between Tom and whoever was inside. Finally, Tom turned to look at Franz, "My little girl, she fell this morning, and I think she may have broken her leg."

"We have a trained army medic with us. May we help you?" Franz asked.

A woman's head appeared next to Tom. "Yes, please, she is hurt badly."

Franz called the others in. "Ed, you and I will go in; if the rest of you could spread out and keep watch."

Franz and Ed donned their masks and gloves and walked up to the trailer.

"Tom, this is Ed Bennet. He has served 20 years as a reserve force medic in the military and is a combat veteran. I assure you he is very skilled. May he look at you, daughter?"

"Yes," replied Tom opening the trailer door, "This is my wife Charlene, our son Riley and our daughter Colleen on the couch." Tom pointed to another couple, "this is our friend Clare Taylor and her son Vaughn."

"We are pleased to meet you," Franz said in his thick German accent. "I wish the circumstances could be better."

Ed passed his rifle to Franz, then took off his pack and removed his medic kit. Colleen was wrapped in a blanket, clutching a stuffed bear. Her eyes were red from crying, and tears ran down her cheeks. She was ten years old, a cute red-haired girl with stunning green eyes, her Irish heritage evident.

"May I look at your leg, Colleen?" Ed asked politely.
She nodded yes, shyly and pulled the blanket aside. Someone had made a feeble attempt to dress the injury, but it wasn't working. Colleen was still bleeding. Ed looked at Colleen, "I will have to cut

away the old dressing. Is that ok?"

She nodded yes. Ed took his scissors from his kit and carefully cut away the dressing. Colleen had a compound fracture of her lower leg; the Fibia bone was protruding through a break in her skin, causing the bleeding. Whenever she moved, the protruding bone would make the bleeding worse.

Ed looked at Charlene, "She must be in a lot of pain. Have you given her any medication?"

She looked at Tom, then replied sheepishly, "We don't have anything."

"I want to give her a painkiller to help with that. Does she have any allergies?" asked Ed.

"No," Charlene replied shyly.

Ed pulled a bottle of Ibuprofen from his bag and handed it to Charlene to examine. "It's a very safe and effective painkiller," Ed informed her.

"Ok, we are fine with this. Riley, please get your sister a juice drink," Charlene asked.

Colleen swallowed the meds and cuddled into her bear.

Ed looked at Charlene and Tom, "This is a severe break. I recommend we take her back to the Campbell's farm for care. Jessica Campbell is our chief caregiver and is much better equipped to address this type of injury. She is not a doctor but a veterinarian, there is little difference between treating animals and humans. She has a treatment centre set up at their home."

Charlene had a worried look on her face, "can we be with her?"

I will have to check everyone for symptoms of the flu," replied Ed. "If you are all clean, we will bring you back so you can be with her."

"Yes, anything for my little girl," Charlene sobbed.

Ed then examined everyone at the camp. They were clean. He radioed Jessica, who was on guard with her father on the west roadblock. Everyone was monitoring the radio, so they all heard.

Ed filled them in on the situation. "I have checked them out, and no one is infected."

Cory then agreed to put the family up in Kara's and Brent's rooms while Colleen healed.

While this happened, Franz talked to Scott and the others camped there. It was apparent they were woefully unprepared to weather the storm, let alone a pandemic, and there were still four months of winter.

There were four families here, Tom and his Family, Scott and his wife Jennifer, plus two children, Andrea and Randy. Clare Taylor, a single mother and her son Vaughn shared the tent trailer. Darlene and Bob Jones were crowded into Scott's trailer. The tent was theirs. They all came from London, three hours south of here. They all lived in the same apartment building and were friends. When all hell broke loose in the city, they gathered all they had, loaded up the campers and fled north. Clare Taylor knew the Conservation area, having hiked here on the Bruce Trail with friends when she was in college.

Franz excused himself and made a phone call to John. He didn't want to bring a large group of people in without clearance. "John, they have nothing," he said as he explained what they had discovered on patrol.

"Give me fifteen, Franz. I will call the others and run it by them."

True to his word, John called back fifteen minutes later. "Ok, Franz, it's a go. I will bring transport to bring them out. Cory will take the injured girl and her family. The others we can put up between our house and the Clary's. Dan is up and around, but he cannot do anything. A few extra bodies there could free up J2 and Sam to come home."

"Excellent," replied Franz, "I will give them the news."

"I will be there with transport in half an hour. Thank you, Franz," John replied.

Franz filled everyone in on the offer. After a few short minutes of conversation, it was agreed. They were all very willing to accept the generous offer.

Ed had Colleen's leg immobilized, the bleeding stopped, and her wound dressed. She was resting comfortably, hugging her teddy. All the kids were enjoying the chocolate bars Ed handed out.

Charlene looked at Franz, "Please forgive me if I ask this, Franz, but who are you, people? You are well prepared and professional." Franz smiled and explained about the friends on the farms and their plans to get through this crisis. He was finishing up when John's convoy pulled in.

The trailers were all hooked up, gear loaded and stowed away. Liz's SUV was the closest thing they had to an ambulance. Colleen was gently loaded in the back, where the little girl could rest comfortably. The convoy pulled out of the park and headed for the Campbells.

Once at the Campbell farm, introductions were made. Colleen was carried into Jessica's treatment room in the basement. She had done a superb job; the clinic was as well-equipped as any they had seen.

With the O'Gorman's trailer parked and gear stowed away, Pauline and Cory helped the family settle in and feel at home.

It was agreed that the Sabovitch family, plus Clare and Vaughn Taylor, would stay with Marg and Dan Clary. That would free up J2, Sam, J3 and Lauren to return to the farm.

John and Liz would put the Jones's up at their farm. After everyone was settled in at the Clary's, they headed back to MacIntyre farm.

The snow started to fall heavily, and the winds were picking up; the storm had arrived. "We made it just in time," Liz announced as they went inside.

Another round of introductions was made. The Jones's were set up in a spare bedroom in the basement. With everyone settled in, they all gathered in the kitchen. Caroline and Kat had prepared a fantastic supper.

"If you gals keep this up, I may just let you move in," John joked.

"In your dreams Dad," Caroline replied."You're a slave driver."

They all shared a laugh and dug in. This was the Jones' first decent meal in two days, and they enjoyed it. The chat was fun and light as everyone got to know one another.

Cleanup was quick with all the help, and everyone gathered in the living room with coffee. Bob Jones was a carpenter, and he worked for a small restoration company in London repairing homes damaged by floods and fires, etc. Darlene worked as a cook at a local restaurant; they had no kids. Both were from Cape Breton, Nova Scotia, and neither had family nearby.

"Bob, a carpenter, could come in handy around here with all the new people. Do you mind if we put you to work?" John asked.

"John, we have nothing, Dar and I will do whatever we have to earn our keep here."

"We sure will," Darlene replied in her finest east coast accent. "I'm an excellent seamstress and a pretty fair cook."

"Excellent," John replied. "We check in at 8 PM with the others, and I will share your talents with them."

At the 8:00 PM check-in, the group went over the patrol Franz led into the Conservation area, the people they met, and the new guests. John had already worked the new families into the duty schedule.

Jess reported Colleen was doing well and her spirits were high. Franz and Hatto were on the east roadblock, while Ed and Glen Bennet handled the west side.

John said he wanted to check up on the Hodgson group still camped in the Conservation Area. J2 and Franz would accompany him. They would leave at 9:00 AM. With that, everyone signed off for the night.

9:00 AM, 24 NOVEMBER 2020

Toronto, Ontario

David and Chantel MacIntyre had finished breakfast and prepared to attend a Condominium meeting in the rec centre. The previous afternoon a note was slipped under everyone's door announcing a meeting of all residents in the rec centre by the Condominium Management at 9:00 AM.

Janet Ashton, president of the Condominium Association, worked as a senior account manager in Toronto's financial district. Janet was a tall, lean woman in her late 40's. She was fit and attractive, always well-manicured and expensively dressed. She and her husband, George, owned the penthouse on the top floor of the condo. David and Chantel lived on the floor below them.

The condominium had ten stories with 12 units per floor for 120 units, including the penthouse suite. Attendance was roughly 20%.

Janet addressed the gathering in her usual aloof style. "Thank you all for coming. I see we are missing some residents." She looked around the room, trying to catch everyone's eye. "Several residents are down with the flu, and some have left to stay with family elsewhere. I called this meeting to address how we could help one another during this pandemic.

"We must stick together and support one another through this. I want you all to know that this Condominium Authority takes our safety and security very seriously here. Given the recent wave of criminal activity in the city, I have asked our security provider to double the staffing at this residence until things return to normal.

"I have listed several ways to assist with our needs until the government gets control. First I want everyone to list any food supplies they have on hand. If another resident is in need, we can aid one another.

"Also, I know some residents own a vehicle, and I am asking those that own one to make the vehicle available to others seeking medical aid or shopping for supplies. Necessary precautions will need to be taken when transporting someone infected. Under the current circumstances, this would be far safer than walking, or God forbid, taking public transit."

David MacIntyre raised his hand.

"Do you have a question, David?" Janet asked.

"Yes, I do. Thank you, Janet. We have all watched what is unfolding in the news, and our limited resources here in the building will not last long. Do you think we should all consider leaving?"

Philip Galvin stood to speak. Philip and his partner Peter Bright owned a very successful upscale restaurant. They lived in the unit beside David and Chantel and had become terrific friends.

"Do you have something to add, Philip?" Janet asked.

"Thank you, Janet. Neither Peter nor I are on good terms with our families. They disapprove of our lifestyle, and we have nowhere else to go."

Both Sal and Anna Cutrara stood next.

"Sal, Anna," Janet said, deferring to them to speak.

Sal Cutrara and his wife Anna lived on the ground floor. Sal was 50 and Anna 45. Sal worked as a lobbyist for PETA and pressed the Ontario government to introduce laws restricting hunting and fishing and programs to reduce meat consumption and promote a vegan lifestyle. Anna was a human rights lawyer.

Sal spoke up, "Anna and I have been talking about this. We think we should stay here. The government will get a handle on this very soon."

"I'm not so sure, Sal," David disagreed. "This seems to be getting worse, not better."

Sal raised his hand in a dismissive wave, "The uncivilized will kill one another off soon enough, and the world will be a better place without them, wait and see. The government has set up distribution centres, and we can send people should we need to restock-"

David angrily interrupted the pompous, Sal, "We have scant few supplies in this building and those food distribution centres you speak so highly of are experiencing plenty of security and supply issues. I must ask, Sal, will you be the one going to these centres to pick up supplies?"

Sal looked at, David indignantly but never answered.

Your silence speaks volumes, Sal. Everyone should have done as the government recommended and stocked up before things got bad," David added furiously.

"David, you are beginning to sound like your deranged father!" Chantel scolded in her French accent. "You went out and bought plenty of supplies, and now we have plenty of food in our unit."

David looked over at his wife angrily. "Maybe I was wrong. Maybe we were wrong," he said. "I know my Dad is a bit out there, but I can assure you they are all warm, safe and cozy right now. We are not."

"David, I will not go there," Chantel snarled. "They are all farmers, and they kill innocent animals. Goodness knows how many PEOPLE your father has killed. You go if you want, and I am staying here with my friends."

Anna and Sal looked at David with disgust. Sal spoke defiantly, "They sound like the kind of people I work against daily."

Anna and Janet nodded with him in agreement.

"David," Sal scolded. "We are safer here. If you want to live with a bunch of hillbillies, suit yourself."

"They are my family, Sal, they are good people. And that is the end of this conversation," David said angrily.

Pasteur Kavaruganda stood next to David in support of his friend and addressed the group. Pasteur and his younger brother immigrated to Canada from Rwanda with their Uncle and Aunt shortly after the genocide in 1993. He and his wife, Giselle, both in their early 40s, met in Canada. Pasteur worked with David at the University of Toronto as a professor in the science department.

The tall, lanky Rwandan called out loudly! "Please, my friends, please. We must get along here. Sal, regardless of your opinion, others have the right to live as they please. You would do well to respect others. In Rwanda, I learned that it's the good guys with guns that always have to come in and fix the mess made by others." Pasteur continued. The same will come to pass here in Canada if this pandemic gets out of hand. You can mark my words."

Sal and Anna looked at Pasteur with disdain.

Pasteur stared back, unflinching as he continued, "I agree with David. We should make plans to leave here. Giselle and I witnessed our share of hate and death in Rwanda. I will loan anyone my copy of General Romeo Dallaire's book, Shake Hands with The Devil. General Dallaire tells the truth about the genocide committed in our home country and how those that could do something stood by while we were butchered,

"Trust me when I tell you, it can happen here. Sal, Anna, Janet, the world is not all ice cream and cake. Evil lives among us."

Sal was unaccustomed to being challenged. He looked at Pasteur angrily, "I don't need to be lectured by you or educated by some - General," he said scathingly. "This is not some backwater in Africa.""

"You are correct about one thing, Sal. This is not some backwater in Africa, that is why this will be so much worse," Pasteur corrected angrily.

"Pasteur is right," Giselle spoke up defiantly. "This will get worse. We have been down this road before, Sal."

Things were beginning to get out of hand. Janet called out for calm.

Philip Galvin walked up to the platform and stood beside Janet, raising his hands for calm. "Please, please, everyone, calm down. Can I have your attention?" When everyone settled down, he spoke. "Peter and I would like to make you all an offer." Philip looked around the room. He had everyone's attention. "Our restaurant is closed due to the pandemic. However, we have a large quantity of food and drink we can share. All we ask for is help to bring it back here."

Everyone turned toward Philip and applauded.

"Thank you, Philip, that is very kind of you both. Are there any volunteers?" Janet asked excitedly.

Chantel looked at David. She was angry with him and wasn't pleased with his desire to leave. She would not leave and made it abundantly clear to him. "David, Philip and Peter are offering everyone food, and we already have plenty. We can all stay here together, and we will be safe," Chantel scolded David.

David reluctantly agreed with her. He put up his hand, nodding at Philip that he would help. In his mind, he feared they were all making a colossal mistake.

Pasteur agreed to help and would bring his vehicle. Two other men did the same; both had cars.

"Excellent," Janet spoke to everyone. "Philip, can you arrange with the others when you wish to begin."

Philip nodded in agreement, "Please come to see me when we finish, and we will set this up."

Janet continued, "If there are no more questions, I will have the lists here for the food, supplies and vehicles to loan. Please come up and add your information."

David stepped aside with Philip while Chantel went to list their supplies. Chantel filled out the form. She wrote out in her immaculate penmanship all the food and water stores they had, roughly three weeks' supply for the two of them.

Chantel looked at what some of the other residents had listed, and there wasn't much. Most of these people are professionals who undoubtedly eat out all the time. *"Thank God Philip has food to share. Our meagre supplies would not go far."*

Janet and Anna walked up to Chantel and briefly looked at her list of items. They both gave Chantel a forced smile. "You and David have a lot of food there," Anna said.

Chantel replied in her best French-accented English, "David's father is one of those crazy doomsday prepper people." "He called, wanting us to come to the farm, and when we refused, he told us we should, at the very least, stock up. David went out and spent a small fortune on supplies."

Janet gave Chantel a distant look, "Chantel, David is a Professor. It's hard to imagine his parents being like those redneck hillbillies pictured on that foolish television program."

"His Mother is nice but his Father is retired from the military. He has been to Afghanistan and God knows where else. I know he has killed people!"
Chantel whispered.

Both Janet and Anna looked at her in shock. "I didn't think you were serious when you mentioned that earlier," said Anna.

"He was some kind of sniper in the army. We all watched the news, and we know they shot many people," Chantel added.

Janet hugged Chantel, "Poor David, growing up must have been terrible for him."

"Thankfully, we are here now. I hate that smelly farm,"

Chantel replied.

9:10 AM, 24 NOVEMBER 2020

Grey Sauble Conservation Area

Overnight substantial snow had fallen. 25 cm of soft fluffy snow lay on the road into the camp, and it was still falling. The morning was cold. The temperature dropped to -25 overnight. John, Franz, J2 and Bob Jones pulled up to the Hodgson campsite.

Ken Hodgson was on guard duty. He recognized Franz from yesterday and waved them in.

"Good morning Ken," Franz said cheerfully.

"Good morning Franz," replied Ken.

Franz introduced John, J2 and Bob. "How are you folks doing here," Franz asked.

"We are doing fine," said Ken. "We do appreciate you, folks, checking up on us. Would you fellows like to come in for a coffee? We could get to know one another," Ken offered.

"Sounds like a plan," replied Franz.

"Brianna," Ken asked. "Would you mind standing watch while I chat with our guests?"

"Sure, Dad," the attractive 23-year-old replied.

The men followed Ken into his camper. One at a time, they removed their winter boots and coats.

The other adult Hodgsons made their way over as well. "Ken, Andy is on his way out to help Bri," Roger said as he removed his gear.

The camper was crowded with nine adults inside; however, introductions were made, and coffee was shared while everyone got acquainted.

Ken was the eldest Hodgson. His family lived in Windsor,

Ontario. Ken was 48 and worked as a Millwright for Ford Motor Company in Windsor. Ken had worked for Ford all his life. Brenda, Ken's wife, was 46. She holds a Master of Science degree in plant agriculture. She worked as a horticulturist for the Windsor Botanical Gardens. Brianna, 23, was their only child. She was working toward her master's degree in business at the University of Windsor.

Roger Hodgson, 46, was the middle child. Roger and his wife Marlene, 45, owned a landscaping business in Windsor. Their eldest was Andrew, 23. He went by Andy. Andy worked as a landscape foreman with his parent's company. Mary Anne was 19 and a nursing student at Conestoga College in Kitchener, Ontario.

Christopher Hodgson, 40, was the youngest sibling. Chris was recently laid off from Chrysler in Windsor. He was using his severance package to study Police Foundations at St. Clair College in Windsor. Penny Hodgson was Christopher's wife. She worked as a legal secretary. Their children, Lynn and Larry, were both students and Sea Cadets.

With everyone acquainted, John filled them in on thier mutual assistance group (MAG). The story about the Clary's shocked them all.

"We have been getting news on the radio," Marlene added. "It's getting scary out there."

John offered them the option of moving the campers to the farm.

"John, that is a very generous offer, Ken replied. We would be wise to consider it. We are fine here, but could we take some time to talk it over among ourselves and let you know in the morning?"

The other Hodgsons nodded in agreement.

"That would be fine," replied John. "We want you all to be comfortable with your decision. Regardless of your choice, we will be here for you if you need us. I will send some machinery in to clear the roads for you."

"You folks are all very kind," Brenda spoke up. "We look forward to getting to know all of you." "We best be going," John said. They all stood, exchanged handshakes and headed out.

John pulled out onto the snow-covered road and gave a wave to the two young Hodgson's standing guard as he drove off.

"Franz, what do you think?" John asked.

"There is an abundance of talent in those three trailers," he replied.

"Son, what do you think?" John asked J2.
"I agree, dad. Those people could be real assets to our group."

"They are quite vulnerable down here by themselves," John added, "I want to get this road cleared ASAP in case something goes wrong. J2 lets you and I fire up the tractors and clear this snow."

"Sure thing, dad."

The men got back home in time for lunch. Franz stayed and ate with the MacIntyre clan. He wanted to check in with his two students, J3 and Kat.

After lunch, John and J2 took the tractors and started toward the Conservation Area. The air was cold and the snow had finally stopped falling. While Cory and Calvin cleared the road between the roadblocks John and J2 cleared the road into the Conservation Area.

Three hours later the tractors were cleaned up, refuelled and parked back in the shop. It had been a productive day. As the sun settled low on the western horizon John and J2 headed inside.

John chatted with Franz about his afternoon. Franz had been teaching J3 and Kat about external ballistics theory all afternoon. He had spent the afternoon teaching them how the Coriolis Effect (the spinning of the earth) affects the path of the bullet to its target in long-range shooting. His young disciples were eagerly eating up this knowledge.

Both John and Franz had the east-end roadblock duty at midnight. Franz excused himself and went back to the Clary's for a nap.

"Caroline," John asked. "Has David called back yet?"

"No," replied Caroline. "He doesn't answer my calls."

John shook his head disapprovingly, "Caroline, I fear this will not end well."

"I know, Dad," she replied. "I will keep trying."

"I know you will, sweetheart. I know you will."

John enjoyed a light supper with the family and then headed to bed. Sleep would not come easy tonight. Many things weighed heavily on his mind.

Those that weren't sleeping gathered to watch the evening news.

> *Good evening, this is Janie Handley with the CBC Evening News.*
>
> *The worldwide death toll continues to grow as infections spread. Hospitals close due to staff shortages, and law and order begin to collapse as looting and chaos spiral out of control.*
>
> *We begin tonight with a pre-recorded statement from the Prime Minister:*
>
> *Good evening. With infections running out of control, I decided today to relocate the government to a secure location. My friends, the situation is dire. Worldwide infections have reached 4 billion, a staggering 50% of the global population. The death toll has climbed to 1.5 Billion.*
>
> *Here in Canada, infections have reached 6 million; the death toll is now 1.5 million. The most regrettable news tonight is that despite the best efforts from the CDC, the WHO and Canada's Health Agency, there is no cure yet available. Hospitals are beginning to shut down as staff succumbs to the*

virus.

The military, police and emergency services are also suffering from staff shortages. Lawlessness will not be tolerated and cannot be permitted to get out of hand. I regret to inform you that I have authorized our security forces to use lethal force to control the situation.

We encourage citizens to use the food and fuel distribution facilities only as a last resort. We regret we have experienced shortages with personnel and supplies resulting in clashes between angry citizens and our security forces. Strict rationing protocols are in place to ensure those that everyone can be taken care of can be taken care of. Therefore we ask for everyones patience while we work through these difficult times. Hoarding and lawlessness will not be tolerated for any reason. The safest thing you can do is to shelter at home and avoid contact with others. I want to ensure everyone that your government is doing everything possible to find a cure for this pandemic and to keep Canadians safe.

Thank you, Merci

The Prime Minister spoke from a secure site near the nation's capital today.

The management of the CBC regrets to inform you that our own Peter Mansfield and Allison McLean passed away earlier today. Michael Anderson has also come down with this virus and is currently in critical condition.

The CBC, as well as other news agencies, are severely understaffed. Management has been forced to temporarily put many of our scheduled programs on hold until staffing issues can be resolved. This decision is regrettable but necessary. The management wishes to assure our viewers that the regular news programs will continue. We are attempting to gather reports from our sources at home and abroad and present them to you from our Toronto location.

The reports from today paint a bleak picture as looting runs uncontrolled and medical facilities close, food and fuel supplies run short. The nation's utilities are also dealing with understaffing. Canadians are being warned to expect temporary brownouts and power interruptions while repairs to the electrical grid are made.

This is Janie Handley with the CBC Evening News, this 24th of November 2020.

Good night.

J2 handled the 8:00 PM check-in. Everyone had watched the news and agreed the situation was spiralling out of control. "What is critical for us here to keep in mind is what the Prime Minister and news media are not saying.

First, lawlessness among those still healthy enough to break the law is getting out of control.

Second, those food distribution centres the PM talks about are few and far between. They have good intentions, but these are turning out to be disasters. Workers have been dropping out sick or failing to show up for work before some of the centres could be assembled and stocked, which leads to the third.

There are very few shipments of food and fuel getting through. The few healthy truck drivers out there can't keep up, and some are refusing to show up for work, fearing infection and prefering to stay home and protect thier loved ones. My sources on the internet confirm that gangs and desperate people are ambushing some shipments, drivers killed, and cargo looted. This is even happening here in Canada.

Fourth, I have been sent pictures of bodies piling up in tents because morgues are overfilled. Lastly, I got word that the government is worried about our nuclear power plants. They fear the staff needed to keep them running safely will either die or not show up for work. They are making plans should they have to shut them down. I don't have to tell anyone what that means."

The entire group was gravely concerned about the situation when they signed off.

10:00 AM, 25 DECEMBER 2020

Toronto, Ontario

David jumped in the SUV with Pasteur, and followed the convoy to the restaurant. They lived in an affluent area; the real crime and looting problems had not gotten this far. They passed a few desperate-looking people as they drove. Other drivers were out, some driving very aggressively as they hurried on their way. Everyone looked afraid.

The restaurant did a lot of catering to high-end functions and owned two large catering vans. The men loaded all the food, bottled water, wine and liquor the restaurant had, filling all three cars and the two vans.

"Wow, we could have some party with all this David joked as he and Pasteur climbed into his SUV.

Yes, we sure could," replied Pasteur, "An apocalyptic wine and cheese. We could all dress as zombies." The two men shared a laugh as they drove off.

Upon return, the food and supplies were quickly unloaded. Philip and Peter organized all the food in the rec centre's two large commercial refrigerators and freezers. They stacked up the canned and dry goods on shelves. What they couldn't fit was set aside to be shared among the residents.

Janet thanked Philip and Peter, saying this should last them for several months, maybe more. She called all the residents to inform them that there were supplies for everyone.

Janet, of course, was there, as was her husband, George, Sal, and Anna, ensuring they got more than their fair share of high-end food and wine. Like many others, they ate out every night and had little on hand at home. Other residents were also looking for a handout; few had any food in their units. David and

Chantel had only asked for some excellent wine, and Philip was happy to give them some.

With the refrigerators, freezers and shelves all stocked up, Janet wanted to remind everyone she was in charge. She posted a note on the door containing her unit and phone number, informing anyone who needed supplies that they would need to contact her. She then locked the door behind her, pocketing the key.

That night David and Chantel ate a nice vegan dinner and enjoyed a bottle of excellent wine as they watched the mayhem unfolding on the evening news.

Watching society break down so quickly was beginning to unnerve David. "I am thankful Philip and Peter brought back all that food. Not many in this building felt the urgency to stock up when they should have. I also think it was wrong for Janet to take control of it; that food belongs to Philip and Peter."

"David," Chantel scolded. "Janet is the President of the condo association. You are so disrespectful."

"I am aware of that," David replied, "Did you happen to notice that neither the Ashton's nor the Cutrara's gave a list of what food items they had on hand? They certainly weren't shy when it came to hoarding the finest food and drink for themselves. I'm willing to bet they had nothing before Peter and Philip helped out."

Chantel gave him a disapproving stare. "David, don't you start in on this again. I told you I am not going to that farm, and that's final. I am, however, going to bed by myself," she growled as she stomped off to their bedroom.

David took a blanket and pillow out of the hall closet and laid them on the couch. He poured himself a large scotch and set the bottle on the coffee table. He scanned the news channels by himself. It was going to be a long night, and right now, David was quietly wondering if maybe his Father was right.

* * *

The condominium residents had no idea they were being watched. Another group had thier eye on that food and they would come for at a time of thier choosing.

10:00 PM, 25 NOVEMBER 2020

West End Roadblock

Calvin and Arlene Emerson were on the west end roadblock. It was just past 10:00 PM, the sky was clear, the air was cold, and the moon was almost full.

Calvin Emerson thought he heard something as he tipped his head, listening. Sound travels so much farther in the cold winter air. He heard it again. He looked at Arlene tilting his head to one side so that he could hear better. "Jacob's engine brake ... on a Cummins engine ... a big Cummins engine ... a 15-litre engine ... 605 horsepower, I'm thinking ... nope, I'm sure, and judging by how it's being shifted, it's hooked up to an 18-speed Eaton transmission.

Arlene looked at her father-in-law, shaking her head in disbelief. "Calvin, it's not hard to tell your Carl's father."

"It's coming this way fast, Arlene, lets light up the tower," yelled Calvin as he jumped into the big green loader. He smiled as big Detroit came to life and switched on all the lights.

Sure enough, a big truck rounded the bend, plowing through the deep snow. It was lit up like a Christmas tree. Upon seeing the roadblock, it started to slow the driver, effortlessly dropping the gears one by one. The big rig stopped about 50 meters from the roadblock.

Calvin and Arlene stood behind the monster loader aiming their rifles at the truck.

After what seemed like an eternity, the driver's door opened, and a big, old white-haired, white bearded man stuck his head out. "For fuck's sake, don't shoot me. Cory, is that you?" He yelled out.

Calvin and Arlene looked at one another. Finally, Calvin yelled back, "How do you know Cory?

Who the fuck are you?" the man yelled back.

"Who the fuck are you? answered Calvin.

"I'm Cory's uncle, Bill Campbell."

Calvin got on the radio to Cory. "Cory, we have a Bill Campbell at the west roadblock, and he claims he's your uncle. Damn, he has one sweet ride."

"Is he a big, ugly, hairy old bastard, Calvin?" Cory asked.

"He most certainly is," replied Calvin.

"Well, I'll be damned," replied Cory. "I'm on my way."

Five minutes later, Cory pulled up to the roadblock. Sure enough, there was his Uncle, Wild Bill Campbell. He was drinking coffee with Calvin and Arlene, his hands and arms gesturing wildly as he relived the tale of his trip here. It was as if Bill had known them forever.

"Uncle Bill," Cory called out.

Bill grinned a big goofy grin, "Cory!" He hugged his nephew, "How is that pretty wife of yours?"

"She is fine, Uncle Bill. I see you have met Calvin and Arlene."

Bill nodded. "That Calvin is a sharp one. He could tell what I was runnin' before I even pulled up and that Arlene, she's a looker."

"Be careful, Uncle Bill; she's small but could whoop your hairy old ass in a heartbeat."

"I would die a happy man," Bill smiled.

Cory smiled at his uncle. "It's been what, seven years? Not a phone call or a text message."

"Ah shit, Cory. You know I don't like to talk." Bill replied.

Everyone gave him a questioning look.

"Well, on the phone, that is," Bill laughed.

"You haven't changed a damn bit. Still trucking, I see."

"Ahh, you know me, Cory. I would drop dead if I weren't

truckin," replied Bill.

They all shared a laugh. "What brings you by here, Uncle Bill?"

Have you seen it out there?" Bill replied excitedly.

"Only what's on the news. We have had our share of drama here, hence the roadblocks," Cory replied.

"Good thing," Bill replied. "As I was so eloquently explaining to Calvin and Arlene. I was on my way to Collingwood with groceries. Bloody good for nothing's tried to ambush me three God damned times. Shit, I had to run a few of the bastards over. I think Big Blue still has blood on the bumper.

"Finally, I said screw this. I may be old, but I'm not checking out like this, no way. I decided my smartest move was to head here. I knew you and Pauline would have things sorted out."

"Uncle Bill, you're not sick, are you?" Cory asked.

"Nope, I'm healthy as a horse," Bill replied. "The last time I was sick was last year, damn flu bug. I was sick as a dog; figured I was gonna croak."

Calvin nodded knowingly, "Oohh ya, we all had that bug. Sick as dogs we were."

"We were too. All of us, flat on our backs," Cory added.

Then Cory tilted his head to the right, and he looked at Bill, then to Calvin and Arlene, a look of serious thought on his face.

"I know that Campbell look, yep, seen it many times. Wheels are a turnin' and a burnin' in that ugly bean of yours. I can smell the wood burning. What the hell are you thinking?" Bill laughed.

"We were all sick last year, but none of us are sick this year, hm," Cory rubbed his jaw. "I will have to run that one past Jess. Come on, Uncle Bill, get Big Blue and let's get you back to the farm and settled in."

Damn, that's a sweet ride, Calvin smiled as he backed the big loader off the road, allowing Bill's semi to roll through. Calvin pulled the loader back on the road and called in the update.

10:30 PM, 25 NOVEMBER 2020

The South Side of the Grey Sauble Conservation Area

T he four young men arrived the day before on the 24th. Their cars running on fumes as they drove up to the south entrance to the Grey Sauble Conservation Area. They had been travelling north with no destination in mind, looking for a place to make their own.

They had lived off the goodness of the system all their lives; neither had held a job for more than a few days. It was far easier to collect welfare, party and have fun.

Since the pandemic began, that plan hadn't worked so well for them. They had tried stopping at a few farms occupied by the living and were chased away. No one was willing to take in four healthy young men who were not willing to work in exchange for food.

They broke into homes occupied by the dead. Unwilling to clean up bodies, they took what they wanted and moved on, siphoning gas when they found it. They had acquired four shotguns and a few boxes of birdshot from the homes they had broken into.

Not a one of them could read a map, so they had no clue where they were, and now they were almost out of gas again. They pulled into the Conservation Area's south parking area and stopped.

They needed a plan; they had no food, gear, gas, decent winter clothing, and little ambition. That's when they spotted the faint flicker of a campfire in the park. The fire was deep inside the park down by the river, so far in that they almost missed it.

Shotguns in hand, the four wandered in to check it out. The

snow was knee-deep; they wore jeans, light jackets, and sneakers on their feet. They were wet and cold. When three trailers appeared, they figured they could travel in style with one of those.

From their vantage spot in the woods, they observed two pretty young women sitting around a warm, inviting campfire cradling shotguns. There were three three sweet-looking pickup trucks and three comfortable-looking fifth wheel trailers, so it was apparent there were an unknown number of people there, and they were armed.

The four cold and wet young men discussed their findings as they struggled back to their vehicles in the knee deep snow.

Late in the afternoon, as the sun set, they sat in thier cars, trying to keep warm; as they cycled thier engines on and off to conserve precious fuel. Full of youthful bravado, several bottles of rye whiskey, a few joints and too many hours playing Call to Duty, they hatched a plan.

They would wait until early morning when everyone was asleep. They would knock out the guard, storm the trailers and tie up the occupants. They would take one of the pickups, the biggest trailer, maybe the girls, and bugger off, spending their days living the RV lifestyle, drinking, partying and having fun.

It had gotten much colder overnight, and the winds had picked up again. At 4:30 AM, the first car ran out of gas, and the engine shuddered to a stop. The four hungover fools grabbed their shotguns and headed back into the park, poorly dressed, half-frozen and under-equipped. They could only see them in a nice RV, a fancy pickup and some pretty girls.

Bullying and bluster had never failed them, so the four were confident it would serve them well one more time. The four crept up to the rear of the first trailer. The pretty girls standing guard were gone, replaced by a young man about their age.

The four poorly dressed, hungover men shivered, the bitter cold clouding their thinking. Between shivers the pack's defacto leader, Reggie, ordered, "We club the guard, rush into each trailer, put everyone out here by the fire, and tie them up. Got it?"

They all nodded, "ok."

Two of the gang snuck behind Andy Hodgson, sitting by the fire. Andy was 23 and well-muscled from hard work, but it wouldn't help him tonight. Andy never saw the club coming. He was hit on the head and slumped to the ground; he landed perilously close to the fire.

Reggie stayed on guard outside while the others each took a trailer. The Hodgsons were caught off guard as the three young men forced them all outside at gunpoint.

One of the young men made the foolish mistake of getting too close to Ken Hodgson. Ken grabbed the man's shotgun, and they wrestled for control of the weapon. Reggie fired at Ken, hitting him in the leg. Ken fell to the ground. Everyone in the Hodgson group either yelled or screamed. The man regained control of his shotgun and pointed it at Ken. The others aimed at the group, shouting, "Freeze, freeze!"

5:15 AM, 26 NOVEMBER 2020

West Roadblock

John and Franz were nearing the end of their shift. It had been a cold night. They had alternated standing watch outside and warming up inside the camper. John was inside warming up, and Franz was on the roadblock when the unmistakable blast of a 12-gauge pierced the cold morning stillness.

John ran out of the trailer, SKS rifle up and ready.

Franz called to him, "John, it came from the park. It must be the Hodgson camp. Let me investigate. You warn the others."

"Agreed," replied John. "Be careful, Franz."

Franz climbed into the pickup, killed the lights and headed into the park. He stopped 300 meters from the Hodgson camp, parked the truck, grabbed his weapon and ran toward the campsite. As he approached, he moved into the trees and stealthily closed in.

All hell was now breaking loose in the Hodgson camp. Ken's wife, Brenda, was beside herself, seeing her husband on the ground, bleeding. The pure white snow was red with blood when she moved to go to his aid. One of the men struck her on the side of the head with the stock of his shotgun. She fell to the snow, bleeding from a head wound.

Fear and panic had fully set into Brianna. Seeing her parents laid out on the ground, bleeding, panicked her, and she ran to them.

Reggie and his gang were now running on adrenaline and fear. This was not how the plan was to unfold; everything was falling apart. He pointed his shotgun at Brianna. Roger jumped to prevent his niece from being shot. Reggie fired, and Roger caught a blast of birdshot in his back. He fell to the ground, the snow around him sprinkled with blood.

Franz was in position now. It was apparent the situation was completely out of hand. He took a knee and fired—two rounds into Freddie, two rounds into the next man, then two into the third. By the time the third man fell, number four had identified roughly where the shots were coming from. He pointed his shotgun and fired.

Franz knew he would be facing at least one shotgun, so he had positioned himself at the edge of shotgun range. The pellets fell harmlessly to ground well to the to the right of his position. Two quick rounds from the SKS dropped the shooter.

John had heard the shotgun blast, followed quickly by the very different sound of the semi-automatic SKS. Three groups of two shots from Franz, a shotgun blast, two more from the SKS, then silence. John had a pretty good idea of how this had just played out.

Franz called out to the Hodgson's, "are there any more bad guys?"

Christopher immediately picked up one of the shotguns and yelled back, recognizing the thick German accent, "I don't think so, Franz, it seems all clear. Come on in. I will cover you."

Back at the farm, the cavalry was on the move.

Franz ran to the campsite, weapon at the ready, scanning the area to be sure. Franz keyed the mic on his radio, "It appears to be clear here. We have four friendlies down, four bad guys KIA."

"Three minutes out," replied Cory over the radio.

Franz went immediately to Roger, the most seriously injured, pulled his IFAK from his vest and went to work. Christopher went to Ken while Mary Anne, a nursing student tened to Brenda.

The backup group pulled into the camp. Hatto, Carl, Calvin and Arlene immediately spread out to check the area, ensuring it was indeed safe.

Jessica took over from Franz, tending to Roger. Ed went to Ken. Mary Anne had Brenda's bleeding under control . She was now sitting up holing Brianna tightly

Andy Hodgson had regained consciousness. He had a nasty bump on the head from the club and a light burn from the fire. Christopher tended his wounds.

Franz got on the radio and gave the group an update. The injured were quickly stabilized, loaded, and transported back to Jessica's treatment centre.

Franz and Christopher gathered the uninjured Hodgsons. They were all in shock as the adrenaline rush subsided. When they were calm, Franz instructed them to lock everything up and follow hi back to the Campbells's farm in the remaining vehicles.

6:00 AM, 26 NOVEMBER 2020

The Campbell's Farm

The convoy wheeled into the Campbell's farm. The injured were quickly carried into the basement for care. Samantha had already arrived; she and J2 had the clinic prepped for the wounded. The others were sent to Cory's shop.

Caroline changed the morning radio check-in at the last minute to an all-available hands gathering at the Campbell's. Pauline, Tom, Charlene and Riley O'Gorman had been hard at work preparing breakfast for everyone. Marg, Dan, Clare Taylor and young Vaughn arrived to help out. Dan was getting around quite well and wanted to help, but Marg quickly put him in his place, ordering him to sit. Relieved from guard duty bt J3, John was the last to arrive.

By 7:00 AM, everyone in the group had arrived except those on guard duty and the medics tending to the injured. Brianna helped her mother into the shop, and introductions were made.

The panic and danger now subsided, everyone enjoyed a fine breakfast of bacon, homemade sausage, fresh farm eggs, and Pauline's excellent pan-fried potatoes. Plenty of coffee and tea were shared, and farm fresh milk and juice for the kids.

With breakfast over, John called the building to order. "I would like to thank everyone for their actions early this morning, and I would like to thank Caroline for seizing the opportunity and moving our morning check-in here at the last minute. We truly have a well-oiled machine here."

Everyone applauded.

"Before we begin, we added a new member to our ranks last evening. Cory's Uncle, Bill Campbell, arrived last evening with his tractor-trailer and a full load of groceries."

Bill Campbell stood and thanked everyone for allowing him to join the group.

John looked around the garage, smiling. "Including the Hodgsons, we have 50 people in our group. That is if you folks want to stay?"

Brenda Hodgson stood with the aid of her daughter. Brenda wiped her eyes and spoke. "We cannot even begin to express our thanks for what you all did for us this morning. I was certain we were dead. I speak for every one of us when I say this. If you are willing to accept us into your group, wild horses couldn't drag us away. We will work hard, pull our weight and contribute to the well-being of everyone."

With hugs and handshakes, the Hodgsons were warmly welcomed into the group.

"That settles it. We now have 50. The Emerson family has agreed to host the Hodgson's until we find suitable housing." Once again, I would like to thank everyone for how professional you were this morning. Your efforts are commendable, and I mean that sincerely. We are proud of you all."

Everyone joined in with hearty applause.

"Now, for our first order of business, I spent some time this morning talking with Franz and Ed. We agreed it was time to begin regular roving patrols. We do not want a repeat of this morning's drama. That could have turned out much worse."

Everyone nodded in agreement.

"Franz has volunteered to organize and execute these patrols. I cannot think of a better person for this task. Those wishing to participate, please see Franz after our morning meeting.

Furthermore, to prevent manning conflicts, Franz will also assume the duties of coordinating our roadblock staffing. With our numbers expanding, we need to start extending our territory.

This afternoon, Franz and I will lead two patrols around

the immediate area to check things out. We could use a few volunteers for this. Again check in with Franz when we are finished. We will depart my farm at 1:00 PM."

"This next bit of news has piqued my interest. Cory was talking with his Uncle Bill when he arrived last night. They all realized everyone was down and out with that flu bug last year, and now not one of them is sick with this recent bug. Could that be a coincidence? How many in this room were down with the flu bug last year?" John asked.

Every hand in the room was raised, and everyone looked around in disbelief.

"Well, now isn't that interesting," said John.

Every head in the room nodded yes in unison.

"Before we get too excited. We must evaluate if the previous infection protects us from this new one. We must evaluate if the previous infection protects us from this one. If this is true it will be a huge blessing. Until we know for sure we must continue being cautious when meeting new folks.

"There is the matter of garbage that needs attention in the park. All of us old buggers have agreed to handle that one. After the meeting, Calvin Emerson, Will Bennet, Bill Campbell and I will assume clean-up duties and bring the Hodgson's trailers back to the Emerson's farm.

"My daughter Caroline will be handling the personal information file. She would like to get together with all our new folks to take down their contact information, list of skills and interests so we can add them to our files.

"Once again, my thanks to our team for an excellent job this morning. We have a hectic day ahead of us. Let's get to it."

1:00 PM, 26 NOVEMBER 2020

The MacIntyre Homestead

The two scouting teams were all geared up. Everyone carried a rifle, a sidearm, ammo and a patrol pack. The packs contained enough rations and gear to sustain each person for 72 hours in harsh winter conditions should something go wrong. Everyone wore their personal Individual First Aid Kit or IFAK. The patrols pulled out of the farm gate at 1:30 PM.

The plan was to visit and scout neighbouring farms and homes to see who was healthy and who wasn't. They needed to ascertain if any remaining neighbours would be willing to join the group and what homes and farms would be available for cleanup and re-occupancy. Valuable livestock needed to be tended to and kept safe.

They also needed to determine if there were any threats in the area. In this current environment, people are either friend or foe. Once past the roadblocks, the snow on the road was getting deep. Very soon, no one would be getting through.

Now was the time to ensure empty homes and farms were identified and reoccupied to prevent winter damage from destroying them. John's team, consisting of John, J2, Samantha, Scott and Jennifer Sabovitch, would scout north. Franz, Hatto, Ed, Anna Bennet, and Arlene Emerson would scout south. Both teams had a medic, people with weapons skills and each team had two vehicles. No one expected any trouble, but nothing would be left to chance after the past few days.

John's first stop was a farm about 2 km north of their area. John had spoken to the new owners in the spring when the Burtons first moved into the farm. John's intention was to introduce himself and get a feel for who they were and if they could be counted on in case things went bad.

John made it his mission to know who lived near his family. He learned that these folks had no intention of farming the land. They were seeking a private, quiet area to live in and were not interested in mixing with people. Both were business executives with no children. John didn't come away with a positive feeling about these two.

The two patrol vehicles pulled through the open gate of the driveway. There were no tracks in the snow as John drove slowly up to the house. He and J2 scanned the area for any threats.

They parked in front of the home's attached garage. Everyone donned their N95 masks and nitrile gloves. John and J2 got out, leaving their doors open and engines running. J2 would go the door, weapon-at the low ready, while John covered him, weapon-shouldered.

The others exited the vehicles, prepared to react. J2 went to the door and rang the doorbell. It could be heard; the power was still on. Receiving no answer, he knocked loudly and rang three more times. There was no responce.

The group paired up to search the barn and buildings. There was no sign of life anywhere. The drive shed contained a newer diesel tractor with a loader, a lawnmower and snowblower attachments. There was nothing in the barn at all.

J2 tried the house door; it was locked. One of the skills J2 practiced regularly was lock picking. In less than 30 seconds, the door swung open. John and J2 cleared the home and gave the all-clear to the others. Scott stood outside on guard while the others searched the home.

No one had been here in days, and it was agreed that the owners were probably still in Toronto. The search of the house provided cell phone numbers for the owners. John called both numbers. There was no answer, and the mailboxes were full.

"We could assume that these folks were still in the city and very likely deceased," John said.

Everyone agreed.

Sam took notes of the owner's phone numbers and what they had found. The house was warm; the heat was still working, as was the electricity. The house had a fair amount of food, and the freezer was full. There were no signs the owners owned a weapon. Inventory complete they moved out. They closed the gate and installed their own lock.

* * *

The next home on the road was not a farm, just a lovely new home on several acres. There was no gate and no tracks in the snow. The patrol repeated the same tactics they did at the first home.

Once the area was secure, J2 picked the lock and opened the door. The stench of death was overpowering. J2 gaged, then caught his breath. "No one alive in here," he said, shaking his head to clear it.

The Albertsons, much like the previous couple, prized their privacy and preferred not to mingle.

John looked at the others. "If you don't want to come in, I fully understand." They all sucked in a breath and went in while Jennifer Sabovitch stood guard. The search revealed one dead woman in bed, obviously overcome by the flu. A poor, dehydrated, starving dog lay in the corner, eyeing them suspiciously.

He was a small dog and did not appear to be a threat. Samantha filled his water bowl; the little dog drank thirstily. A search of the kitchen revealed plenty of top-quality dog food, she filled his bowl, and he devoured it hungrily.

The search of the house revealed the power and heat were still on, and the home had plenty of food.John picked up a cell phone by the bed. It was still plugged in and fully charged. He checked the recent calls. There were plenty of unanswered calls to a number in Collingwood, calls to a Doctor, 911 and other numbers that appeared to be family with no answer.

They wrapped the body in the bedclothes and carried it to the garage to freeze. They would return tomorrow and give her a proper burial.

This was another empty home with supplies that could be utilized by the group once sanitized and cleaned up. They took the little dog with them. It sat next to Sam, cuddling up to her.

"I think you have a new friend," said J2.

"I know," she replied, "the kids will love him to death." They all chuckled

* * *

The next on the list was a small hobby farm. John had spoken with these folks, and they seemed like good people. They had attended several meet-and-greets that John and Liz hosted at the farm. John had phoned them several times in the past few days but got no answer, and the voicemailbox was full.

As the team pulled into the driveway, they noticed tracks in the snow.

"They look at least two days old, judging by the fresh snow in them," John said as he looked thracks over.

The group went on full alert. J2 went to the door, John covering. He looked inside; the home had been looted. Scott stood sentry while the others searched the buildings.

The external search revealed many footprints in the snow. Like those in the drive, they had fresh snow, meaning they were old. The drive shed contained a small tractor. The battery had been removed, and empty fuel cans were thrown around.

Next was the barn. It wreaked of death as soon as they opened the door. The family's chickens and goats were excited to see humans. They were hungry and suffering dehydration.

Dad!" J2 called from the rear of the barn. "You need to see this. We have two deceased people here."

Sam had seen enough death in the past few days; she opted to go back outside.

"I'm with you, Sam," Jennifer announced. I will relieve Scott.

Scott joined John and J2 in the barn. The two bodies of the owners lay face down in the stall. Their hands were zip-tied behind their backs, each with a single bullet wound in the back of their heads. John was upset as he took in the scene of these innocent people who had so violently met their end.

J2 and Scott fed and watered the animals while John contacted Franz. John was pissed and immediately got on the radio. "Franz, come in," John called into the radio, urgency in his voice.

"Go for Franz," came the reply.

"Franz, we are at our third location. We found both homeowners in the barn, a single gunshot wound to the head execution style. The mutts we cleaned up this morning only had shotguns; there are still bad guys out there somewhere."

"Got it, John. We have cleared one farm; we found two deceased from the flu. One home where there hasn't been anyone around for days. We are just headed to number three now," replied Franz.

"Be careful," John replied. "If you see anything out of sorts, hold back until we get there."

"Will do, John," replied Franz.

Franz halted his group well back and out of sight of the next farm. "Ok," Franz said to the others, "I am going forward for a look-see. Ed, you come with me. Hatto, Anna, and Arlene remain out of sight and cover us."

Franz and Ed got out their binoculars and scanned the area closer to the farm. Four SUVs were parked in front of the garage.

Smoke from a wood fire was coming out of the chimney, yet there was no sign of any guard.

"Hold your position, everyone. Ed and I are going in for a closer look."

Franz and Ed moved into the woods and stealthily approached the house. Five minutes later, they were concealed in the trees parallel to the house. A row of evergreen trees planted behind the house formed a windbreak and would provide cover for Franz and Ed to get to the barn unseen. The distance from the trees to the barn was roughly 100 meters.

"Ed, you cover me, and I will run to the barn. When I get there, I will cover your advance."

Ed nodded his approval.

Concealed by the trees, Franz ran, weapon ready to the corner of the barn. Ed then followed. The two men were crouched beside the barn, listening. Over the noise of the animals, they heard two men talking inside.

The side door to the barn was open and not visible from the house. "Ed, cover me while I slip over to the door, then I will cover you." At the door, Franz looked inside. There were lights on, but no one was close to the door. So far, so good, he thought. Franz quietly slipped inside, followed by Ed.

The humidity and scent of the barn assaulted their senses as they waited for their eyes to adjust to the darkness, they listened. Two men were talking about hitting other farms and making raids into town.

"This is a great hideout; it's out of the way and well off the road," the first man said.

"For sure, a much better location the last one," the second man answered.

"Let's off these old coots and get back inside. I have a beer waiting," said the first voice.

"I've heard enough," Franz whispered. They crept forward,

weapons at the ready and stopped outside the stall the men were in. Franz looked through a gap in the stall fencing, two fit-looking armed with handguns stood over an older man and a woman, zip-tied and lying face down on the floor of the dirty stall.

Franz looked at Ed and whispered. "We have to act now, Ed. I'm going in there. You cover me."

Ed nodded.

Franz hung his SKS by the single-point sling and pulled his Ka-Bar knife. Both men had their backs to Franz. The younger man was getting ready to execute the two, taunting them—the older man standing back two paces smiling.

Franz moved swiftly and silently in behind the older man. In one swift movement, Franz grasped his head, pulling it sideways to the left as he brought up the big blade and slit the man's throat. He silently lowered the body down.

The younger man had sensed the movement behind him and started to turn. Franz drove his elbow hard into the man's nose. The man's fell to the stall floor face down, stunned and bleeding.

Ed followed Franz into the stall and covered the barn door while Franz had a chat with his new friend. The elderly couple looked wide-eyed at the events unfolding before them. Franz knelt hard on the man's back and held the K-Bar to the side of the man's neck. "Do I have your undivided attention, asshole?" Franz asked angrily.

"Fuck you," the man mumbled.

Franz made a shallow slice in the man's cheek with the bloody Ka-Bar knife. The man started to squirm and yell, and Franz punched him in the head with his knife hand, briefly stunning him. Franz rolled the man onto his back, and pressed the razor sharp knife into his throat.

"Feeling more motivated to talk now?" asked Franz.

The man nodded yes.

Franz eased the pressure on the black blade. "How many in the house?"

"Seven," the man grumbled.

"How are you armed?"

"Handguns and AK 47's."That got Franz's attention,

"How many AKs?" asked Franz.

"Four," came the reply.

"All men?" Franz asked.

"Three women," came the reply.

"These people meant you no harm. Why were you going to kill them?" Asked Franz sternly.

"Why do you give a fuck?" answered the man arrogantly. "The world has gone for a shit, and you will die right along with them." Regaining his nerve, he started to struggle.

"Big mistake," stated Franz.

The man's eyes widened as the big Ka-Bar sliced through his throat.

Ed released the elderly couple from their bonds while Franz quickly searched the bodies. Franz turned to Ed, "Metropolitan Toronto Police Detective badges."

Franz immediately keyed up his radio. "John, we need help ASAP. We have a group of renegade police officers who have taken over this farm."

What is your name, Sir?" Franz asked the elderly man. "Handley, Raymond and June Handley

"I got that, Franz. I know the Handleys. We are on the way, and I will have back up en-route as well," John answered.

"We will hold in the barn until we get your signal John," Franz replied.
"Agreed," added John.

John's crew pulled up behind the others waiting on the road. Everyone gathered around John. "Ok, everyone, we are dealing with seven adults, four men and three women. At least some of them are rogue police officers. They will be well-armed and well-trained.

We have had no opportunity for training. We are nowhere near where we should be before going into a battle like this. I will give you my plan of how I see this going down. I need everyone to stay cool and concentrate on their assigned task.

We do not have enough radios, so if something changes, I may not be able to communicate with you. Remember these words 'no plan will survive the first contact with the enemy.' No matter how well we plan or how many contingencies we plan for, we do not know how the bad guys will react. They could do something unexpected. We need to be prepared to adjust our tactics on the move. Does everyone understand that?"

They all nodded yes.

"No heroics; that only works in the movies. We will rendezvous back at the vehicles if something goes bad and you need to retreat. If this location is compromised, head for the home next door," John pointed to the house. "And wait there. If that fails, you go home, ok?"

Everyone nodded yes.

"First and foremost, I do not want to act until we get more backup. If we have to act sooner, I will initiate contact by firing at the bad guys. Until then, no one shoots. Are we clear?"

They all said "Yes."

"Ok, Sam, I need you and Anna to move through the woods and cover the rear of the house. Again, please wait for me to initiate contact. If any bad guys come out, you drop them.

Scott, you and Jennifer take a vehicle and drive by quickly. Don't look in at the house. When you're out of sight, park, then move through the woods to get yourselves in a position to cover the front of the house. Again, please wait for me to initiate contact, then drop any bad guys that come out the front and pose a threat. Can you do this?" John asked.

"Yes, John, you can count on us," they both replied.

"Thank you," John continued. "The signal will be the first shot fired. Stay still and out of sight. Everyone clear?"

"Yes," they all agreed.

"Hatto, Arlene, you come with me. We will head through the bush behind the windbreak and rendezvous with Franz and Ed at the barn. Let's move."

Within five minutes, everyone was in position. After a quick discussion, John and Franz agreed that it would be best to draw them outside, where they could pick them off from concealed positions.

Then it happened! The one thing no one ever expected; a blue Toyota Four Runner drove up the road and turned into the driveway. There was a lone occupant in the vehicle, a woman.

"Shit, so much for that plan," John announced. "She will be walking right into a trap. Quickly, while they are preoccupied with watching her drive up. Franz, you and I storm the patio door. Ed, you, Hatto and Arlene storm the side door. Let's go."

"Shit," Scott said to Jennifer. "This is exactly what John was talking about." As they watched the woman in the Toyota drive up.

Both Scott and Jennifer Sabovitch were hunters. They had taken their share of wild game and were both excellent shots, but this was different. How would they react when the targets were humans? Then they noticed John and the others move on the house. "Let's get ready, Jen; looks like it's game on."

John and Franz shot through the patio door just as Ed, Hatto and Arlene burst through the side entrance. Then all hell broke loose.

John and Franz were both armed with SKS rifles, their red dot sights were already tracking targets, and they started firing as two men with AK 47s reacted to their entry. Both men went down. One of the women pulled a pistol and swung it towards

John. As soon as she moved, John had the red dot on her chest, a quick two-shot burst, and she fell.

A big man with an AK47 and a short, muscular woman with a handgun ran out the front door. From the front step, the man swung the weapon firing wildly in full automatic into the house. The rifles bolt locked back indicating an empty magazine and he reached into his pocket for a fresh one. Scott had already lined him up with his hunting rifle. Scott's heart was pounding wildly. He tried to calm himself. This is just like hunting, he told himself over and over. Scott fired, and the man fell.

The woman in the Toyota froze, her parent's home had become a war zone, and she had driven right into it. The short, muscular woman with the pistol ran toward the Toyota, hoping to make her escape..

I must save her. I must." Jen quickly aimed and fired, and the woman fell. Jen's shot had hit her in the right shoulder, knocking her to the ground. The wounded woman then aimed her pistol toward Jen who fired again, finishing her.

A bearded man with an AK 47 ran for the side door, followed by two blonde women. One of the women picked up an AK47 that landed beside her when John shot her comrade, and they both started firing wildly as they ran down the hallway toward the side door. Ed and Arlene jumped into a bedroom on the right, and Hatto into a bedroom on the left.

The bearded man with the AK 47 swung into Hatto's room, firing as he entered. Hatto was waiting in a low crouch. He came off his knee and swung at him with the Katana, disembowelling him. The man fell to the floor, watching his internal organs spill out before him

A blonde women followed her partner into the room. Seeing him fall, she stepped over him and turned, pointing her handgun toward Hatto. Before she could line up the shot, Hatto had severed her arm at the elbow. The woman looked in shock at the spot her arm used to be. She looked toward Hatto in amazement as the Katana severed her head.

The blonde woman with the AK47 turned into the other room, firing wildly. The breach of her AK-47 locked back; she was out of ammo. Ed knocked the gun out of her hands, and Arlene tackled her. She met Arlene's elbow as her forward momentum carried her into the room. She fell to the floor, stunned.

Arlene was immediately on the womans back, wrapping her right arm backward and dislocating it at the elbow. The woman screamed in pain. Arlene pulled out her Ka-Bar knife, yanked the woman's head back by the hair and held the big knife to her throat. She stopped screaming.

Ed yelled. "Bedroom clear. We have a prisoner."

Hatto yelled. "Bedroom clear, two KIA."

John yelled. "Main rooms clear."

Franz did a quick count, "Five bad guys KIA for a total of eight."

The entire battle was over in less than 90 intense seconds.

John went out front and waved to the Sabovitches to come in. Franz waved the rear group in, then went into the barn to get Raymond and June Handley.

Just then, the backup came rolling up the drive.

The woman in the Toyota looked on in horror at what had just transpired in front of her. She gripped the wheel, her eyes bulging, mouth wide open, talking, but no words were coming out. John and Sam walked up to her vehicle. She just kept on looking forward, talking but not speaking. John knocked gently on the window; she jumped, then looked at him. She raised her hands and begged, "Please don't kill me."

John talked gently to the woman in the Toyota, got her to relax and shut off the vehicle. She then slowly exited the Toyota. She looked at the two bodies in front of the house, bent over and vomited. Sam comforted her while she collected herself. The hysterical woman then turned to John and stammered, "Who are you, people? Who are those people? And where are my parents?"

"Please relax, you and so are your parents are safe. Franz has gone to get them."

"Are my parents ok?" She asked, crying.

"Yes, they are," Sam said, comforting her.

"Can I see them?" she asked.

"Of course," John said as he and Sam led her to the barn. They met at the barn door just as Franz brought Raymond and June Handley out.

The Handleys remembered John from a meet and greet at the MacIntyre's last summer. "Now I know what you were talking about when you told us we should work together if something went wrong." He shook John, Franz, and Sam's hands happily.

Franz excused himself to go back inside.

Cory and Carl Emerson helped the Sabovitchs drag the bodies out back. Jessica went to check on the Handleys.

Ed and Hatto were searching the bodies for information. "Franz," Ed called him over. "We have four more cops!" "Interesting," Franz replied. "Let's talk to the prisoner."

The woman was zip-tied and sitting on the floor, the dislocated elbow and broken nose causing her considerable pain. Arlene was guarding her. The woman would often glare at Arlene with hate in her eyes.

Franz walked up to her, "Who are you, people?"

"Fuck you," the woman replied defiantly.

I will ask you once again, "Who are you, people?"

"I already answered, fuck you."

Arlene unsheathed her Ka-Bar knife, pulled the woman's head back by her hair and let the blade dig in just far enough to draw blood from her neck. "The man asked you a question," she said in the woman's ear.

"We are from Toronto," she said.

"I gathered that much from the Toronto Police badges we found," said Franz. "I'm listening."

"We got here last night; we needed a place to stay," she spoke.

"So, you decided you would kill the owners and just take it did you?" Franz questioned.

Fuck you," she said. "The world has gone to hell, or are you people too stupid to see that?"

John excused himself from the Handleys and went inside to talk with the prisoner. John looked at the woman, "Did you people raid a farm near here and kill the occupants?

"What if we did," the woman answered scornfully.

Franz spoke to her again, "Some of you are police. What are the police doing, invading homes and killing people?"

Fuck you," the woman screamed.

"Answer the question," Franz ordered."
The woman glared at him. "What are you, a fucking Nazi?" She spat.

"I think we have learned all we need to know, Arlene," John said as he gave her a knowing nod.

Arlene changed her grip as the woman's eyes went wide. Arlene broke her neck.

"We will dump her with the others and bury them out back," John added. ED and Arlene carried the lifeless corpse out back and threw it next to her comrades.

John and Franz walked back out front to Sam and the Handley's, "You folks can't stay here. I'll get Sam to drive you back to our farm, and you can stay with us until we get your home repaired."

Thank you," Raymond replied. Sam helped the shocked family into the Toyota and drove them back to the farm.

John gathered the others around. "Excellent job! I want to

thank everyone for their part in this. You all did well. Frans, Hatto, Ed, Arlene and I will bury the bodies." John looked at Bob Jones, "Bob, could you stay with us and help patch up those broken windows?"

"Sure," replied Bob.

Tom O'Gorman, Glen Bennet, Andy Hodgson, Calvin Emmerson Bill and Cory Campbell offered to help Bob with the repairs.

Everyone else searched the house and discovered a huge stock of looted goods that they inventoried.

"These characters had been looting other homes in the area and I wonder how many innocent people they have killed." Anna Bennet remarked in disgust.

"I am sure we will find out in the coming days," Sam answered sadly.

With the burials complete, John, Franz, Ed, Hatto, and Arlene gathered up the weapons. The group added four full auto AK47s, eight 9MM pistols, a huge cache of ammo and four late-model SUVs to their inventory. Duties completed, the group returned to their respective homes and cleaned themselves and their weapons.

* * *

Back at the MacIntyre home with an excellent meal complete, Raymond Handley asked if he could speak to everyone.

Liz replied, "Our home is your home."

Raymond Handley looked solemnly at everyone seated, "I wish to convey my sincere thanks to all of you for what you did today. If you hadn't arrived when you did, we would all be dead right now. You have invited us into your home, and we are very thankful."

June and Ruth Anne had tears running down their cheeks as

they nodded in agreement.

Over coffee, John and Liz got to know the Handley's. John discovered that Ruth Anne was a nurse and she would be happy to work with Jessica Campbell. The Handley's also had another daughter Janie, who worked for the CBC as a reporter. She had assumed the news anchor position because everyone else was either ill or deceased. The Handley's had been pleading with her to come home, but Janie wouldn't. She said she was needed there because everyone else was either sick or passed on. John agreed to let them tell her what happened today, but under no circumstances were they to give any details or mention names.

Later that evening John settled in to watch the news before the 8PM check in..

Good Evening. This is Janie Handley with the CBC Evening News.

Death tolls rise sharply from an out-of-control pandemic as society collapses around an ever-darkening globe.

The worldwide infections are now 4.1 billion, while the death toll has risen to 2 billion. Here at home, infections stand at 10 million. This pandemic has now claimed 5 million Canadian lives. There is hope this evening; infection rates have slowed worldwide. The CDC released a statement today that confirms this. They have also confirmed that testing has proven that anyone stricken by the 2019 flu epidemic is immune to this recent pandemic. A similar thing happened with the Hong Kong flu pandemic of 1968. People who contracted and survived the Asian flu pandemic in 1957 were not affected by the Hong Kong flu. Immunologists at the CDC still have yet to develop an antiviral that is effective with this new mutated H5N1 flu. They are now working day and night to find the connection between last year's flu and this one, hoping it leads to an effective antiviral.

The good news tonight is wholly overshadowed by the bad.

The rule of law has now completely broken down worldwide, and Canada has not been spared. As society crumbles around us, raping, pillaging and killing are now out of control in all major centres.

Small towns and rural communities are also reporting incidents of violence. My parents' home near Owen Sound came under attack today. Fortunately for them, some neighbours came to their aid. Tonight, I am pleased to report they are safe and sound.

Public utilities worldwide and here at home are also losing the battle. Personnel shortages have skyrocketed due to the flu. Failures are not being repaired, coal shipments to coal-fired plants have virtually stopped, and equipment failures at natural gas pipeline facilities are beginning to affect the flow of gas to fuel power plants and homes.

The CBC has also received an unconfirmed report that the government is ordering the military to bolster the security duties of all the nation's nuclear plants. Further, the government is asking any retired personnel still healthy to return to work at all the nation's power plants and critical utilities. With winter getting a firm grip on the entire northern hemisphere, over a billion people will be at risk of freezing to death if the electrical and natural gas grids fail.

Even here at the CBC, a nationwide shortage of journalists and reporters has reduced news programming. Please be assured we will always keep you posted with breaking news on this global crisis.

This is Janie Handley with the CBC Evening News for the 26th day of November 2020. Good evening.

With everyone tuned into the 8 PM check-in, John began by thanking everyone for their actions today. "Tonight, he continued. We have added three new members to our team. Raymond and June Handley are farmers and will work with us to provide for the group. Ruth Anne Handley is a registered nurse. She would like the opportunity to work with Jessica and our medical team.

If you haven't already heard, the discovery that Cory and Bill Campbell made has been proven true. The news this evening has confirmed for us that anyone stricken with the flu bug in 2019 is immune to this current virus.

"This is fantastic news; it provides hope that humanity will pull through this pandemic. Remember, we cannot let our guard down when meeting new people. So, stay focused, everyone.

Today we scouted out three unoccupied farms and two homes we need to occupy and secure. The Handley's will also need help securing their farm and repairing the damages.

We will need to discuss the moving of our roadblocks and how we will secure our extended area. There is much to go over, many of which require immediate action; therefore, I would like to convene a meeting of everyone not on guard duty tomorrow at 9:00 AM here at our farm in the shop.

"Tonight, I ask everyone to talk amongst your groups and bring your ideas and concerns to the meeting."

Everyone agreed and signed off for the evening.

8:00 AM, 27 NOVEMBER 2020

Camp Thunder

Martin LeBlanc studied the lodge and cabins through his binoculars. He had been surveilling Camp Thunder for the past two days now.

The bitter man smiled slyly to himself. *There is no one here but that stinking Indian and his bitch. Before long, this place will be mine.* Martin packed up his gear and strapped it securely to his snowmobile. During the long cold trip back to the cabin, he hatched his evil plan. Martin took a long pull of whiskey from the bladder that hung around his neck, the stong drink felt good as he swallowed it down.

9:00 AM, 27 NOVEMBER 2020

The MacIntyre Homestead

L iz, Caroline, Kat and Darlene Jones had prepared coffee, tea, milk, water and juice. John, J2 and Bob Jones arranged the shop while Greg stood guard.

People started rolling in at 8:30. They were all enjoying hot beverages while getting to know one another better. At 9:00 AM sharp, John called the meeting to order, and everyone that wasn't seated found one.

John introduced the Handleys and welcomed them to the group; everyone applauded.

Raymond Handley stood."On behalf of my wife, June and our daughter Ruth Anne, we wish to convey our sincere thanks to everyone for coming to our aid. Without your intervention, we would all be dead now. Thank you, thank you so much."

Everyone applauded, and Raymond Handley sat down.

"Good morning, all," John continued. "As of this morning, we have 60 souls in our community. We have many things to discuss and many things that require action.

"First up is the matter of our expanding area. We need to move our current roadblocks and add a new one on Moles side road. We need this done today, and Calvin Emerson has agreed to lead this up. He has already arranged for the help and equipment to do this. They will begin right after the meeting this morning. Thank you, Calvin and crew, for this.

Once the roadblocks are in place, we will have three farms and two homes that need occupying and once settled, the farms need to be worked, animals cared for, and they need to be secured.

It was decided that the Hodgson group would occupy the Burton farm. The Sabovitch family will occupy the Poole farm.

The O'Gorman family will occupy Albertson's home; it's a large home, so Clare and Vaughn Taylor will live there with them. Bob and Darlene Jones will occupy the Greene's home. The Greene's home is a small 2-bedroom house. The home is well in the centre of our expanded territory. Since there are just two of them, it will make security more manageable. Ben Greene, like Bob, was also a carpenter. He had a nice wood shop behind their home. Bob can make good use of that for everyone's benefit.

"In the coming days, we will keep expanding our patrols outward. We need to keep looking; people who are still healthy will need security and assistance. We need to identify unoccupied farms and put our people in them to care for the livestock before they die. Tomorrow, Franz and I will lead two more patrols to search more farms and homes. We need a few volunteers to help out here. See us when we are finished here.

As our community grows, we see the need for clothing for our people. We need to organize a group to go out and gather supplies. I'm still in the thinking stage, but I would like to do this the day after tomorrow. Please give this some thought.

"Finally, with our community as large as it is now, it's time we start considering how we will govern ourselves. I have been our defacto leader, and it's becoming more than I can handle. We don't need a dictatorship; therefore, it's only fitting that we democratically elect members of our group. We have many talented people in our group who can share decision-making. I am suggesting some type of council that could manage our day-to-day affairs, with chairpeople representing the administration, security, housing, education, agriculture, medical, transportation, and maintenance.

"The takeaway from this meeting is to give this some thought. We can sit down again in a few days and discuss it more. We are all part of this community; everyone's participation is encouraged here. That's all I have. Are there any questions?"

Will Bennet stood, "John, this is not a question but an observation. I like what I hear you saying, and I know I am speaking for everyone here that you have done an exemplary job of preparing us for this day and bringing us through this. John, you brought us together and gave us hope and strength to carry on. We, as a group, are thankful for your leadership."

Everyone stood and gave John a standing ovation.

ohn managed to get everyone to settle down and spoke. "Thank you, everyone, for that vote of confidence, but I cannot take credit for this. I had an amazing team backing me up all the way. My wife and best friend Liz and our entire family are my strength. Many of us worked hard and planned this mutual assistance group together.

"Many of you were dropped into our midst and hit the decks running. You put your lives on the line for strangers. I am proud to call you all my friends, and I thank you all.

"Ok, friends," John continued."Let's get to work and get these folks settled into their homes."

The meeting ended on a high and positive note.

* * *

The day passed quickly and without a hitch. Everyone got moved to their new locations. With most of the group pitching in, the homes were all disinfected and checked out. Food supplies were inventoried, and deficiencies were noted for restocking. The barns were all cleaned, and animals were fed, watered and checked out. Fuel tanks were checked.

Since all the homes had backup wood heat, firewood stocks were also checked. Those that didn't have a winter's supply of firewood would be restocked ASAP. Everything was going well.

The weather cooperated, providing clear skies and temperatures just a few degrees above freezing.

One of the first things Brenda Hodgson noticed after moving into the Burton farm was the fantastic fire pit way back by the forest. It was well sheltered with an inviting circular seating area surrounding a central fire pit made from a 36" round steel pipe set into the ground.

This would make a beautiful setting for a backyard wedding, or how about a meet and greet party for the group's singles? That would be an excellent way to thank everyone. Brenda ran the idea past her sisters-in-law, Marlene and Penny. All thought it was an excellent idea.

"We have a lot of very nice, young, single people in the group. It would be a great icebreaker for them," said Penny enthusiastically.

"We could provide hot drinks and snack foods, and Brianna and Andy can play guitar. It will be super," Marlene added.

"It's a plan, then. I will run it by the group at tonight's radio check-in and see if we can do it before we tell the kids," Brenda said, smiling.

* * *

After supper, Franz, Hatto, Arlene, Christopher Hodgson and Ed Bennet pulled into the MacIntyre farm. They would meet with John and J2 to discuss setting up the group security force. Everyone helped themselves to a fresh coffee and sat down.

John began the meeting. "Thank you all for coming. Franz and I were scheming today about setting up a group security force. We wanted to invite you because we see you folk as the most capable people for this task. More would be nice, but you folks would make an excellent start.

"We feel a group our size needs a dedicated security force that would always be on standby to act. The past few days' events have made it abundantly clear that we must train as many people as possible. We can hone our skills by working and training together and utilizing each other's strengths. We would also utilize our specialties to train the other group members in weapons handling, self-defence, marksmanship, awareness, and navigation. What do you think?" John asked.

"Thank you for asking me to be part of your team," replied Arlene. "We have a lot of young people in the group, and they would be ideal candidates for self-defence training."

"I agree," added Hatto, "Arlene, you handled yourself extremely well yesterday. I have been giving much thought to this and would be honoured to work with you."

"I would like that very much, Hatto. Thank you," Arlene replied.

"That would be amazing," John agreed. "You set it up and we will make it happen."

"Back in Japan I trained students in situational awareness, I would be happy to train our people here," offered Hatto.

Everyone agreed this would be a benefit to the group.

"John, Christopher, Ed, and I would be able to take on the weapons handling and marksmanship," added Franz.

Again the group agreed that this was urgently needed.

"J2, Sam, Christopher and I have already discussed giving training on first aid and trauma care, so our people can handle gunshot wounds and serious injuries," added Ed.

"I like that, Ed," John replied. "The better our people are trained, the better it is for all of us."

As the evening progressed much was discussed. John and Franz wanted to set up training for the security force in close-quarters battle skills, room clearing, sniper skills, shooting, and potential handling of hostages. Hatto and Arlene talked about hand-to-hand fighting, training with knives and improvised weapons, stick fighting and stealth. Ed, J2 and Christopher shared ideas about first-aid skills and trauma care. "It was a great meeting.

I'm happy," John announced, "There is a lot of synergy in this group. We make an excellent team."

Once the meeting ended the newly formed security team tuned into the evening news. The most apparent was the lack of pizzaz and special effects that usually introduced the evening news. Everything was plain and straightforward; even Janie Handley looked worn down and lacked the makeup and prep typical for TV hosts.

> *Good evening; this is Janie Handley with the CBC Evening News*
>
> *The rule of law fails tonight; rising death tolls and massive power outages rock the globe.*
>
> *Worldwide infections have slowed to 4.6 billion, but deaths are still increasing and now stand at 3 billion. Here in Canada, infections have soared to 15 million, almost half the nation's population. The death toll this evening stands at a shocking 7 million. People are dying in their homes with no help coming, morgues are overflowing, and bodies lie frozen in the streets.*
>
> *As power outages roll across the land, people will soon be freezing to death in their homes. As of tonight, roughly 25% of the nation is without electricity. Worldwide the figures are worse at 35%.*
>
> *Crime is completely out of control as surviving gang members battle for control of the cities. Police and military control has collapsed in many areas due to personnel losses. Gangs are looting, raping and murdering at will as they work to consolidate their control over humans, food, fuel, water and drugs. It is just not safe to be caught outside alone.*

The effects of an early Canadian winter with heavy snowfalls and cold temperatures have restricted gang activity primarily to the nation's urban areas. Please make no mistake; gang activity and crime are also up in our rural areas.

Many viewers have sent in cell phone pictures and videos. We will air them at the close of the program. Please be advised that everything is disturbing and unsuitable for young viewers. We at the CBC regret we cannot provide a weather forecast this evening as our entire Meteorology department is down with the flu.

We wish to thank everyone who has contributed by sending in the news via Twitter, email and text. We ask that you continue to do so as long as you can. Please stay tuned for extended video and Twitter feeds.

This is Janie Handley with the CBC Evening News for the 27th of November 2020.
  Good evening.

"That is very grim," said Franz, shaking his head sadly.

"It sure is," added Arlene. "John, how long do you think we will be safe from the worst of the gangs?"

"Good question Arlene. If we are lucky, they will kill each other off or freeze to death before spring."

"I think I am going to take up praying," added Ed. "It may just be time to renew my faith."

Everyone nodded in agreement.

❋ ❋ ❋

The 8:00 PM check-in was short. John confirmed that everyone had watched the news and shared his concerns. The scouting mission was still a go for tomorrow, and everyone attending was to meet up at John's farm by 9:00 AM.

Everyone was settling into their new homes and thanked the group for all they had done to make the day a success.

Excellent," John said. "Does anyone have anything to add?"

Brenda Hodgson explained about the fantastic fire pit area at their new home. She then pitched her idea about a single's meet and greet and said Marlene, Penny, and herself would host the event.

Everyone agreed it was an excellent idea. John's only concern was security, and he insisted that at least two armed adults must be present. Scott and Jennifer Sabovitch volunteered to handle security.

"Ok," John replied. "Brenda, I like this. When you set a date, we will make it happen."

With that, everyone signed off for the evening.

8:00 AM, 28 NOVEMBER 2020

The MacIntyre Homestead

With all the morning chores completed and the 8:00 AM check-in finished, John and Franz made preparations for the scouting mission.

The weather was clear and mild; the temperature right on the freezing mark. Today, they were going to expand the area just a little wider.

They had three main concerns. Firstly, if they extend too far, they would not have the manpower to patrol and keep the area secure. Secondly, they didn't want to leave surviving farmers and homeowners alone and unprotected. Thirdly, they could not allow valuable livestock to die from dehydration and starvation.

Today, John was joined by J2, Arlene and Christopher Hodgson. Franz would have Hatto, Ed Bennet and Scott Sabovitch. John searched east along Concession Road 14, then carried on down Linton side road, while Franz searched south along Grey Road 17 to the bottom of the Grey Sauble Conservation Area. They were as equipped as they were on the previous patrol, with rifles and scout packs. Each group had two vehicles.

Several beautiful homes on acreages were built against the conservation area's east boundary, and John's team pulled into the first driveway. There were no fresh tracks, and a snow-covered late-model Lexus SUV was parked in front of the garage. The team exited John's pickup and spread out for a look around. They took their SKS rifles and were all alert for any trouble.

J2 had been instructing Arlene and Christopher in the fine art of lock picking. Arlene pulled out the tools her husband Carl had made for her yesterday. "Let's check out Carl's handy work," said Arlene. It took Arlene four tries to open the lock before it clicked open.

"Super," praised J2, "It takes a bit of practice to get used to the feel of different locks. You did great, Arlene."

"Thanks, J2. I will tell Carl these tools work great and get him to make us a batch of these."

As soon as the door opened, the stench of death hit them like a hammer. "Whoa," J2 gaged as he stepped back, shaking his head.

"I will stay out here on watch; you guys can go in there," Christopher announced grimly.

"A smart man," replied John. As he put on his mask, took a deep breath and walked inside. "Whoa," John gagged. "This is bad," his eyes started watering.

This home had two dehydrated and starving Shih Tzu dogs. They made an effort to get up and bark but quickly gave up. Arlene went to the kitchen and found them a bowl. She tried the taps in the kitchen and was pleased that the water still flowed. The little dogs lapped it up eagerly while she searched for some food for them.

John and J2 checked the master bedroom. A couple in their late 50s that had lost the battle with the virus lay in bed. They appeared to have been dead for about five days. "Let's crack the windows and air the place out while remove the bodies," John ordered. Once the windows were opened John and J2 wrapped the bodies in bedclothes and carried them out to the garage one at a time so that they could freeze

Arlene checked the owner's phones; they were plugged in and fully charged. She checked the call list. Some calls were placed to 911, the Owen Sound Hospital, and several numbers in Vancouver. Arlene called them all no answer; all went into a full mailbox.

It was a beautiful home with plenty of food and supplies. The power was still on and the propane tanks were full. The team secured the home, making a note to come back and collect the bodies for a proper burial, loaded up the little dogs and then moved on to the house next door.

❋ ❋ ❋

There were no tracks in the driveway when John pulled in; however, there were tracks around the house. "Let's be careful," John ordered.

Movement behind the living room curtains caught J2's attention. "A woman is alive and well in there," he warned.

John stopped the pickup and waited for a few seconds. "Arlene, would you step out with me? The presence of a woman may make us look less threatening."

"Sure, John," she replied, and they stepped out, leaving both doors open, appearing as non-threatening as possible.

The front door opened, and a woman in her late 50s stepped out, pointing an over-and-under shotgun at them. A Jack Russel terrier barked at her side. "Please leave," she ordered sternly. "I have nothing for you."

"Ma'am, we mean you no harm. My name is John MacIntyre, and I own a farm on County Road 14. This is Arlene Emerson, one of our neighbours. My son and a friend are in the pickup."

"I recognize that name," the woman replied, "Do you have a booth at the farmers market in town?"

"Yes, we do," John answered.

"I have bought eggs from your lovely wife, Elizabeth, am I correct? The woman asked as she relaxed her posture."

"Yes, Liz is my wife. May we come forward, ma'am?"

"Yes," the woman replied, "Please come in. Smedley, you go lay down."

Christopher assumed guard duty again while the others went

inside.

"My name is Karen Wood, and I just made coffee. Would you all like some?" she asked, smiling.

"Yes, thank you," they all cheerfully replied.

Arlene made a cup for Christopher and took it out to him. Then joined the others at the kitchen table.

"My husband passed away from the flu," Karen told them as tears formed in her eyes.

"We are so sorry to hear that," John replied. "Please accept our condolences."

"Thank you," Karen replied sadly. "I called 911, and no one answered. I called the police, the hospital, and the funeral home, but no one answered," she continued shakily. "I wrapped him up in the bedding and dragged him into the garage where it's cold."

Arlene stood and walked over to comfort her.

"Thank you," Karen sobbed. "It was something I never imagined I would have to do."

"We are so sorry," John said. "Karen, did you get sick with the flu?"

"No, I didn't," she answered. "I figured I would soon be meeting the same fate as Arthur, but so far, I am healthy."

"Karen," John asked. "Did you, by any chance, have that nasty flu in 2019?"

"Oh yes, John, I did," she replied while looking around the room. "I was flat on my back with that one, but Arthur didn't get sick at all."

"We all had that one, too, and we are all healthy. This virus doesn't seem to have any affect on those that caught the 2019 bug," John added.

"Karen, you're all by yourself. Do you have any family coming?" J2 asked.

Once again a sad look again crossed Karen's face, and a tear appeared in her eye, "My daughter's family and my grandkids, they all got sick; none survived. My son Maurice and his family didn't get sick, and I think they were all sick back in 2019, like me. They have left Kingston trying to get here, and it's a long way away."

"Karen, you have lost so much. When was the last time you heard from Maurice?" John asked.

"Yesterday," Karen replied. "He calls every day, and this morning he made it to Shelburne and was looking for gas. It's been slow going, and they had to make many detours. Some people have been cruel to them."

"We have had our share of trouble, too, Karen," John replied. He explained the attacks on the Clarys and Hodgsons, leaving out the gore.

"I have had people stop in. I chased some off; she paused, looking down. "John, I shot a man. I had to. He wouldn't leave. When he figured out I was alone, he tried to break in. He kicked Smedley hurting him badly. I'm so sorry, but I had no choice. I was terrified."

Again, Arlene comforted Karen. She was crying again.

"We understand, Karen. Some in our group have had to do the same thing, Liz included," John replied. John then explained the mutual assistance group and asked Karen if she would like to stay with them until Maurice arrived.

"I don't want to burden anyone, John, but I am terrified to be alone," she replied shyly.

"Karen, you will be safe with us. We don't have enough people to ensure your safety here by yourself."

"Thank you all for your kindness, John. That would be a wise move, and I can come back when Maurice gets here, and things settle down? I will have to tell Maurice; he will be worried sick if he doesn't find me at home," Karen added.

"Excellent," John replied. "You call Maurice and fill him in, so he can stay in touch with you."

Don't worry about, Arthur, we will come back and give him a proper burial," J2 said to promised.

"John, we can pack some food and things. I have plenty, and I want to contribute," Karen offered.

"Thank you, Karen, that would be helpful," John replied.

"I will help you pack up some things," Arlene added.

John contacted Franz for an update.

"We checked three homes that were close together, all empty, the heat and power still on. We found names and phone numbers for all the owners, but no one answered the calls, and all mailboxes were full. The homes all contained food. We found some weapons, and we took those, don't want them falling into the wrong hands," Franz replied.

"Good work, everyone. At our first stop, we found a deceased couple. The home still has heat and power, along with plenty of supplies. The second has a lady living there. She is alone and has had trouble with intruders. We will bring her back with us until we can secure her property," John replied.

Franz continued, "We just pulled into an acreage on the west side of the conservation area. This will be our last stop for the day. The property looks empty, no fresh tracks around."

"Ok," John replied. "We will circle south of the conservation area and meet you at your location. John out."

Franz stopped the pickup in the driveway of a home set back off the road, about 300 meters. Old snow-covered vehicles and machinery littered the yard. Wood smoke drifted lazily from the chimney of the house.

Franz advanced slowly. "Be alert, everyone; this place looks occupied."

They noticed tracks in the snow around the house. A late-model Chey pickup parked in front of the garage was covered in snow; it hadn't moved in quite a while. The team noticed the curtain move, and a young girl's face appeared and then disappeared.

Franz turned to the others, "I think we should wait until Arlene is here. A group of men approaching this young girl will terrify her."

They all agreed.

Franz radioed John and filled him in.

"We are about five minutes out, Franz. We stopped to look at a construction yard just south of your location. No one has been here in a while. We should have Calvin, Carl, and Cory come back and check it out. There may be some useful equipment in there, John out."

A few minutes later, John pulled in behind Franz. John, Arlene and Karen walked up and John introduced her to Franz.

Karen looked back toward the road, her eyes stopped at a small vegetable stand at the end of the long driveway. "I have spoken with these folks before. They were selling vegetables on the side of the road. Art and I used to stop once in a while; maybe they would recognize me."

"Excellent, Karen, let's walk up slowly," Franz suggested. "If she recognizes you, she may come out."

The door opened just a little as they approached the house, and a teenage girl shyly walked out. She had a double-barrel shotgun in her hands, but she held it low, not threatening. The poor girl looked dead on her feet like she hadn't slept in days.

"Hello," Karen called. "Do you remember me? My name is Karen Wood. I bought vegetables from you."

The young girl nodded shyly. She never spoke.

"May we come forward?" Karen asked.

The girl nodded, ok. She was clean and well-dressed but terrified.

"We mean you no harm," Arlene spoke softly to her. "What's your name?"

"Sheila," she replied, "Sheila Carr."

"Are your parents home, Sheila?" Asked Arlene softly.
Sheila hesitated, not knowing what to say.

It's ok, Sheila," Arlene added. "We are here to help you. May Karen and I come up there with you?"

Ok, she nodded.

Arlene and Karen walked up onto the front porch of the house. Sheila stayed in the doorway, she started shaking, and tears appeared in her eyes.

"It's ok, Sheila, we are here to help you," Karen said softly. "Are your parents' home?"

"My parents and little brother got the flu and died," Sheila replied, sobbing. "I'm alone."

"Oh, my poor dear," answered Karen. "We are so sorry. I lost my husband Art to the flu. Do you remember him?"
Sheila nodded yes.

"Sheila, can Arlene and I come inside? Our friends will stay outside. Is that ok?"

Sheila nodded yes and opened the door.

The house was clean; there were no dirty dishes or messes anywhere. There was plenty of firewood stacked beside the wood-burning stove.

"You have kept everything immaculate and tidy," Arlene praised. "Good for you, Sheila."

The young girl looked up at Arlene sadly. "I wrapped my family in their bedclothes and dragged them outside. I called 911 over and over again, but no one answered. I had to do something. I dug a grave for them with the tractor and buried them out back."

"We are so sorry, Sheila, that must have been terrible," said Arlene.

"It was," Sheila started to cry. Karen hugged her closely and let her grieve.

When she settled down, Arlene made her an offer. "Sheila, we live close by. Would you like to come back to the farm with us? There are lots of girls and boys your age; it would be much safer for you."

"I can't leave my livestock. How will I care for them?" Sheila asked anxiously.

"We will bring you back daily and help you feed and care for them," Arlene reassured her.

"Ok then, I want to stay with you," she nodded. "I'm so afraid. Some boys were here a few days ago. They wanted to come in, but I said no. They kept coming and wouldn't stop, and I shot at them. They told me they would be back and said they were going to," Shiela stopped talking and sobbed.

"It's ok," Arlene said, hugging the terrified girl. "You don't have to say it, we know.

Karen will help you pack some things, and I will tell our friends. Don't worry; we will keep you safe."

"Can we take our food with us?" Sheila questioned.

"Those boys will be back; they will take it."

"Yes, we can, Sheila. I will get the others to help, ok?"

She nodded yes.

The teams looked over the stock of food and supplies. The home was full of food, vast stores of preserved items, dry goods and two large freezers full of meat. Both the power and heat were still working.

"Wow!" John exclaimed. "We will need another vehicle for this." He radioed back to the farm. Caroline and Kat would come out with Liz's Suburban and a trailer.

The guys got busy draining all water lines and the tanks, preparing the home for when the electricity shut down. This way, it would be ready for Sheila when it was safe for her to return home.

Sheila and Kat were the same age, hitting it off immediately. She quickly decided to move into the MacIntyre farm to be close to Kat. Karen, too would be staying with John and Liz. With everything loaded up, they returned home with plenty of food and supples. There were now four more vacant homes that could be reoccupied once the group could secure the area.

That evening dinner was excellent as usual. The new guests were welcomed and settled in. Caroline, Liz and Kat sat down with Karen and Sheila and got them to write out the events that happened to them. Law and order will be re-established someday, and the information should be recorded while it is still fresh in their minds.

* * *

John wanted to check on Karl Hanson at the Farmer's Co-op, so he excused himself and made the phone call.

Karl answered immediately, seeing John's name appear on the call display. "Hey John, how are you?" He chirped.

"The shits, but thanks for asking, Karl. How are things at your end?"

"It's been a real struggle, John. We have had attacks by looters nearly every day. We have partnered with several other business owners and friends to secure the Co-op and their businesses," Karl replied.

John filled Karl in on the events at his end and their actions.

"I'm impressed, John. The people we are dealing with here appear to be a large group of thugs and seem somewhat organized. It's only a matter of time before we are overrun here. I have talked with the others here they are deeply concerned about our collective safety. John, this may be asking for a lot, but would you consider letting us relocate to your group?"

"That would be an excellent idea, Karl. With all the new people we have here, we need to add to our supplies and need suitable clothing for them. We could move you into one of the empty homes we scouted today and extend our roadblocks out to provide security for four families. If your people are willing to work with us, I am confident we can come to an agreeable arrangement."

"John, give me fifteen minutes; I will call you back."

Right on cue, John's phone rang. "John, if you will have us, Anita and I would love to join your group. After Liz called me and told me you were worried, I rounded up every barrel and container I could find. I have emptied all my fuel storage tanks and filled three fuel trucks. The store has lots of food, clothing, hardware, and tools. We can move as much as we can to your place. I just don't know how we can move it all."

The vision of Bill Campbell's big blue rig appeared in John's head, and a huge grin crossed his face. "You leave that to us, Karl. We got that covered."

"John, Tim and Simone Henderson are also willing to join us. They are a nice couple. They have three young children. Simone is also a teacher, and they said they would pitch in and help with any needed work. They own the snowmobile/ATV store here in Owen Sound. Tim says we can move all his inventory of machines out and put them to work. There are no buyers out there. If we don't use them, these assholes will take them. Tim also has a large inventory of clothing, plus parts, tools, etc."

"Wow," John replied. "That's a bonus."

"There is more, John. Tim's head mechanic, Darrel Boersma, has been helping us keep the looters away. He is a hell of a mechanic. Darrel's wife, Victoria, is a dentist. They would like to join the group as well. Darrel and Victoria are our friends, and Victoria is our dentist."

"That would be great, Karl. We don't have anyone here with dental skills, and Victoria would be a real asset. Karl, I have to run this by the group, but I don't see a problem. I will call you back at 8:30 tonight. Thanks, Karl."

"Thank you, John."

That evening at the 8 PM check-in, Karen Wood and Sheila

Carr were introduced. John filled the group in on the details and the four vacant homes.

Progress was being made on setting up a group council, and it was agreed they wanted to have the committee established before Christmas.

John filled everyone in on the Hansons, Hendersons and Boersma's. Everyone was on board. Plans were made to head into Owen Sound with all available help and vehicles to move them out first thing in the morning.

It was agreed that the three new families would reoccupy three of the four vacant homes. Calvin and Carl Emerson would relocate the roadblocks tomorrow to encompass the four newly added homes. When that was complete they would check out the construction site and the Carr's for usable equipment. Sheila told them everything on their property worked, and the group was welcome to use it.

With all the work ahead, it was agreed that the singles meet and greet would be set for an evening the first week of December.

Everyone signed off for the night. Tomorrow was going to be a busy day.

5:00 AM, 29 NOVEMBER 2020

The MacIntyre homestead

J ohn was up well before dawn. The group had a big day ahead with plenty of unknowns that made John uneasy. He had called his security team last night and informed them of the criminal gang activity that had haunted Karl and his group. "I want everyone to be fully armed and prepared with body armour and full patrol packs, just in case we have unwanted guests," John cautioned.

The group had never been close to a major town since the world went for a dump. The small city of Owen Sound surrounds an inlet on the south side of Georgian Bay, at the mouths of the Potawatomi and Sydenham rivers.

The city is the county seat of Grey County; it had a population of just over 21,300 before the pandemic, and there were bound to be many desperate people around. The businesses were all located on the northwest outskirts of town, which was perfect.

The convoy was all formed up and ready to roll into town with every available vehicle and trailer for the first of two trips. At the east roadblock, Bob and Darlene Jones wished them luck as they went through.

Twenty minutes later the convoy arrived at the Co-op, where they met with the Hansons, Hendersons, and Boersma's. After introductions and a quick meeting, they split into two groups, half going to Hendersons business next door and loading up. The remainder of the group stayed at the Co-op. As Bill Campbell backed his tractor-trailer up to the Co-op's loading dock, the security team took up positions around the facility. Three hours later, and loaded to capacity, they headed home.

The convoy was larger on the return trip, with three

fully loaded Co-op fuel delivery trucks and two more Co-op flatbed trucks loaded with seed, fertilizer and livestock feed. Bill Campbell's trailer was filled with all manner of food. The Henderson's had three pickups with large enclosed trailers loaded with new snowmobiles, Quads and gear. Plus, two cargo vans full of clothing and inventory from their store.

Back inside their security barrier, the group took advantage of a large building as the new stores area. The merchandise was quickly unloaded and stowed away. Perishable goods were distributed among all the group's homes.

The group met no interference on the first run and hoped thier luck would hold out as they arrived in Owen Sound for the final run. As on the previous trip, the group split up between the two businesses and began loading up.

Franz, J2, Ed, Arlene, Christopher and John were on sentry duty. Halfway through loading up, five vehicles started up the road toward them.

"Battle stations, everyone," John spoke into his two-way radio.

When John's call came in over the team's radios, Franz was already up on Bill Campbell's trailer with his favourite Remington 700.

J3 and Kat, standing guard on the Co-ops loading dock, went upstairs and took up positions on the store's roof. They each had a Remington 700.

Others grabbed weapons and took up concealed positions around the two properties.

John could hear the heavy bass from the punk music well before the vehicles pulled up and stopped. Four big burly tattooed men stepped out of the lead vehicle, and one, obviously the leader, angrily looked the group over.

John, Tim Henderson and Karl Hanson stood behind John's pickup.

The big man looked at John, Tim and Karl attempting to intimidate them. "You fuckers are stealing my property."

"I beg to differ," John replied confidently. "This belongs to these two people here." Gestureing calmly toward Karl and Tim. "These people own these businesses."

"This is my turf now, and I call the shots here." He boasted as he pointed his thumb defiantly toward his chest. "Lucky for you old fucks, I'm feeling merciful today, so I'm giving you five minutes to fuck off out of here," the big man scowled menacingly.

"Or what?" John replied calmly as he placed his hand on his 45.

More goons started getting out of the other vehicles. "Don't fuck with me, old man," the leader yelled as he pointed at his watch. "The clock is ticking."

John clicked the radio mic twice. Franz fired one round from the Remington 700. The 338 Lapua magnum's full metal jacket round entered the engine block of the lead car; it chugged then stalled. Franz immediately chambered another round and lined up his next shot. *Now, if this stooge's giant head isn't as hard as it looks.*

Some of the goons jumped, but the leader didn't flinch. He turned to look at his now disabled vehicle, then looked back at John. "Big fuckin mistake, old man," he snarled. "The clock has now stopped ticking."

John looked the big, burly man in the eye. "You call me old man one more time, and the next round will impact in the centre of your ugly head. I suggest you jerk wads load up, and screw off before we kill every one of you."

The big man's face went red. He was furious, and moved for his gun. Before his hand touched the automatic pistol tucked into his waist, his head exploded. The powerful jacketed round carried on, passing right through the chest of the man standing behind the vehicle.

Franz grinned a sadistic grin, *two for one.* He chambered another round and fired, dropping another goon.

Kat already had the forehead of one in her crosshairs. This was not a moose; it was a human. She had seen the evil that evil people can do, and these were threatening her grandfather and her friends. Kat squeezed the trigger, and the head of the goon standing next to the leader exploded.

J3 having similar thoughts as his cousin, didn't hesitate, and another goon fell as a 338 round hit him between the eyes.

The remaining men ran behind their vehicles for cover as round after round slammed into them and their vehicles. The battle was over within 10 seconds. The groups' concentrated fire and the accuracy of the three shooting the powerful 700s eliminated the bad guys and disabled all their vehicles.

The security team checked over the bodies retrieving any weapons and identification carried by the goons. Everyone gathered around. "They appear to belong to some kind of biker gang," J2 said, showing John some IDs and biker wear they had with them.

"That was excellent shooting you two," Franz said proudly, hugging his two young disciples.

John looked sadly at his grandkids, J2 and Greg, at their children. They all hugged. Finally, John spoke, "That was intense. You are both so young and supposed to be doing teenage things."

"It's ok, Poppa," Kat said. "We are living in a different world now. These dirtbags threatened you, and they threatened all of us. I have no remorse," she replied.

"Neither do I," J3 replied. "They deserved it."

John proudly looked over his team. "We best finish up here," John said. "That noise may attract more unwanted attention, be alert, everyone."

Two hours later, they were all loaded up. No one else had shown up, but John was certain they hadn't seen the last of these dirtbags.

As the convoy pulled out. John, Franz, Hatto, Arlene, Ed and Christopher remained. "I suggest we beef up the guard at the roadblocks, John recommended.

"Yes, I feel we should position a sniper near each roadblock to provide covering fire should anyone try to run the roadblock," Franz added.

Agreed," replied John.

If I may, John," Hatto spoke. "We haven't seen the last of these people. A blind man could track us in this snow, and they will send people searching for us."

"Agreed, Hatto. We should plan a wee surprise for them, and I know just the place," John smiled

4:00 PM, 29 NOVEMBER 2020

Owen Sound, Ontario

Bull Darlington stomped around the bodies of his crew. He was raging. "Twenty good men wiped out, tons of my goods stolen. Burn these fucking places to the ground," he yelled. "Those fuckers are going to pay for this. I will hunt them down and kill every one of them."

Bull turned to face two of his men, "Darren, you and Frankie, follow these assholes and don't get too fucking close. Find out where they live and report back to me, understood?"

"Yes, Bull, we're on it."

John, Franz, Ed, Christopher, Hatto, and Arlene waited one kilometre south of East Linton on County Road 1. They were parked at two abandoned properties, expecting a scouting party, and they weren't disappointed.

The sun had fallen below the horizon as John and Franz studied the snow covered road through binoculars. An SUV with no lights on and two men inside slowly appeared. "It's show time, everyone," John announced over his radio.

When the men entered the zone, Ed pulled one vehicle out in front of them, and Christopher pulled out behind them, blocking the road.

Darren attempted to turn around and escape by smashing through the car behind them. He misjudged the shoulder of the snow-covered road and dropped a wheel into the ditch.

Darren made a feeble attempt to get free but the SUV was stuck. He and Frankie jumped out of their car and stood, pointing two AK47s around in every direction.

Armed with the powerful Remington 700s, John and Franz shot each man in the right knee, dropping them both as their knees collapsed. Arlene and Hatto ran up and disarmed the two while the others covered them.

"Well, now," John said as he walked up to the two. "Start talking."

"Fuck you, old man," Darren balled, screaming in pain.

"I trust you witnessed what happened to the last bunch of jerkwads that called me old man," John said, smiling.

"Fuck you," wailed Frankie.

John nodded, and Hatto and Arlene went to work on the two breaking every finger on their right hands, one at a time. The two were screaming in pain, bleeding from knee wounds and now trying to nurse their broken fingers.

"Feel like talking now, or will we do the other hand?" John asked as Hatto and Arlene grabbed their other hand bending back one finger.

The two started screaming again, and both got a kick in the nuts for their trouble.

Darren puked, and Frankie pissed himself.

"Start talking," John ordered as Arlene bent Darren's finger back further.

"Ok, ok," he yelled, "I'll talk."

"Who are you two working for?" John asked.

"Don't tell him, Darren. We'll be dead meat."

Hatto broke one of Frankie's fingers, and he screamed.

Darren started talking, "Bull Darlington is our boss. We are members of a biker gang, and we run the north end of Owen Sound. You fuckers are going to be sorry you fucked with Bull," Darren said scathingly.

Arlene broke a finger.

"Fuck, fuck," yelled Darren. "I told you what you wanted."

"You didn't answer nice. Don't do that again," Arlene warned.

"Keep talking," ordered John. "How many in the gang?"

"Fuck," Darren howelled as Arlene bent back another finger. "We have," he paused. "Had 80 until you cunts killed them."

"I warned you, Darren," Arlene smiled as she broke another finger.

"Ahhh," Darren screamed, "fucking stop that."

Arlene bent back one more finger, "When I run out of fingers, Darren, I'm going to cut your dick off and make you eat it." She smiled a sadistic smile.

"Better keep talking, Darren. Where do you hang out?" John asked.

Darren said nothing.

Franz pulled out his Ka-Bar and showed it to him, "You have three fingers left, asshole. I would start talking unless you want to eat your dick."

Darren looked at Arlene, and she winked at him smiling.

"We live in a condo building on the waterfront," Darren groaned.

"Address?" asked John.

"Fuck Darren, don't tell them," Frankie yelled.

Hatto broke the remaining fingers, one at a time, and then he dislocated his right elbow. Frankie was now crying in pain.

"345 Eddie Sargent Parkway, right next to the marina," a panicked Darren yelled.

"Was that so hard, Darren? Now, what kind of security does this Bull Darlington have?" John asked calmly.

"Fuck," Darren wailed. "You're killing me."

Arlene broke another finger. Darren wailed again.

"One more finger left, Darren, then your dick comes off," Arlene said, grinning.

"Three gunmen on the roof, more inside the lobby and more outside Bull's door."

"Excellent," John replied. "Now Darren, what unit does Bull

live in?" "The penthouse," answered Darren, sobbing.

"Bull wants you people dead. He will come for you," Frankie screamed. "You don't fuck with Bull Darlington."

"We will see about that," John replied, smiling. He then nodded one last time, and Arlene and Hatto snapped both men's necks and tossed the bodies into the ditch.

"That should keep the coyotes happy for a few days," John smiled. "Christopher, can you drive that SUV back to the farm?" John asked.

"Sure thing, John," He replied.

7:00 PM, 29 NOVEMBER 2020

The MacIntyre Homestead

J ohn made several phone calls, and within 15 minutes, six vehicles pulled up to the shop. "Thanks for coming," John said. "We must go on the offensive tonight before these mutts get over the shock of our first encounter and regroup. They can find us easily in the snow; our tracks are obvious and lead to our door. No one will be safe here with them on the loose.

The team all agreed.

"I printed these pictures of the condo at 335 Eddie Sargent Parkway, Owen Sound from Google street view. Franz will hand pictures out to everyone while I fill you all in on what we know as of now.

"There are approximately sixty members left in this gang. The filth has obviously taken over the entire condo. They have three armed men on the roof, an unknown number in the lobby, and many more in the building. The leader, Bull Darlington, lives in the penthouse.

"Franz and I are heading there right after this meeting. We will recon the building and make a plan. We need you all to arrive at 0300.

"Ed Bennet will lead from this end and organize your teams. We will be in touch via the radio. Check out your COMMs; you should all be on 154.100 Mhz. Ensure you have three days' worth of food and gear in your packs to get you back home if this goes for a dump. Try and get some sleep. It's going to be a long night."

The night was overcast, with a light snowfall coming down as John and Franz drove to Owen Sound. Nothing was moving when they passed the smouldering remains of the CO-OP and the Hendersons business. Some homes had lights on; most were dark. John took back streets and parked several blocks from 345 Eddie Sargent Parkway.

John and Franz both wore white ghillie suits, and with the falling snow, they were virtually invisible as they approached 345 Eddie Sargent Parkway. 335 was the middle of a three-condo group. They were all low-rise units, six floors overlooking the yacht club. 345 was well lit up, these people were obviously the dominant power in the neighbourhood, and they feared no one. 343 and 347 were both dark.

The two old soldiers stealthily approached 347. The lower floor windows and doors were busted out, making entry easy. The building was empty, with no soul to be found and no security for the bikers.

345 was the same, unoccupied. John and Franz positioned themselves on the roof of 343 and studied the comings and goings of 345 Eddie Sargent Parkway. They noted three armed men on the roof, walking around, smoking, drinking and making no effort to conceal themselves. The lobby was no different, well lit up and the guards appeared half-drunk.

John lowered his binoculars and turned toward Franz. "These mutts are pretty confident."

"They are a bunch of fools," Franz replied, "No effort to conceal themselves. They are drunk, undisciplined and ruining their night vision."

"Agreed," answered John. "Let's watch a bit."

Several SUVs came and went, gang members dragged women in and out, and they treated them like trash. It was 0230 when things started to slow down. One of the men on the roof had passed out, the other two staggering around smoking and talking. The lobby was still lit up. One of the guards was on the couch having sex with an unconscious woman while the other three goaded him on.

"Observations?" John asked.

"They are not expecting any trouble," Franz replied.

"Agreed," answered John.

John made a phone call to Ed. "Hi Ed, update, please."

"We are ten minutes out, John," Ed replied.

"Excellent!" John gave Ed directions to where he had parked. Ten minutes later, six vehicles pulled in, and the team gathered in a small park.

John laid out the plan. "There are condos on both sides of this one. Franz and I have scouted them. They are empty, but take no chances, be alert as you get into position.

"I want team 1, led by Franz, on the roof of 347, the north condo. Team 2, led by Ed, on the roof of 343, the south condo. I will locate on the south condo with Team 2. It has the best view into the penthouse. I am hoping to take down Bull Darlington. I don't know what the man looks like, so I will be taking out every target of opportunity I see in there.

"Team 3, led by Christopher Hodgson, will spread out around the north and east of the condo. Team 4, led by Scott Sabovitch, will spread out around the south and west perimeter of the condo.

"Arlene will distract them by running the SUV they were so kind to loan us into the lobby. She will jump clear and join up with Hatto; they will hunt for runners.

Carl Emmerson filled the vehicle with fuel and placed a nice fertilizer bomb it in the trunk. It will be like the 24th of May when that goes off," John smiled.

"When the vehicle enters the lobby, we take out the rooftop guards, then any other target of opportunity. Once the building starts to burn, the smart ones should come running out. The fire teams spread out all around the building will strike them. We hit them fast; we hit them with extreme violence. If we are lucky, no one will escape.

"There will be some women in that building. Some are bikers; they are fair game. However, I believe these pigs have captured local women. Try not to hit any.

"Questions?" John asked.

Everyone answered, "no."

"Arlene will start the ball rolling at 0330 by clicking her radio mic three times to signal the start. Take no chances. We are outnumbered 3 to 1, but we have the element of surprise on our side, and we will prevail. Let's get this done!" John smiled. Everyone had their game faces on and moved into position.

Ed Bennet was armed with his AR15, with a Trijicon ACOG 4 X 32 scope. He would provide cover for his shooters. His team consisted of Kat armed with her Remington 700, 338 Lapua magnum. Andy Hodgson armed with his scoped hunting rifle, a Sako 85 in stainless steel, chambered in 30-06. They were his main shooters. John was on his own, armed with the powerful MacMillan TAC 50.

Franz was armed with a Remington 700, 338 Lapua Magnum. His team consisted of J2 providing cover armed with an SKS and J3 armed with his Remington 700, 338 Lapua Magnum.

Scott and Christopher's fire teams would surround the building. They were armed with the AK47s confiscated earlier, SKS rifles and hunting rifles. Each team had seven shooters.

At 0330 sharp, everyone heard three distinct clicks from Arlene. Two seconds later, the SUV came speeding toward the building. Carl had done a masterful job rigging it, so Arlene could aim it straight into the lobby and lock the steering wheel and accelerator. Arlene lined it up, locked the wheel and accelerator, then bailed out. She was dressed in white and disappeared before anyone could see her.

All the guards were passed out when the SUV smashed through the lobby doors. Carl had set the bomb to go off 15 seconds after the SUV stopped, plenty of time for the fuel load to spread out and vaporize.

As soon as the SUV entered the lobby, the three rooftop guards woke up and started running to see what was happening. Franz,

Kat and J3 dropped all three, one shot each.

John studied the penthouse through the powerful Carl Zeiss optic. It was like he was standing right outside the window. A young girl ran into view. She was naked and couldn't have been more than 12 years old. She fell, shot by a bullet from inside the room. That pissed John off.

Then a giant half-naked man came into view with a pistol in his right hand. John followed him, his big ugly head centred in the crosshairs of his optic as he raged across the room, shouting orders to his guards. *That must be the Bull.* "Here's a little something from that innocent little girl," John cursed. The massive 50 BMG bullet hit Bull in the side of the head and Bull Darlington fell to the floor. John smiled a sadistic grin, *Payback is a bitch Bully Boy.*

Two bodyguards with AK47s fired wildly out the window. John hit one squarely in the chest slamming the big biker against the wall. A bloody red smear stained the wall as the body slowly side to the floor. Kat took out the other shooter with her 338 just as the SUV exploded in the lobby.

Fire alarms that would never be answered rang into the night as bikers and girls ran from the burning building. The fire teams picked the bikers off one by one. A black Suburban came around from the back of the condo, sliding sideways in the snow as the driver attempted to pick up speed. One round from Johns TAC 50 took out the driver and another seated behind him. Three men jumped from the moving SUV only to meet the swords of Hatto and Arlene.

The shooting lasted five minutes. When no more ran from the building, everyone held their positions and waited. Three white SUVs rolled slowly up the street, and John followed them in his scope. They were Owen Sound police vehicles.

"Hold your fire," John called over the radio. "This may be the good guys."

The lead vehicle stopped 100 meters short of the burning

condo, and a man dressed in a police uniform stepped out. He wore a bulletproof vest and carried a shotgun. Others followed, and six police officers stood by their vehicles and surveyed the carnage.

"All teams disengage, but do not stand down. I am going to approach them, cover me," John called over the radio

John was closest to where the police were parked, and Franz was on his way. John remained behind cover and called out. "Hello, Police, this is John MacIntyre. To whom am I speaking?"

The six officers spoke among themselves for a few seconds. The officer from the lead car replied, "Hello, John MacIntyre, this is Miles Davis. I am acting chief of police."

"May I approach?" John asked.

"Yes, John, come forward."

John walked toward the police. He had the MacMillan slung over his shoulder.

Miles extended his hand. "John MacIntyre, you taught my son and daughter first aid at Army Cadets."

John shook his hand, "Pleased to meet you, Miles."

Another familiar face walked up. "Gordon Cameron," John said and extended his hand,

"I am happy to see you here. John, I owe you and Liz a great big thank you. She came to the bank to withdraw some money and warned me. Am I glad I listened."

Miles put his hand on John's shoulder, "John, the city of Owen Sound owes you and your people a huge debt of gratitude. This vile den of vipers has been looting and killing for far too long. Only the six of us are left, trying to keep the remaining residents of this city safe, and we haven't been doing very well."

"Miles, let me call my team in. They will all be pleased to meet you."

Miles agreed.

John keyed his mic, "Listen up, everyone, Scott, keep your

team on watch? The rest of you stand down and come to the police vehicles. John out."

A few minutes later, most of the team had gathered around the police. Introductions were made as Miles shook everyone's hand and personally thanked them.

Gordon was wearing his Army uniform and assisting the Owen Sound police. Miles's son, fifteen-year-old Andrew Davis, was the youngest police officer and wearing a uniform that was too big for him. He walked up to Kat and J3. They shared a hug. They were all aquatinted. Andrew and Kat were both cadets with 42 Grey & Simcoe Foresters in Owen Sound. J3 from 2919 Grey & Simcoe Foresters from Barrie, Ontario. Both Cadet Corps often trained together.

Franz had phoned Caroline back at the home farm and shared the news about a successful operation and meeting the police. Everyone was thrilled when Caroline passed the good news to the group over the radio.

John, Franz, Ed, Christopher and Miles agreed to help one another out and share training. Miles needed new police officers, and with the biker problem now under control, he could go into the community and seek recruits.

Miles informed them about the conditions in Owen Sound. Roughly half of the 12,000-plus residents remained alive. The city had electricity for now, and Miles feared Lake Huron's Bruce Nuclear Power plant would be shut down, leaving many cold and dark. The Mayor and many of the council had died, leaving Miles to keep the city operating. With the bikers dealt with, he could concentrate some of his efforts on getting the city back on its feet.

John shared what his group was trying to do by keeping the farms occupied and operating. If all went well, a food source would be available to provide the area with food. They all had a long hard winter ahead of them and plenty of time to plan for their collective futures.

The body count of the bikers was 54. The team was sure none had escaped. The team searched through the rubble and collected what bodies they could find. Miles would send a truck in the morning and a crew to load them up and bury them.

While the teams searched, eight poorly dressed young women and girls walked up to them and thanked everyone for saving them. Miles and his officers would escort them home and ensure they were adequately cared for.

The two groups shared phone numbers and agreed to set up a meeting sometime next week. Handshakes and goodbyes were shared, and the team loaded up and headed home.

The team arrived back at the MacIntyre farm to a hero's welcome. Everyone had chipped in and prepared breakfast. Hugs and handshakes were shared, tears were shed, and everyone ate and enjoyed one another's company.

After breakfast, the exhausted team members retired for some well-deserved sleep.

8:00 AM, 30 NOVEMBER 2020

Toronto, Ontario

T The power had gone out in the building that his gang had called home, it was getting cold, and for that, Drago Cuz was pissed.

The word on the street was that Bull Darlington and his entire gang of bikers had been wiped out. Bull had long held the number two spot in The Kazankov Boys gang, Drago a distant number five. *One man's misfortune is another man's opportunity,* Drago smiled.

Drago prided himself as a tough, skilled fighter and big-time dealer. His gang specialized in human trafficking but also peddled drugs and guns.

Drago himself was 26 years old, 6'2", lean and mean. He was covered in tattoos and had his namesake dragon tattooed on his shaved head. He had a scar on his forehead; Drago earned that in a knife fight with a big black man from Chicago. The other guy earned himself a notch on Drago's Karambit knife and was added to Chicago's extensive file of unsolved deaths.

Drago carried a Beretta PX4 Storm, 9 MM pistol tucked into the waist of his pants. He was a skilled knife fighter and preferred the Karambit over the gun.

A master manipulator, Drago got off by terrifying his prey. This skill earned him his reputation as the "go-to guy" when humans were needed. He liked to smoke, loved his booze and had a serious drug habit.

Arnie Davis was Drago's right-hand man. Arnie was 26, at 5'9", shorter than his boss but more sturdily built. Arnie loved the look of a shaved head and tats. He was a heavy smoker, drinker and drug user.

Arnie packed a Beretta, PX4 Storm, but like his boss, he was a skilled knife fighter and preferred to use his Karambit knife over the handgun. Arnie was ruthless. He enjoyed cutting people and watching them slowly bleed to death while he beat on them.

Melanie Prop was Arnie's squeeze. At 19; she was stunningly beautiful and well-built. She was from a good home but had run away because she didn't want to be told what to do by her parents.

Mel met Arnie in a club one night, and she was immediately attracted to his tough guy image. Mel could see people feared and respected him, which turned her on.

Technically she was his girlfriend, but if he needed money or drugs, Mel would be whored out to pay for it. Three years ago, Arnie offered two American gun dealers a night with Mel in exchange for the Beretta PX9s. They didn't disappoint, and neither did Melanie. However, she spent two weeks in the hospital for her part. Despite several well-meaning social workers' interventions, Mel returned to Arnie.

Drago's other six inner circle members were petty thieves and drug pushers. Gary Smythe, Harold Katz, Ralph Heston, Chad Hurt, Tyler Stone and Tony Milan. These six were the group's muscle, all in their thirties, big on brawn but short on brains. They all had shaved heads and wore plenty of tats. All six were heavy drug users. They all carried handguns and folding knives.

Three days ago, Arnie and Mel had watched the restaurant owners and a group of friends load the food from the restaurant into two catering trucks. They followed the vehicles to the condo, then watched as the food and booze were unloaded into the rec centre of the building.

That food was supposed to be the gang's food, and Arnie would see they got it back. He and Mel had staked out the building. There were two ageing men providing security, one overweight, the other wore a turban and could hardly walk; they would offer zero resistance.

Drago had big plans, and now with the power was out in the gang's building, Drago informed his crew they were moving up. They were now in the market for a new place to call home and a group of sheeple had been kind enough to move all the gangs food and supplies in for them. "After we thank these kind fools for their service and get settled into our new diggs, I will report to Kazankov and assume my long overdue role as his number two-man," Drago bragged to his people.

The gang assembled outside the condo. "The plan is simple," announced Drago. "Mel will go up and knock on the door, beg for help, get them to open up, and when they do, we rush them. We know where the goods are; we go there first and check them out, then we look for some nice new apartments," he smiled.

They all nodded.

"Ok, Mel, head for the door," Arnie ordered. "And for fuck's sake, show your tits that will get the old pricks attention."

Melanie was a superb actress. She staggered up to the door and fell to her knees. Her hair was a mess, and she was crying. Mel's shirt was unbuttoned and pulled out of her jeans, her ample breasts on full display. "Help me," she called to the overweight man inside. "Two men are after me. They tried to rape me," she sobbed, banging on the glass.

The guard was beside himself; he had a granddaughter that age. He went to the door, carefully looked around then opened it up. As soon as the door opened, Gary, Harold, and Tony rushed the man, and he was quickly overpowered.

Arnie strutted up, pulled his Karambit and spun around his finger to the horror of the guard lying helpless on the floor. He bent down and smiled a sadistic smile, then slit the guard's throat. "One down, one to go," whispered Arnie.

The elderly Indian man was making his rounds of the lower floor. He was caught entirely by surprise by the six thugs and didn't stand a chance. He was hit on the head, knocked down, kicked and beaten to death. Arnie used the man's turban as a football and kicked it down the hall while they all shared a silent laugh. Arnie removed the keys from the guard's belt and walked proudly to the rec centre door.

Drago held his hand up for Arnie to wait. He eyed the notice that Janet taped to the door. He looked at the others, smiling, "the penthouse," he mocked. "This Janet sounds like a real take charge kind of woman. Probably has a really tight ass, my kind of bitch. I should move in with her."

The gang smiled and nodded, knowing what Drago was thinking.

"Arnie, you and Mel, come with me. The rest of you fuckers gather up some booze and food. We are going to check out my new penthouse."

Arnie pulled Mel close and squeezed her breast, "That was a sweet performance, baby. You ready for part two?"

Mel smiled back while she rubbed Arnie's crotch. They had watched Drago perform and wouldn't miss it for the world. The three made their way to the penthouse.

Mel opened her shirt, mussed her hair and rubbed her eyes to make them red. Mel rang the doorbell, "Janet, help me," she called out, sobbing.

George Aston was awakened by the doorbell. He could hear a woman calling for Janet.

Janet sat up in bed. She, too, heard a female voice crying, asking for her by name. "Oh, my God," Janet gasped. "Who could that be?"

They both got up, put on their robes and walked to the door. George looked through the peephole, but all he could see was the top of a woman's head.

"Janet, I think it's Chantel," George said, unlocking the door and pulling it open.

Arnie sprang at George, elbowing him in the nose, shattering it. Janet started to scream, but Arnie quickly grabbed her and covered her mouth, stifling it. George stumbled back, falling to the floor and holding his bleeding nose. He was stunned by the powerful blow, trying to comprehend what had just happened.

Drago confidently swaggered in, followed by Mel and the boys carrying the food and booze. "Well, now," Drago said mockingly, looking Janet up and down. "You must be Janet."

Janet was horrified. She stared in shock at the tall bald man with the dragon tattoo on his head as he grinned at her.

"We were downstairs, Janet and we were feeling a little peckish. That's when we noticed your kind invitation and I thought, yes, I like this, Janet. We should get acquainted."

Janet started to sob, "Take whatever you want and leave us, please," she cried.

"Janet, you misunderstand me. I am moving in here," Drago mocked as he looked around approvingly. "I could get to like this penthouse."

Janet's eyes opened wide; she was terrified.

Janet," Drago said softly, smiling. "Don't worry; the good news is that you don't have to leave. I would be lonely here all by myself. You see, Janet, I don't have a steady girl like Arnie, and I would like to try out this cougar thing I have been hearing about.

Drago walked up to her. Janet's eyes widened. Arnie held her arms tightly behind her back.

"Now don't you scream," Drago spoke quietly, almost sweetly, to her. "How old are you, Janet?"

"4...48," Janet replied, sobbing.

"Nice," said Drago. "Very nice. My name is Drago, and this is Arnie and Mel. Now we all know one another; we are friends."

Janet stood shaking, afraid to speak.

"Now don't you scream, Janet. I don't want to hurt that pretty face," he said, pulling his Karambit and moving it back and forth in front of her face.

Janet was horrified, but she nodded ok.

"Good," said Drago. "Good girl. Now Arnie is going to release you.

Drago reached out and untied her robe. He then pushed it off her shoulders.

Janet's eyes widened in fear as her robe fell to the floor.

"It's ok, Janet," Drago smiled, holding the karambit close to her face. "We are all friends here, right? I won't hurt you as long as you cooperate, understood?"

Janet nodded.

"Now, Janet, I have very high standards. If you and I are going to be lovers I have to ensure you make the cut."

Janet sobbed and shock with fear fully aware of what was coming.

"The pyjamas as well, Janet. Don't make me angry," Drago added, grinning sadistically.

Janet slowly removed her pyjamas and then covered herself with her hands.

"Good Janet, now, show me what you have to offer," Drago said quietly.

Janet looked over at Mel, hoping for some female sympathy, but she didn't get any.

Drago took his time examining the terrified woman. "I am impressed, Janet, you look very nice for 48. Now, are those boobs real?"

Janet nodded yes as she sobbed uncontrollably.

Drago licked his lips then reached out and caressed her right breast in his hand. He gently squeezed, rubbing his thumb on her nipple. "They feel very nice, Janet." He then reached down to put his hand between her legs. Janet continued to sob. "It's ok, Janet, relax and open up just a little for me."

Janet moved her right leg just a little as she shook from fear.

"Good girl, Janet," Drago said and gently rubbed her vagina.

"Nice," he said. "Very nice. I really like a shaved pussy."

Janet was shaking, tears running down her cheeks.

George attempted to get up, but Arnie kicked him three times in the ribs. George lay still after that.

Drago held the Karambit in front of Janet and his other finger to his lips in a 'shh' motion. He then pointed his Karambit at George. "Janet, I don't like this fellow, he is not much of a man, but I fear he would try to come between us."

Janet was sobbing uncontrollably.

"Janet, turn around and touch the floor for me."

She did as instructed.

Drago squeezed her butt cheeks one at a time. "Nice," he exclaimed. "Arnie, tell me if these are as nice as Mel's."

Arnie squeezed Janet's butt cheeks one at a time, smiling as he did. He looked at Drago approvingly, "Nice, Drago, they are equally as nice as Mel's."

"Janet, you can stand up now," Drago whispered to her. "You should consider that quite a compliment; Mel is only 19."

Janet never spoke. She slowly stood and turned around. Tears streamed down her cheeks as she feared what would be next.

"Janet, do you like anal?"

"I, I never," she sobbed.

"I do, Janet, I am very good at it, and I know I am really going to enjoy your tight ass." Drago led a sobbing, naked Janet into the bedroom and closed the door.

Arnie looked at the boys, "You fuckers grab some beers and go down to the front desk. See if you can find out who is still here and what units they are in."

The six knew they weren't wanted, they grabbed some beers and left. The whole show had given Arnie one hell of a hard-on. Mel, too was horny, rubbing her crotch.

Arnie walked over and quickly slit George's throat. "Drago

doesn't like him, and we don't want that old pervert watching us, do we baby?" He smiled, grabbing Mel. They fell on the Aston's couch and fucked wildly.

Half an hour later, a smiling Drago led a defeated Janet from the bedroom. "She was perfect, Arnie, and she likes anal. I love this penthouse, and I think I'm going to enjoy this cougar business," Drago said, smiling at Janet.

Arnie and Mel quickly dressed, then called Tony, "Did you boys get the information?"

"Sure did," replied Tony.

"Good, come on back up, fellas; we need to make a plan."

Five minutes later, the six walked back into the penthouse.

"Grab another beer and pull up a seat," ordered Arnie.

Drago sat Janet on a loveseat in the living room. She was dressed in her robe and was heavily sedated.

"Ok, boys, what do you have for me?" Drago asked while he gently stroked Janet's inner thigh.

"There are only five units besides this one that is occupied, Boss," Tony replied excitedly. "Two on the floor below us, two on the second floor and one on the ground floor."

Drago thought for a minute, then looked at the gang, smiling, "Ok, we pull the fire alarm. When all these idiots come running down to the bottom floor, Tony, Harold, and Gary will be waiting. The elevator is right beside the stairs, which makes it so easy

"Chad, Tyler, and Ralph wait up here and check their rooms, make sure we got them all.

"Arnie, Mel and I will visit the people in the ground floor unit. When we are inside, Mel will signal you to pull the alarm and spring the trap. Bring our guests to unit two. We will be waiting, easy peasy, right?" Drago questioned, a huge grin appearing on his face.

They all nodded in agreement.

9:00 AM, 30 NOVEMBER 2020

Toronto, Ontario

Sal Cutrara was awakened by someone ringing his doorbell and banging on the door. He heard a woman's voice calling his name. Sal was still groggy from sleep; was he dreaming? No, someone was banging, ringing and calling out for him. The voice said it was Janet Ashton.

"What is it?" Sal's wife Anna asked.

"I, I think it's Janet; something must be wrong," Sal replied. They both got up, put on their robes, and went to the door.

Sal looked through the peephole; Janet was outside sobbing. "Oh my God," he gasped. Janet was standing outside their door, dressed in her robe, and looked terrible. Sal unlocked the door and pulled it open.

Arnie was fast, moving in as Mel pulled Janet back. He burst through the door and pointed his Beretta at Sal and Anna. "On the floor, both of you."

Neither Sal nor Anna registered what was going on. "You can't come in here pulling guns on us, ordering us around. Get out!" Sal ordered defiantly.

Anna Cutrara stood defiantly beside her husband, "Get out of here, you filth," she yelled. "We have laws here, get out," she ordered, pointing at the door.

Then the fire alarm went off, and Drago walked in smiling with his arm wrapped around a drugged and defeated Janet Ashton. Drago walked right up to Sal, looked him in the eyes and smiled. Then he locked eyes with Anna. The room went silent at the sight of the tattooed man holding Janet.

Anna gasped in disbelief.

"I am terribly sorry," Drago asked softly. "Are we invading your safe space?"

No one spoke, and no one moved.

"What's your name?" Drago asked Sal in his soft, friendly voice.

Sal looked at Drago defiantly, "My name is Sal Cutrara. Just who the hell are you, and why are you here? What have you swine done to Janet?"

Drago ignored him, shifting his gaze toward Anna, "What is your name," he asked?

"She is my wife," spoke Sal boldly. "She will not speak to the like of you," and he moved to push Drago aside.

Drago moved with lightning speed before anyone could so much as blink.

Sal was unsure of what had happened. He clutched his throat and tried to speak but couldn't, as he fell to the floor with a massive gash in his throat.

Anna screamed and looked on in horror, finally realizing the trouble they were now in. She stood there and started to sob, looking down while her husband bled out from the massive gash in his throat.

Drago held his finger to his lips in a 'shh' motion to Anna as he spun the bloody Karambit around the finger of his other hand.

"Now, is there any question regarding who is running this show?" Drago asked softly.

Anna continued to sob, the tears running down her cheeks.

The boy's started marching the dazed and confused residents into the room. "Everyone over there on the floor," Tony ordered.

The stench of death and blood was overpowering. All the residents gasped in horror at the sight of Sal's body bleeding out on the floor, his throat slit open.

Chantel MacIntyre gagged and vomited.

David MacIntyre went to his wife's aid. Harold intercepted and punched him solidly in the head. David stumbled.

"David!" Chantel screamed.

The other gang members pointed their guns at everyone, "sit and don't move.

Arnie fired his Beretta 9MM into the ceiling, and everyone complied.

Through the mayhem, Harold continued to work over David. Harold kicked him hard in the stomach, and David fell to the floor. David tried to get up, and Harold kicked him again. The powerful kick drove David through the patio door. David landed on his back in the snow. David tried to get up once again. Harold went out after him,

"You don't know when to quit, do you asshole?" Harold kicked David with a roundhouse kick driving him through the wooded privacy fence. David lay unconscious as the heavy snowfall started to cover him.

Drago spoke again in his calm, quiet voice, "Now, let's not see a repeat of that. Are we clear?" As he looked around the room smiling.

Drago looked back at Anna. "Where were we? Oh yes. What is your name?"

"An, An, Anna," she said between sobs.

Drago then addressed the residents in his calm, quiet voice. "Look around," he said. "Do I look like someone who gives a fuck about your laws?"

No one answered. Anna stood there sobbing.

"Anna, you look like someone who supports gun control. Would I be correct?"

She nodded yes.

"Good," said Drago. "I knew we would have something in common. What about the rest of you?"

Everyone looked on in shock, but no one answered.

"Me and the boys support gun control, don't we boys."

All of Drago's gang smiled and nodded in agreement.

"Do you know why we would support gun control, Anna?"

She shook her head no.

"Please allow me to enlighten you, Anna, with gun control, only people like us will have guns, and that's how we like it. We don't give a shit about the law, and we don't give a shit about your safe space or your fucking rights." Drago smiled at everyone, "You fuckers are living in my world now. The only laws that apply here are my laws. Do I make myself clear, Anna?"

She nodded yes and sobbed.

Drago looked around the room, stopping at Janie Handley, "You look familiar," Drago said, grinning. "Ah yes, you're the news lady, aren't you?"

Janie said nothing. She sat on the floor and started to sob.

"Well, now, isn't this special," Drago smiled an evil smile, "The big boss will like you. He needs someone to report his propaganda to the public."

Drago looked at the women again, one by one smiling. "I am looking for some new whores. The world is changing, and we will need the means to barter for food. You bitches will soon become the new world currency.

Anna, let's have a look at you. We need to assess your worth. Take off your robe and show me your breasts," Drago ordered.

Anna said, "No."

Drago showed her the bloody Karambit, then gestured to Sal's lifeless body lying on the floor in a pool of congealing blood.

Anna slowly removed her robe, then her pyjama top and stopped.

Drago looked at her, smiling, "You are a feisty old bitch aren't you, Anna? All tough and mouthy when you think you are in control."

Anna just stood silently, looking at the floor.

Drago used the bloody Karambit to slice open her bra. Her breasts spilled out in front of everyone in the room. "Hmmm, Anna," Drago said disappointedly as he reached out and picked up her left breast. "This will not do, it will not do at all. Those are a little saggy now, aren't they?

Anna stared at the foor shaking.

How old are you, Anna?"

"45," she said, sobbing.

Drago looked Anna in the eyes, shaking his head in a no gesture, "I am very disappointed, Anna. No one wants old floppy tits. I may have to kill you."

Anna, started to shake and sob, waiting for the strike from Drago's Karambit.

All the women were sobbing, fearing they were next.

Drago loved the performance. He enjoyed terrifying people, and that was how he got control over them. Fear and intimidation are powerful weapons.

Arnie had his eye on Chantel, he heard her French accent, and it turned him on, he wanted her bad, but he stayed behind his boss. A wise man would never interrupt Drago when he was performing. Drago was not one to be trifled with.

* * *

Pasteur Kavaruganda held onto Giselle, sweat running down his face. He was transported back to their childhood in Rwanda when Tutsis ran through the country in a bloodlust, butchering every Hutu they encountered.

The Tutsis didn't discriminate, male, female, old, young, or infant; they slaughtered everyone in their path, hacking them to death with machetes.

Pasteur and his little brother were huddled in the corner

of the family kitchen when a Tutsi man kicked in the door. Pasteur's father held up his hands in surrender.

The Tutsi man showed no mercy. He hacked at his parents with his machete until they both lay dead.

Pasteur was frozen in horror. He cannot recall where he found the courage to run, but he grabbed his younger brother and ran, never looking back.

Pasteur now held Giselle, frozen in fear like he had his younger brother long ago.

With everyone preoccupied with watching Drago's performance, no one noticed David crawl back into the yard.

David had to do something and do it fast. He could visualize Chantel being assaulted by these criminals. He cursed himself for not having a way to defend Chantel and his friends, and he cursed himself for not listening to his parents.

David had no weapon, but if he could distract them, maybe Chantel and the others could escape. David threw a patio chair through the window. The unexpected crash caught everyone by surprise, covering Harold and Gary in broken glass.

Chad and Tyler turned to the window just as David threw another chair through. Chad and Tyler ducked, but it struck Harold knocking the gun from his hand. Dan Brown then grabbed Harold and started fighting with him.

Pasteur saw his opportunity. He grabbed Giselle and Chantel and then ran out the patio door.

Drago threw Anna against the wall with such force she fell unconscious to the floor.

Arnie was pissed seeing Chantel escape and ran out the door in a blind rage. David hit him squarely in the head with another patio chair, and Arnie went down.

Harold quickly overpowered Dan Brown, stabbing him six times with his knife and killing him.

Gary and Tony ran for the door, but David cut them off. The

three men fell to the floor, tripping Harold, who then fell, hitting his head against the coffee table. The impact made a terrible crack.

Peter Bright seizing the opportunity ran out with Janie Handley and Patricia Brown.

Drago swung his Karambit at David's throat, narrowly missing him. David kicked at him, catching a surprised Drago right in the nuts. Drago fell, screaming in pain.

David quickly turned and ran outside. He was hurt badly by the beating Harold gave him.

Chad, Ralph and Tyler ran out the door in pursuit only to be met with another chair thrown by David.

David ran, slipped in the snow and fell. Philip Gavin helped David to his feet, and they ran.

Chad was now back on his feet. He emptied his gun, all his shots missing their mark as the escapees slipped and slid in the snow.

Ralph fired, his weapon jammed, "Fuck," he yelled, throwing it to the floor.

Tyler emptied his gun as he gave chase, all the shots going wild. Meanwhile, Gary had reloaded and resumed firing.

Philip Gavin was hit in the shoulder and stumbled, falling to the ground. Now, it was David's turn to help his friend.

Another of Gary's rounds hit Peter in the back, and Peter fell face-first into the snow. Chantel and Patricia each grabbed an arm and began dragging him.

A Chevy Suburban came screaming around the corner with Pasteur at the wheel, it stopped, and the rear door flew open. Giselle jumped out and helped David get Peter and Philip inside. Patricia and Janie climbed in on top of Chantel. Pasteur hit the gas, and the big SUV spun around and headed out of the lot.

Gary emptied his pistol striking the Suburban twice in the right rear corner. Then it was gone.

Drago was fuming. He stepped out onto the patio and knelt beside Arnie. Arnie was bleeding badly and was out cold. "Mel, watch these women, Tony, Gary, Ralph and Tyler. Take two cars and go after them. Find out where they went," Drago ordered as he and Chad picked up Arnie and carried him to the couch.

Drago then went to check on Harold, who lay on the floor, his neck at an odd angle, blood drooling from the corner of his mouth. Drago checked his pulse. Harold was dead.

"Fuck," Drago yelled, "Fuck, fuck, fuck. Nobody fucks with Drago Cuz. I will find them, and when I get my whores back, I will slowly kill the men in front of them."

2:00 PM, 30 NOVEMBER 2020

Toronto, Ontario

Tony and Gary went one direction, Ralph and Tyler another, as they searched for the Chevy Suburban and its occupants. They knew that two of them were wounded, so they searched the areas near any medical facilities.

The first Suburban they found turned out to be a dead end; it was not the one they sought. "Fuck," said Tony. "If we don't find them, Drago will skin us alive, and I do mean that literally. He calls every twenty fucking minutes."

Another hour passed before they spotted the next Suburban outside another closed medical facility. "That's them," said Gary excitedly. "I recognize the tall black dude."

"Fuck," said Tony. "Those pricks must have bled to death by now. Nothing is open, and no one will take them. They should have just beaten it away from the city."

"That's the thing about dumb fucks," added Gary sarcastically. "They are predictable. I better call Drago before he calls again; this should cheer him up."

* * *

After the escape, the group drove around to find a medical facility to take the injured, but no one would. They were either overfilled with infected and injured or closed due to a lack of staff. The best anyone would offer them was to drop the wounded off; they may get looked at tomorrow.

"Unacceptable," David said. "Our friends will not last that long."

"David, our only hope is to get to your parent's farm," Pasteur replied out of frustration. "They may not have a doctor, but they must have medical supplies."

"You're right, Pasteur," David said, looking at the others. "Both my brother and his wife are trained paramedics. Any objections?"

Fully aware of the situation they were in, Chantel reluctantly agreed, and so did everyone else.

"Excellent," replied a relieved Pasteur. "David, point the way."

Toronto was like a living hell; the signs of looting were everywhere. Even in this snowstorm, buildings were burning, and people were still looting—the smart ones running away with food. Most, however, still thought big-screen TVs were valuable. *What fools*, thought Pasteur to himself as he drove.

Large areas of the city seemed to have lost power, and there were not enough maintenance workers to get it back on. There were plenty of vehicles stopped everywhere, out of fuel and abandoned.

At one point, a group pushed a shopping cart in front of the Suburban, hoping it would stop. Three men with baseball bats ran out and stood on the road when it didn't. Pasteur stepped on it, hitting one and sending him flying over the hood. There was no sign of police, medics or military anywhere; they were on their own.

* * *

Arnie had finally come to. Like Drago, he was furious. He paced back and forth, drinking the Cutrara's 20-year-old Scotch. Chad was guarding Janet and Anna, who, despite being sedated, they hugged one another.

Drago's phone rang, and Arnie listened intently as his boss got the news. Well done, boys, well done," Drago replied, smiling.

Drago looked at Arnie, "Now, I wonder where they are headed?"

Arnie thought for a minute, then looked at his boss. "Maybe they know a place where there are lots of supplies."

"Hmm," Drago replied, "Tony, stay with them but don't try and stop them. I want to know where they are going.

"Will do, boss," replied Tony knowing what his boss was thinking.

"Arnie, load up the women; we have people to kill."

"Drago, when we catch them, let me have that Frenchy," Arnie pleaded.

"Don't worry, my friend, you will be in her tight little pussy before this night is through, that I promise. You can fuck her while I torture her man in front of her."

They piled into Drago's Escalade, Arnie driving, Mel riding shotgun and Drago in the back with Janet and Anna. Chad followed in another SUV.

Drago was happier now; he could taste revenge. He closed the privacy screen separating the driver's compartment from the back and looked at Anna, smiling.

"Anna, your friends, have caused me much distress today, and you, Anna, will have to make amends." Drago opened his pants and took out his penis, "Anna, you will give me a blowjob."

Anna moved away as far as she could from the tattooed man. She looked at him in shock. Then she looked at Janet sitting there staring off into space.

Drago pulled out the still bloody Karambit, "Anna," he said, smiling. "With those saggy tits, there is only one thing you could be useful for. If you can't give a good blowjob, I may as well kill you right now," Drago smiled. "Now, Anna, I will not ask again."

* * *

Pasteur and Giselle always carried extra clothes, food and a decent first aid kit. Pasteur never let the gas tank fall below ¾;

the lessons learned so hard in Rwanda saving them today.

Patricia was still traumatized; she had lost her husband. Giselle tried her best to comfort her.

Peter was laid in the very back of the Suburban. He was injured severely. David was no medic, but he remembered some of the first aid training his father had insisted they all have; today, he was thankful for the lessons.

David then went to work on Peter, who had received a gunshot wound in his back. He had lost a lot of blood. The first thing he noticed was that there was no exit wound, meaning the bullet was still inside Peter.

David had found Celox in the first aid kit and remembered his father telling him, "Celox is the cat's ass to stop a bleeding wound." Sure enough, it worked as advertised. David then applied a military-style trauma dressing to cover the wound. He then wrapped Peter snuggly in a blanket. He needed to be kept warm to prevent him from going into shock.

David then went to work on Philip's shoulder. He noticed the bullet went right through the shoulder. Again, David applied Celox to the wound and taped on gauze dressings to stop the bleeding.

David then immobilized the arm in a sling. He was amazed he remembered how to make the sling. The knowledge just came right back after all these years.

The Suburban was crowded as they drove north on Hwy 10, leaving Toronto behind. It was snowing heavily now; snowdrifts were piling up on the road, and visibility was only 20 meters at best.

Pasteur had the 4-wheel drive set on auto, and the big Suburban rolled along. David had moved to the front with Chantel and aided Pasteur with directions to the farm. They were all completely unaware of the danger behind them.

4:00 PM, 30 NOVEMBER 2020

The MacIntyre Homestead.

John woke up with the wonderful aroma of dinner in his nose. *Smells like roast beef.* John quickly dressed and headed to the kitchen. He hugged Liz for a very long time, then hugged all his other children.

He pulled J3 and Kat into a big hug. I am very sorry for what you two have had to do. You are both so young. You should be playing sports and getting into teenage mischief."

"We are living in a different world now, Poppa," J3 replied. "We have to do our part to make it safe."

Everyone shed a tear.

Dinner was excellent, as usual. After everything was cleaned up, John went to his study to scour the internet. As he searched, he wondered how long the internet and phone would last. The news and pictures were horrific; the world was coming unglued. *What will be the end of this, and what future will my children and grandchildren face?*

At 6:00 PM, John made coffee, filled two thermoses and drove to the west roadblock. Carl and Arlene Emerson were on duty.

John gave both Carl and Arlene a big hug, "Thank you both for everything. Arlene, you are a competent warrior and Carl, that was a sweet bomb you made."

They spoke of the previous night's success while John poured them a coffee from the thermos.

Next, John drove to the east roadblock arriving just as the O'Gormans relieved Glen and Christine Bennet. John poured them all coffee. "How is young Colleen settling in, Charlene?" John questioned.

"She is doing very well, John. Jessica tells us she is young and strong and will be back on her feet in no time."

"That is wonderful news indeed," John replied happily. Are you making progress restoring the newly secured homes to live-in condition?" John questioned.

"This morning, we completely disinfected two homes. It will be announced during tonight's radio check-in," Charlene cheerfully replied.

"Good work," John praised.

"Glen, how are you and Carl making out with the communication base?" John asked.

"We have all the pieces in place, John. We have contacted Ham operators worldwide and are working to build a network to share information on events in our respective areas," Glenn Bennet proudly replied.

"Excellent, Glenn. How long before you fellows can conduct comm's training?" John asked.

"John, we have everything we need. It's just a matter of scheduling the training," Glenn replied.

"Super, I will get right on the scheduling," John replied happily.

"What have you been up to, Tom?" John asked Tom O'Gorman.

"John, I have been a busy boy. I have been working with Karl Hanson to secure the fuel supplies and put the fuel trucks into short-term storage," Tom replied.

"That's comforting, Tom. We will need that fuel over the winter," John praised.

"How is our future school coming, Christine?" John asked Christine Bennett.

We had been planning diligently. We hope to have our school up and running by Christmas," Christine replied"

John was pleased.

His last stop was the new roadblock north of the Hodgson's farm where Marlene Hodgson and her son Andy were on duty.

John poured them each coffee. "How are Ken and Roger healing?"

"Both were doing well, thanks to Jessica, Sam and Ed. They are both up and moving around," Marlene replied.

Marlene and Andy had spent the day with Calvin Emerson moving machinery and equipment from the construction site into the secure area.

"We have all the construction equipment secured. Tomorrow Calvin, Cory and Darrel Boresma are going to check everything over and identify things needing repairs, Andy announced cheerfully.

"We have an excellent team here, and I am impressed. Everyone is gelling together very nicely," John replied proudly.

John arrived back home to more good news. Karen Wood informed him that Maurice and his family had spent the night at a farm south of here. He had traded his skills as a welder in repairing the farmer's damaged snow blower in exchange for enough fuel to get them here. They should arrive this evening.

"That is excellent news, Karen; soon, you will be reunited. We should have them stay here for the night, then see if we can get you moved back into your own home," John offered.

"That is very kind of John, thank you."

7:00 PM, 30 NOVEMBER 2020

Flesherton, Ontario

The sleepy town of Flesherton sits on the junction of Provincial Highway 10 and Grey County Road 4 in southern Grey County.

Recently, strangers passing through were stopping and harassing the town folks. One man had been shot, and other people had been robbed. Six men from the town had set up a roadblock from the south to protect the residents. All six were at the roadblock that evening. Despite the worsening weather, vehicles were still heading north.

Maurice Wood approached the barrier slowly and carefully; some armed men were blocking the road. "Look sharp, everyone. We have a roadblock just ahead." *How do I handle this?* He didn't have a gun or anything to defend his family with. They had made it this far with good luck and the aid of some very decent people.

One of the men waved Maurice up to the roadblock. Maurice stopped and lowered the window in his Ford Explorer. His heart was in his throat.

"Good evening," the man said. "Where are you folks headed?"

"Good evening," Maurice replied, "We are going to my mother's. She lives just north of Owen Sound."

While Maurice and the man spoke, high-beam headlights approached from behind Maurice and stopped about 50 meters back. Two men got out of the approaching vehicle.

The man talking to Maurice shielded his eyes from the intense beams. "I don't like the look of this," he said to Maurice as he stepped back, signalling the men to lower the lights.

Suddenly automatic gunfire erupted. The man beside Maurice

jerked by the impacts of the bullets and fell to the ground. The other men on the roadblock started firing back.

Two shots hit the rear of Maurice's Explorer, and Donna and the kids all screamed.

Maurice stepped on it, turning his 4-wheel drive Explorer off the road and into the ditch. He had enough momentum to drive up the other side and onto Grey Road 4. Maurice kept his foot to the floor, fishtailing as he tried to escape the gunfire.

"Mom," Beth screamed, "Jordan's hurt. He's bleeding."

Jordan sat slumped forward in his seatbelt; his back was covered in blood.

"Maurice, we have to stop," Donna screamed.

Maurice pulled into the first driveway he saw and stopped, rushed out, and went to Jordan.

No sooner had he opened the back door of the Explorer when Maurice heard someone behind him.

"You move, you die," a voice warned.

Maurice jumped back in fear. Then everything went black.

7:20 PM, 30 NOVEMBER 2020

Flesherton, Ontario

After Tony and Gary shoved the six bodies aside; they drove the vehicles blocking the road into the ditch.

A few minutes later, Arnie drove up, and lowered his window, "What the fuck happened here?" He said, looking around.

"Just some hillbillies with a roadblock," Tony replied. "We took care of it, boss."

"Let's top up the fuel tanks since we are stopped," Drago yelled up from the rear of the Escalade.

Tony had loaded extra fuel, and five minutes later, the gang's three vehicles were topped up. Then they proceeded on Hwy 10, following their prey.

8:00 PM, 30 NOVEMBER 2020

The MacIntyre Homestead

A t the 8:00 PM check-in, John passed on his thanks once again for the success of last night's mission.

"Tomorrow, we begin our training sessions. Franz and I will hold a basic firearms course for new shooters tomorrow at 10:00 AM.

At 1PM, Ed Bennet, Sam and J2 are holding first aid training at the Campbells all afternoon. We need as many people as possible to attend this training. We have been very fortunate in the skirmishes we have had to date. We need to upgrade our skills and readiness ASAP.

"There is a vacant building on the property occupied by the Hodgsons to set up a clothing store. Karl Hanson will organize this operation and will be looking for able bodies to help out. Please get in touch with Karl.

"Tim Henderson and Darrel Boersma have been working with Calvin and Carl Emerson to set up his shop in a vacant machine shed on their farm. It needs renovations, but they hope to have a functioning shop in a week or two. Bob Jones is heading up the renovations and needs volunteers to work on the building. Once complete, we will have all our mechanical talent housed in one location.

"Victoria Broersma has been talking with the Campbells about setting up her new dental practice beside Jessica's medical clinic. This is a super idea, and soon we will have one-stop healthcare.

"The two Shih Tzu dogs we rescued yesterday have a new home with the O'Gormans.

"In conclusion, I am impressed at how everyone pulls together and tackles projects that would secure their collective futures. Thank you all for your continued hard work and dedication."

The group then signed off for the night.

8:30 PM, 30 NOVEMBER 2020

Chatsworth, Ontario

Pasteur had been watching the fuel hand fall lower and lower. The low fuel light had been on for a while, and he was worried. The driving around looking for an open medical facility and the poor road conditions had drained his tank.

They were approaching the small town of Chatsworth, where Hwy 10 and 6 intersect. "David," Pasteur asked. "We are on empty. How much further?"

"Owen Sound is about 15 minutes north on a good day; then the farm is another 20 minutes from there," he replied.

"We will never make it, David. We will have to find fuel."

"There is a gas station on the south side of Chatsworth. If it's open, we should be able to fuel up there," replied David.

The electricity was still on in Chatsworth, the lights visible as they approached the town, and the closed gas station appeared on the right. Pasteur pulled in and parked at the fuel island. "We can't go any further, David," Pasteur said anxiously

David got out to look inside. There was a sign posted on the door. Sorry, no fuel. "Shit," David cursed. "Why didn't we leave earlier?" He returned to the Suburban, "Pasteur, they have no gas. I will look around and see what I can find."

The wind was cold, and the snow was over his ankles and continued to fall. David, like the rest, was dressed only in their bedclothes. He wore loafers for shoes and had no coat, he shivered as he looked around.

Pasteur called to him, "David, vehicles are coming. I am worried I am going to pull around back." The big Suburban pulled around the back of the fuel station. Pasteur shut off the engine, and the lights went out.

David looked around the corner as the two vehicles drove slowly by. A late model BMW SUV led, and a man that looked like one of the gang members that attacked them in Toronto rode in the passenger side. A minute later a Suburban and a pearl white Cadillac Escalade followed closely, and he immediately recognized the pretty blonde girl riding shotgun in the Escalade.

A sickening feeling of dread fell over him. They had followed them. David ran over to Pasteur and told him what he had seen.

"This is bad, very bad," replied Pasteur.

Chantel started to cry, and Patricia Brown wanted to get out and run, Giselle held her fast.

Pasteur looked at David, "We can't outrun them. We have no fuel."

David thought for a minute, "let's hide the car and get ourselves inside."

"On it," Pasteur replied as he hid the big vehicle behind a dumpster.

David tried the door, but it, of course, was locked. He searched for a way in and found a side door with a window leading into a shop area. Several wheel rims were lying against the wall, and David used one to break through the glass. He reached in and opened the door; to his surprise, no alarm sounded.

David ran back and called the others. He and Pasteur carefully removed Peter from the rear of the Suburban and carried him inside. Patricia and Giselle helped Philip.

Pasteur pulled out his cell phone and activated the light. They were inside an automobile service bay connected to the store that serviced the gas station. There was one car inside, the hood open.

The store was not looted and still had food and snack items on the shelves. "I hope we are safe here," said David.

Pasteur looked around, a bead of sweat forming on his

forehead, the memories of Rwanda flooding back again. He could see himself and his little brother hiding in the corner, terrified.

David touched his shoulder gently, "Pasteur, are you ok?"

Pasteur looked at David, then pulled him aside out of earshot of the others. "My friend, I am afraid they will not give up if they followed us this far. Like the Tutsis from my home country, they will hunt us down and kill us."

David felt the blood drain from his face as he thought of Chantel and the other women being raped by these people. He pulled out his phone and called his Father.

8:30 PM, 30 NOVEMBER 2020

The MacIntyre Homestead

The MacIntyre family were seated around the living room watching the CBC Evening News. Caroline had recorded it so they could watch it after the 8:00 PM check-in.

June Handley was visibly upset; *where is Janie? She wasn't at the anchor desk tonight and the fill-in anchorman never even mentioned her.* June called several times, but Janie never answered her phone, and her mailbox was full.

Raymond and June Handley were upset with worry.

Liz went to comfort them when John's phone rang.

David and Chantel's wedding photo appeared on the screen, and the name David MacIntyre in the call display.

"Hello, David," John answered happily.

Everyone looked at John, surprised that David was calling this time of night.

David spoke in a hushed voice, "Dad, we are in big trouble."

David, what's happening?" John asked.

"We are hiding inside the Petro Canada in Chatsworth. We are out of gas, and so is the gas station. Dad, there is a gang after us. In my wildest dreams, I could never imagine people more evil.

"There are seven of us, two wounded. Peter has been shot in the back, hurt badly, and has lost a lot of blood. We have done all we can, but he needs a hospital. Philip has been shot in the shoulder. It's bad, but we have patched him up, and he is ok." David continued filling his father in on what happened at the condo.

"You bloodied their noses, David. They will be angry, and they will be seeking revenge. Let's hope they wait until it's late or you're asleep before they strike, it will give us time to organize a rescue. You have no gas, so you will have to hunker down and gather what you can to defend yourselves. Is your phone charged?" John asked.

"Mine is ok; Chantel's is dead. She did all the calling to the hospitals and police."

"Good, put it on vibrate and keep it close. I will gather a few friends and head your way. Conserve your battery, and only call if the situation changes or it's an emergency ok. We should be there within an hour," John added.

"Dad," David said sheepishly. "Thanks for not saying I told you so."

John paused, "I love you, Son. I will call you when we are five minutes out."

"I love you too, Dad. I'm sorry for all this."

❋ ❋ ❋

Everyone was sitting quietly, awaiting the news. "This is the situation," John said, filling them in on what he knew.

J2 stood, "I'm with you, Dad."

"Me too," replied Sam. "You're not leaving without me."

"Or us," both Kat and J3 added.

John smiled, "Go gear up, and I will call Franz."

Franz picked up when he saw John's name on his call display. John wouldn't call this late without reason,

"What's up, John?"

John quickly filled him in on the situation. "Hatto and I are with you, John. We will leave Scott Sabovitch on guard here and gear up. We will be there in five."

John called Ed Bennet, Arlene Emerson, and Christopher Hodgson. They would all gear up and be ready.

"J2 and I are scheduled for guard duty at the east roadblock. Caroline can you and Liz fill in for us, John asked?"

"Yes, Dad," Caroline replied.

"Mr. Handley, can you keep watch on the ladies?"

"Will do," Raymond replied.

"I will help him," Sheila Carr added. "I can shoot."

After John returned from gearing up, he and Liz shared a hug. "Be careful, John MacIntyre, you come home to me," Liz whispered.

"I will, my love. I love you," he promised.

"I love you too," Liz replied.

They were outside loading up when Franz and Hatto rolled in with Dan's pickup.

"Ok," John said. "The weather sucks. I will lead. They are about a fourty minutes away on a good day. I have extra gas for their vehicle. Jessica is picking up Ed. Jess converted her Suburban into an ambulance; the girl must be physic. Christopher is picking up Arlene, and they will be waiting for us when we drive by the Campbells. Franz, I want them to tuck in between us."

"Agreed," replied Franz.

As they approached the west roadblock, the big loader started up and moved out of the way. Carl and Calvin Emerson were manning the post, Calvin filling in for Arlene. They gave a thumbs-up as the convoy drove through.

8:40 PM, 30 NOVEMBER 2020

Chatsworth, Ontario

Tony had driven through town and was heading north on Hwy 6 when he realized the tracks in the snow were gone. He stopped, pulled out his phone and called Drago, filling him in on the bad news.

"Shit," Drago replied. "They either stopped in town or went south on that other highway. Head back into town. We will split up and see if we can pick up the trail,"

They drove slowly back into Chatsworth, there were quite a few tracks in town from people moving about, but the heavy snowfall and strong winds quickly filled them in, making it impossible to distinguish one from another.

After fifteen minutes, Tony called Drago, "Fuck boss, the tracks are filling up so fast I can't find them."

"It's a small town," Drago replied calmly. "They are in a white Suburban and must have stopped here somewhere. We will find them, be patient, my friend."

* * *

After talking with his father, David told the others that help was coming.

"They will be here in half an hour," David said. "My Father is never late. We must look for anything we can use to defend ourselves and hide."

After resting Peter as comfortably as they could in the store, David, Pasteur, and Philip went to the shop in search of potential weapons.

Giselle searched the store and found six folding knives on display behind the cash. Giselle was terrified of knives; she knew too well what they were capable of. Pushing her fears aside, she forced open the display and removed the knives.

Returning to the other women, she handed one to each. "If they come for us, we must kill them. I would rather die than be taken by them," Giselle added in a shaky voice.

"I can't believe this is happening to us," Chantel sobbed as she pocketed the knife.

Ten minutes later, the men returned to the store carrying large wrenches, screwdrivers and a hardwood handle about a meter long.

"I will keep watch," David offered. "If anyone has a phone with them, turn it off. We don't want anything giving us away."

Everyone silenced their phones and then huddled together at the back of the small store.

David took up position behind the store counter, where he had a clear view of the road outside. "Someone is coming," David announced quietly as the BMW slowly drove by.
"There is only one," David whispered. "They must have split up."

John and the team headed south to Chatsworth; the weather really did suck. The night was dark, with the snow falling heavily and the wind blowing it around. Visibility was limited to no more than 50 meters.

All three vehicles had 4-wheel drive engaged and proceeded cautiously. Some abandoned vehicles were on the road, and who knows what other hazards may be hidden under the snow.

9:00 PM, 30 NOVEMBER 2020

Chatsworth, Ontario

Tony took the Hwy 6 turn and started to go further south through town; there was no sign of any tracks. "They didn't go this way," he said to Gary as he turned the BMW around.

They drove back to the intersection of Hwy 6 and 10, then went back south on Hwy 10 the way they came in. Their tracks were covered but still visible. "Now we're getting somewhere," Gary announced cheerfully.

David could see the lights heading back their way and watched the BMW drive slowly past again.

"Stop!" Gary yelled.

Tony stepped on the brake and looked at Gary.

"There is a gas station back there, a single set of tracks pulled in there," Gary said excitedly.

Tony turned the BMW around and headed back. David went white when the BMW slowly pulled in and stopped.

David's phone vibrated, and he picked up.

"David, we're five minutes out," John said.

"Dad, they just pulled in," David replied nervously.

John radioed the others and filled them in. Despite the poor visibility, he pushed a little harder.

Drago's phone rang, "We found them, boss; the Suburban is parked behind a Petro Canada, south end of town."

"Wait for me," Drago ordered. "I want to enjoy this."

Arnie spun the Escalade around and stepped on it, fishtailing as he drove. Minutes later, Arnie pulled into the Petro Canada and stopped beside the BMW, followed quickly by Chad and then by Tyler and Ralph.

The men quickly got out of their vehicles. "Chad, Tyler, you two spread out and keep an eye on things out here," Arnie ordered.

Tony walked up to his boss, "Drago, they broke into the shop through a side door."

Drago smiled, "we go in the same way."

Arnie looked menacingly at Tony, Gary, and Ralph, "Whatever you three goons do, don't hurt that Frenchy or you will answer to me."

"I want all the women alive," Drago ordered. "Let's go."

The boys led the way in; they were muscle and expendable. They each had lights mounted on their handguns. They stepped into the shop; Tony first scanned left, Gary on his heels checking right. They circled the car, looking inside and underneath.

"Nothing in here, boss," Tony announced.

Tony then walked up to the door leading into the store. Tony and Gary knew someone would be standing on each side of the doorway if an ambush was set up. He turned to Drago smiling, nodding his head and pointed his thumb toward the door.

John stopped just north of the Petro Canada, and the team got out. John told Jess to stay here until he called her. Four vehicles could be seen parked in front of the store, the engines running.

John and Franz studied the scene with binoculars. "I see a woman in the Escalade, looking rearward, possibly guarding hostages; two goons are standing guard, no one in the other vehicles," John reported.

"I confirm that," replied Franz

John addressed the team as they gathered close, "We have a woman guarding hostages in the Escalade and two goons outside standing guard. We have seven people in the store, and all the women inside should be ours. David said eight bad guys, so there could be as many as five inside."

John had to think quickly. "This is the plan, myself and J2 will go in through the shop. Hatto, Arlene, I need you two to quietly take out the two goons outside. When you finish, be ready to head inside to help us out.

"Franz, as soon as Hatto and Arlene do their magic, you and Christopher get into position to bust through the store's front door.

"Ed, we need you to get into a position to neutralize the woman in the Escalade. Sam, Kat, and J3, you three position yourselves across the street and spread out, taking out any runners.

"I need everyone to give me two clicks from your radio when you are all in position. When we are all in position, I will give three clicks as a signal. Ed, you will provide the distraction we need by taking out the woman in Suburban. Are you ok with that?"

"Yes, John, I can. These people are evil; no problem there," Ed replied.

"Good. As soon as Ed fires, Hatto and Arlene will dispatch the two sentries. J2 and I burst in through the back, and Franz and Christopher through the front.

"We hit them hard, we hit them fast, hit them decisively," John smiled. "Watch for friendlies and watch your arcs of fire. That's a small store.

"When the shooting stops, Sam, you check the Escalade for hostages. Ed, we will need you inside."

John looked at Franz, and Franz nodded his agreement. "Let's move," John ordered.

* * *

David and Pasteur waited, one on each side of the door. Each held a large wrench, waiting to swing at whoever entered the door. Philip stood back with a large wrench in case someone got by, he only had one good arm, but he would do his best to defend the others. They were as ready as they could be.

Suddenly bullets came ripping through the wall, hitting both David and Pasteur. They both fell to the floor, and the women screamed.

Tony turned to Dago and grinned at his boss. "Amateurs."

Gary then kicked the door hard, and it flew open. He and Tony ran in, scanning left and right, followed quickly by Ralph. Upon seeing Philip with the wrench ready to swing, Ralph shot him twice, and Philip went down.

Arnie walked in, followed by Dago, "Everyone on the floor. Anyone moves, you're dead," Arnie ordered.

"Well, now," Drago said, smiling. "We meet again, ladies. All of your loyal male guardians are down. Who do you think will save you now?" A big smile crossed his face as he stared at the terrified women huddled together on the floor.

Arnie licked his lips and stared at Chantel. She started to shake and sob uncontrollably.

Drago walked over to Chantel. "On your feet," he ordered.

Chantel slowly stood, pulled the knife and swung it at Drago angrily.

Drago quickly disarmed her. "She has real spirit, Arnie; do you think you handle a spirited woman like this one?"

"Oh, yea, Drago," Arnie answered, rubbing his crotch. "I know how to handle her."

Holding Chantel's head up with his hand, Drago looked into her eyes, "My friend Arnie wants you for himself. He is my most loyal companion."

"Arnie, would you like to fuck her right here and now?"

Arnie smiled, "I have been thinking of her tight little French pussy all day, boss."

Drago smiled menacingly at Chantel, "Arnie really likes you."

Terrified, Chantel started to sob uncontrollably.

Drago looked over at the other women. "There is going to be a lot of fucking in here tonight," he said, smiling. "When we are done, you ladies can watch as we skin your men alive, and when we are done that, all you bitches will be my whores," he grinned sadistically.

John, Franz, Christopher and J2 opted to go in with the Mossberg 500 Tactical shotguns. The laser sights and lights would be an asset inside. They loaded Winchester PDX defender slugs. The side saddle held another 3 PDX Defender slugs brass up and two rounds of 00 Buckshot brass down.

Ed carried his AR15, and Sam, Kat and J3 had the Remington 700s. All wore tactical vests with armour plates, and Hatto and Arlene carried only their swords and tantos.

The team quickly moved into position.

Drago looked over the group of captives, smiling as he held Chantel firmly. "So you thought you could get away, did you?" He didn't expect an answer. "This is what's going to happen," he announced.

John had received confirmation that everyone was in position. *I hope we are not too late,* he clicked his mic three times.

Ed was fifty meters away from the Escalade; Melanie's head centred on the reticle of his Trijicon optic when three clicks sounded in his earpiece, and he fired.

The burst hit Mel's head, showering blood, bone and brain matter all over the inside of Drago's Escalade. The women in the back screamed in horror. It was game on!

The two goons outside turned to react to the gun blast; their necks met Arlene and Hatto's blades, and two headless corpses hit the ground. Hatto and Arlene ran toward the building.

At the same instant, John burst through the door with J2 on his tail.

Franz and Christopher smashed the glass to the front door

and burst through

John went high, and J2 went low. John immediately had his laser dot on Tony and fired, the one-ounce lead slug catching Tony squarely in the chest. At the same instant, J2 took out Ralph, and Franz took out Gary.

Arnie, his pistol in one hand and his Karambit in the other, escaped through the store's front window. He tucked in as he went through the glass, rolled and came up standing outside, face to face with Hatto.

Drago pulled Chantel tightly into himself and put his Karambit to her throat. Chantel was much shorter than Drago. She turned her head as far to the right as possible, let her weight pull her lower, and closed her eyes. She was terrified.

John had the red dot of his laser right in the centre of the cross-shaped scar on Drago's forehead.

No one moved.

Drago knew he couldn't win this fight. The doomed gang banger spoke scathingly at John, "Who the fuck are you, old man?"

John smiled at him calmly, "the old man who is going to kill you." The blast from the 12-gauge was deafening, and Drago's head exploded as the slug entered dead centre of the cross on his scar.

Outside Arnie moved on Hatto. Arnie was fast, but before his foot came off the ground, Hatto severed the hand holding the Berretta, followed by the other that held the Karambit.

Arnie looked back and forth between his bleeding limbs, then to Hatto in disbelief. "What the, a fucking Chinaman," Arnie stammered.

Before he knew what hit him, his severed head hit the snow-covered ground.

"I am Japanese, big difference," Hatto spoke.

John keyed his mic, "We are clear in here, Jess, Ed; we need you

ASAP."

Chantel jumped into John's arms. Franz, Ed and J2 immediately went to the fallen men while Arlene came inside to aid the women on the floor. Hatto, J3 and Kat stood guard outside.

"Dad, Chantel," David called. He could barely speak.

"Everyone is ok, David," his older brother informed him as he pulled off his IFAK and went to work. David was hit twice in the left shoulder and was bleeding badly.

Franz was working on Philip, Ed on Peter. Jess went to Pasteur. Pasteur had the most severe injuries, with two bullet wounds in his shoulder and one in his chest. He was bleeding badly. Sam went to help Janet Aston and Anna Cutrara.

A small reunion of sorts was happening when a pickup pulled in, and two men with hunting rifles jumped out. Franz and John had red dots painted on their chests before their feet hit the snow-covered ground.

They both looked down at the red dots dead centre on their chests, then back at the gunmen. "This is my store. We, we heard gunshots," the driver said as he cautiously lowered his rifle.

John and Franz lowered their weapons. Christopher Hodgson stepped in and filled the men in on what had happened.

"Shit," replied the owner. "Remind me never to piss off you people."

Christopher smiled, apologized for the mess and promised they would return and repair the damages.

"You get your people home safe. We will look after the mess," the store owner told him.

These were the people Chantel, Anna, and Janet despised, yet here they were, including two teenagers, laying their lives on the line to rescue them. They were safe now, the effects of the day's events had drained Chantel, and she felt weak, confused and traumatized.

Pasteur and Philip were loaded into Jess's improvised ambulance, where she could monitor them, and Christopher would drive. Once Pasteur's Suburban was refuelled, Peter and David were carefully loaded inside. Ed would look over them while J2 drove. Arlene and Sam would comfort the rescued women while Hatto drove.

Franz looked at John, then at the shiny new black BMW X5 SUV, "What do you think, John? I could use some wheels of my own."

John put his hand on his friend's shoulder and smiled. "Well, it is German. I think it's a good fit," he replied.

They both laughed.

Franz threw his gear in the BMW, and Kat and J3 jumped in with him.

John pulled back onto the snow-covered road and followed the others home. *The last three days had been non-stop action. What will be the end of this.*

10:00 PM, 30 NOVEMBER 2020

50 Kilometres Northwest of Camp Thunder.

Charlie Redbird and his son Gabriel had been working their trap line. Charlie's line was 120 kilometres in length. It stretched from his home on the Wabauskang First Nations reserve and ended close to Camp Thunder.

Like Charlie, Joseph and Pamela Thunder belonged to the Wabauskang First Nation. Charlie and Joseph grew up together as boys; they explored, hunted, fished and trapped in the vast forests surrounding their reserve. While Joseph went off to join the army, Charlie remained on the reserve, married, and raised a family.

It took Charlie and Gabriel four days to run the trap line using snowmobiles. This evening the two approached their trapper's cabin northwest of Camp Thunder. Today was long but fruitful; 80% of their traps were full.

They were both tired and looked forward to a restful sleep. Tomorrow they would drop into Camp Thunder for some of Pamela's excellent cooking and catch up on the news.

Charlie was in the lead, breaking trail toward the cabin on a Skidoo Tundra-wide track. Gabriel followed on a similar machine. He pulled a sled with gear and their catch. Charlie was visible from the light of Gabriel's Skidoo when he raised his right hand in a halt signal. Gabriel slowed his machine and then pulled up beside his father. There was light visible in the windows of their cabin and a hint of wood smoke in the air. This was not good.

Martin and Albert LeBlanc had taken over the cabin, moved in and were enjoying Charlie's supplies and burning his firewood. The men were sitting around the cabin table with their crew of six; they were drinking and playing cards.

Both Martin and Albert had a grudge to settle with Joseph Thunder. Three years ago, Joseph caught Martin and his brother Albert poaching moose. Joseph called the Ministry of Natural Resources and reported the act. Game Wardens caught Martin and Albert with the moose still in their pickups.

The men were arrested and went to trial. Joseph's video of the act was used in court, and Joseph was a witness. The men were each fined $100,000 and 2 years in jail. They lost their pickups, rifles and hunting privileges, and both men were forced into bankruptcy.

This flu pandemic allowed both men the opportunity to exact their revenge against Joseph Thunder.

"Shut up!" Martin yelled. "I hear something." The faint sound of a snowmobile engine could just be heard approaching the cabin.

"Fuck," Martin yelled. "It's them fucking Indians, and they're headed to the cabin."
The men grabbed their rifles and set a hasty ambush. The two snowmobiles had stopped 100 meters from Martin's ambush site; the two riders were talking.

"Fuck this," Martin said. He raised his rifle and fired, hitting Gabriel squarely in the right shoulder. Gabriel fell off his machine into the deep snow.

Charlie jumped off and grabbed Gabriel pulling him onto his snowmobile. He quickly climbed back on, turned sharply to the right and opened the throttle. The powerful machine spun around, dragging the sled containing their gear.

Albert fired once, missing Charlie. Martin fired, hitting him in the back. The wounded man slumped over the handlebars, the pain was intense, but he kept moving. In a matter of seconds, they were back in the shelter of the forest, headed directly to Camp Thunder for help.

Martin was pissed, "Those filthy bastards got away," he

screamed.

"Timmy, go fetch that Skidoo; at least we got something from those heathens," Albert ordered.

"I know where they are headed, and we will be right behind them. Load up, you assholes. We got us Indians to kill," Martin screamed angrily.

4:00 PM, 1 DECEMBER 2020

Toronto, Ontario

Even in a collapsing world, news travels fast. The deaths of Bull Darlington and Drago Cuz gangs meant that the Kazankov Boys had lost their first and second number two man in as many days.

Big Boris Kazankov, the gang's leader, was furious. He would extract his pound of flesh for this insult, and he would extract it at a time and place of his choosing.

1 DECEMBER 2020

Everywhere

The world that was at the beginning of November is no more. As the month ended, the planet's human population had fallen from 8.2 billion to 4.5 billion.

Society had come unglued; the thin veil we refer to as civil society quickly dissolved. All around the globe, desperate people were making plans to survive.

Many would survive by taking from the weak. Some would survive by seeking power, using others to do their dirty work and provide for their pleasure. Many more would perish during the harsh winter, freezing to death in their homes; they were the lucky ones. Many would slowly succumb to dehydration and hunger or die at the hands of the evil ones. Countless innocent women and children would be violated. Many desperate people would commit unspeakable acts just to survive, and many more would become unwilling slaves.

While small groups struggle to restore order, a dark new reality dawns as the planet enters December and the world descends into chaos.

A MESSAGE FROM THE AUTHOR

I hope you enjoyed Antigenic Shift as much as I enjoyed writing it. I encourage you to continue the series with "Descent into Chaos, book two in the Pandemic Series."

I intend to write this series to open your eyes to the possibilities of a deadly global pandemic. Many in the science community warn that the world is long overdue.

I hope this series shocks you into thinking about the "what if" and prepare for the unexpected. To critically examine your skills and take action to improve them. I hope it forces you to examine yourself, your attitude and how you would respond in a given situation.

The rule of three's teaches us, "You can survive three minutes without air, three hours without shelter, three days without water and three weeks without food."

What would you do if your family had no supplies and were thirsty and starving?

Would you resort to violence, taking from those that had? Would you resort to murder to acquire what your family needed?

How would you provide clean water once the municipal supplies were cut off and bottled water was no longer available? Will you be forced to drink from contaminated sources because you lack the knowledge to purify water?

How will you treat injured and sick family members when you can't drive to the hospital or call 911? Do you have first aid gear and the necessary training or medical skills to come to people's aid?

How would you stay warm in the winter if your heat source is cut off? Where would you find shelter for your loved ones if you were forced to abandon your home?

How will you protect your loved ones from the world's

predators when police are unavailable?

Modern people have lost the skills that served humans so well for centuries. Few modern people have the necessary skills for survival. Few have the skills to hunt for meat or the know-how to process and preserve it. The skills required to grow food, raise livestock and process the bounty for safe storage have been lost on so many. Very few know how to acquire clean water or how to purify it. Before long, dysentery and cholera would run rampant throughout the surviving population.

Many that couldn't find sufficient shelter would swiftly die from exposure. Many women would die in childbirth, and many newborns would perish because people lacked the medical skills and the knowledge to help them through their first hours.

Many more would pass away because their prescription medications ran out and could not be replaced. Most medical facilities would shut down. Even if help could be found, the shortage of modern antibiotics medicines would lead to the demise of many from what was once considered third-world diseases. Simple cuts and scratches would quickly become infected, necessitating amputation.

What would you do? How would you act?

---

2 Timothy 3 New King James Version (NKJV)

Perilous Times and Perilous Men

But know this, that in the last days perilous times will come: For men will be lovers of themselves, lovers of money, boasters, proud, blasphemers, disobedient to parents, unthankful, unholy, unloving, unforgiving, slanderers, without self-control, brutal, despisers of good, traitors,headstrong, haughty, lovers of pleasure rather than lovers of God, having a form of Godliness but denying it's power. From such people stay away!

The second book in the Pandemic Series, Descent into Chaos, will be available in 2019

I sincerely hope you will follow John MacIntyre, his family and his friends as they struggle to survive and restore normalcy to their country.

I am an indie author and rely heavily on the comments, referrals and reviews on Amazon, Kindle and Facebook from you, the reader, to provide necessary exposure and to promote my work. A few simple words go a long way to help promote my work and to inspire and teach me. I thank you in advance for your support. I encourage you to like and follow me on Facebook to get updates on this series and future book releases @ Terry BlackmoreAuthor

Once again, I thank you for purchasing my work and your needed support.

I leave with some immortal words of wisdom from Benjamin Franklin.

By failing to prepare, you are preparing to fail

Benjamin Franklin 1707-1790

One of the founding fathers of the United States

ABBREVIATIONS AND TERMS

- (CJIRU) Canadian Joint Incident Response Unit, part of Canadian Special Operations Forces Command (CANSOFCOM)

- (CANSOFCOM) Canadian Special Operations Forces Command is a high-readiness organization, ready to deploy Special Operations Forces on short notice to protect Canada, Canadian Forces, and Canadian citizens at home and abroad.

- (CDS) Chief of Defense Staff, the most senior ranking military officer in the Canadian military. The CDS is the only officer to hold the rank of a full General.

- Colt, C7 rifle. The Canadian variant of the Armalite, AR15 rifle.

- Celox A blood clotting product, it comes in granular form. When Celox comes into contact with blood, Celox swells, gels and sticks together to form a plug. The product is used for treating severe trauma wounds

- COMM'S communication, radios, hand-held radios, base station.

- Health Agency of Canada. The lead national health agency in Canada.

- IFAK individual first aid kit.

- (KSK) Kommando Spezial Krafte, the army component of German special forces.

- Ka-Bar knife. A military issue fighting knife with an 8" blade.

- Karambit Knife. An Indonesian fighting knife with a curved blade and finger hole at the head of the handle

- Katana. Japanese sword. 60 to 70 CM or 23 to 28 inches of blade length.

- MAG Mutual Assistance Group.

- National Microbiology Lab. The only level 4 microbiology lab in Canada. Canada's version of the CDC, Center for Disease Control in

Atlanta, Georgia.

- NATO North Atlantic Treaty Organization. An alliance of western power formed to counter the old Soviet Union and Warsaw Pact alliance, Headquartered in Brussels, Belgium.

- Ninjato. Ninja short sword approximately 48 CM or 19 inches in blade length.

- The 338 Lapua Magnum, a modern centerfire rifle cartridge, was designed in the 1980s as a military sniper cartridge. The calibre. was used extensively in Afghanistan and Iraq.

- Spetsnaz Russian special forces.

- Tanto. Japanese knife used for stabbing or slashing typically has a blade length of 6 to 8 inches.

- WSM. Winchester Short Magnum. A modern centerfire rifle cartridge. Designed a sporting or hunting cartridge. Available in .270 and .300 calibre.

RECOMMENDED READING

Shake Hands with the Devil, by Lt. General Romeo Dallaire

Where there is no Doctor, by Jane Maxwell

Where there is no Dentist, by Murry Dixon

Bush Craft by, Mors Kochanski

Survival Medicine Handbook, by Dr. Joe Alton and Nurse Amy Alton

Survive by Les Stroud (Survivor Man)

How to Survive the End Of The World As We Know It (TEOTWAWKI) by James Wesley Rawles

The many books by Christopher McGarry

After it Happened Series, by Devon C Ford

Once Upon an Apocalypse Series, by Jeff Motes

SOME VERY GOOD PEOPLE

Ontario Preppers Survival Network OPSN .ontariopreparedness.com

Annual Preppers Meet

Prepper Logic Youtube channel.

The Canadian Prepper Podcast on Podbean

Sheepdog Survival, Brian Opdenkelder

Canadian Prepper YouTube channel

City Prepping YouTube Channel

Viking Preparedness YouTube channel, Pastor Joe Fox

Made in the USA
Middletown, DE
30 May 2023